What reade

«A thought-provoking meditation on the future, with enough adventure to make readers stop and cheer.»

-Thibault Worth, Reporter, NPR, BBC, KQED

«With futurist sensebilities and deft prose, Rafidi extrapolates the ecological concerns on today's horizon over four generations. A truly interesting and entertaining read.»

-Justin Dossey, Founder, PodOmatic

«A masterpiece from science fiction's newest champion.»

-Seth Rosenblatt, Senior Editor, CNET

«TJ & Tosc's protagonist, Raymond, leads the reader on a wild ride through personal transformation atop the colossal machinery of cybernetic technology.»

-Ross Pruden, Infinite Distribution

«I can't wait to see what's next.»

- Rene Breton

12/2012

Dear Steven

way to put a mark on it!

thank you,

TJ & TOSC

A Field Guide for Life After Western Culture

TJ & TOSC

A Field Guide for Life After Western Culture

SUHAIL RAFIDI

San Francisco

Thank you to my editors,
Ryan Hurtgen and Suzanne Sweidan,
whose keen eyes and discerning tastes
brought this tale to light.

First Shelldive Paperback Edition, 2012
San Francisco, CA

www.shelldive.com
contact@shelldive.com
@shelldive (Twitter)
facebook.com/shelldive
shelldive.tumblr.com

Book design by Lara J Designs
www.larajdesigns.com

ISBN 978-0-9883389-0-6

Printed in the United States of America

10 9 8 7 6 5 4 3 2 1

TABLE OF CONTENTS

PART I:
THE QUEST FOR MEMORY

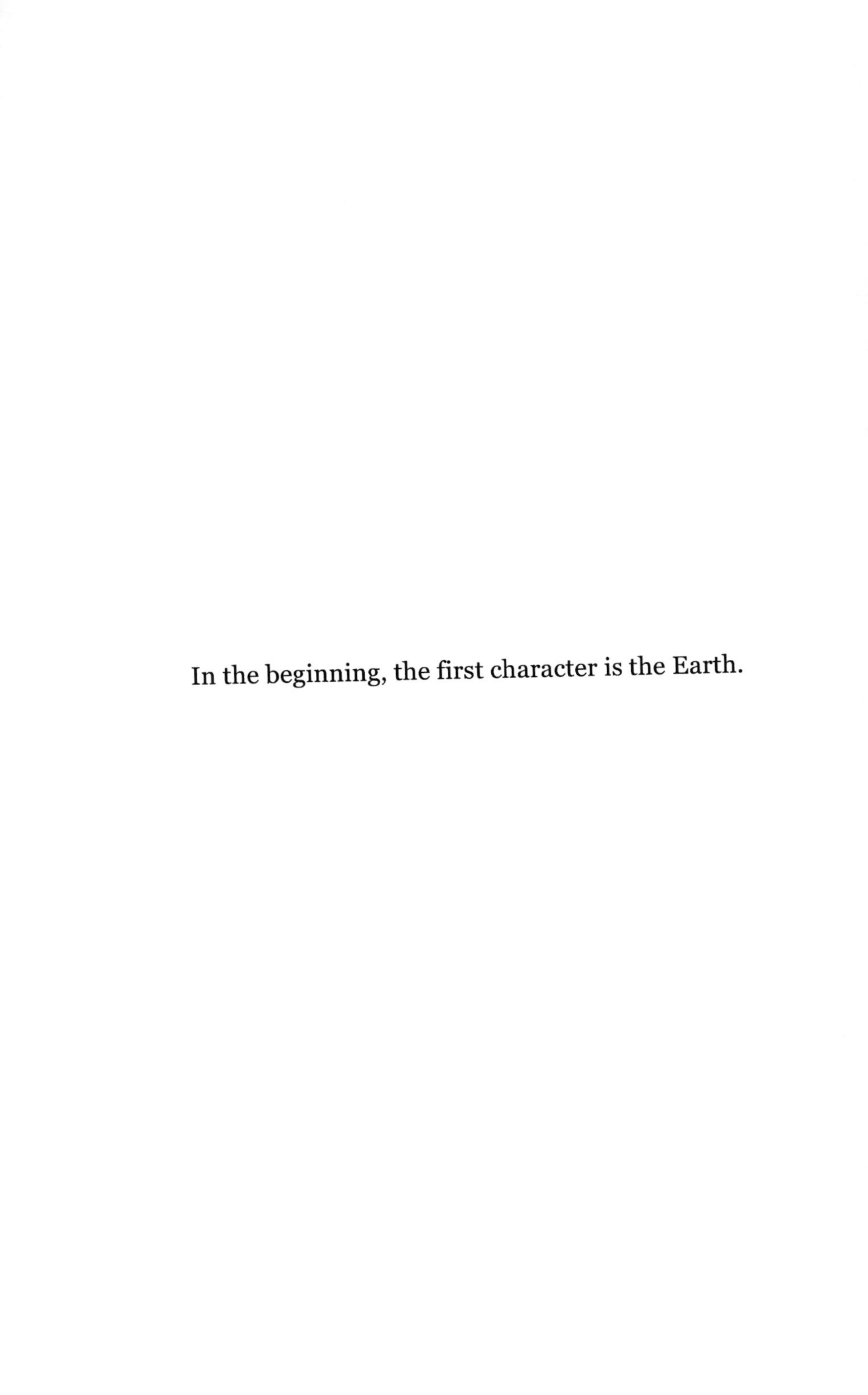

In the beginning, the first character is the Earth.

CHAPTER 1
SALT LAKE CITI

Raymond opens his eyes. Charmin again.

"How will I know which one?" asks Raymond.

"You don't have to know. The bank is a mainframe node. Tomorrow morning, just go to the bank and mash this processor putty into any bank terminal. The virus we wrote will do the rest. Our target safe deposit box will unlock. Empty it and leave."

The citi's public address system chimes in. By virtue of the PA's volume and obtrusiveness, conversations cease.

#ping#

Citizens! The water ration season is in effect! Shower at your allotted times or earn penalties. Protect the sanctity of the citi.

#ping#

"What's in the safe deposit box?"

Charmin has become accustomed to Raymond's absentmindedness. He's lost count how many times Raymond has asked him that question. "It's a unique, and very expensive, computer processor, shaped like a huge gem. It's worth a fortune to the right people."

#ping#

Citizens! A reminder to only purchase trusted, engineered, human-produced foods or earn penalties.

#ping#

Raymond looks down into his food tray. He spoons a morsel of red beans and rice into his mouth. Raymond never gets the meats, floating in their watery gravy. They are boiled and tough and take forever to chew. The beans taste chalky and vitaminized. Last years beans tasted better, but that's always the way, the past always seems better. It seems to Raymond like the beans were different sometime before. Soft, delicious brown beans with salt. What were they called? Some horse name. But these armored red beans with their firm starchy insides aren't as good as those beans. We had these red beans last year, too, thinks Raymond. When did we have those tasty brown beans?

He's been changed by the citi, thinks Charmin. In Appalachia, Raymond was a plucky genius, but he's been buried and erased under amnesia and the citi's constant surveillance. Raymond, like his fellow citizens, is always worried he's being watched, even in his most private moments. In this worry, he condemns his own ideas before he even finishes having them, second-guessing his most inspired thoughts.

#ping#

Citizens! Rejoice! Our mechs are winning! We've engaged PAGsor on a diplomatic dispute.

Images of smoking wreckage illuminate the food court's video screens.

Praise our victory!

#ping#

"Praise!" chorus the collected diners automatically, including Raymond, as if monotonously answering a roll call. The rows of bench perched men and women resume their repast.

Charmin looks across the table at Raymond, remembering Raymond for a moment as he once was, before the identity chip. He had an insufferable smile, a more animated cadence in his speech, and alert, twinkling eyes. But now his face hung dark, lifeless, and bored. The identity chip, besides being a tracking and purchasing device, doctors memories. Chipped citizens lose a week of their oldest memories for every new week of memories they gather, never remembering more than the most recent year and a half of their lives. This measure was implemented after the depression plague, to curtail the spread of the epidemic.

"These poor chipped dopes," he mutters. Charmin is protected by interests beyond the citi, he does not have to wear a chip. He may move freely through the citi, even out of it, like an invisible man. Mr. Z makes sure of that.

Raymond fiddles with his spoon.

"Nervous?" asks Charmin, knowing the answer. He reaches into his pocket. "Here, take this tonight." He hands Raymond a small pillbox. Charmin was instructed by Mr. Z to make sure Raymond takes this pill. When asked why, Mr. Z said he did not pay Charmin to be inquisitive, only to execute plans. Charmin let it drop. The pay is damn good.

Raymond shakes the pillbox. He opens it. It contains a pink tablet. He smiles briefly to himself, imagining whatever altered relaxation this pill has to offer. Of course, the citi stigmatizes drug use. The Bachelor's and Spinster's Association is constantly giving talks around the citi on the evils of recreational drug use. They urge what they call "lost souls" into the rehabilitative fold of the BSA facilities.

Raymond has met a few people after they've undergone a rehabilitation program at BSA, usually leading the talks. None of them ever gives a straight answer about what goes on in the program. And every year, it seems, the citi gets tougher on drug crime, adding new sniffing technology to the dawgs and increasing the penalties for possession. If Raymond were caught with these pills, he could lose his job and his home. The fear that comes with holding the drugs is much of what makes taking them so gratifying for Raymond.

#ping#

Citizens! This luncheon shift has been brought to you by Gibraltar Services, Jeweler's Division. Are you feeling that love bug? Don't bite without a wedding band. Gibraltar Services, procurers of all your citi needs.

#ping#

"Now get back to work," instructs Charmin, reaching out with a lanky arm and patting Raymond's shoulder from across the long, narrow table. "Act natural. Get some rest tonight. It's your last day in this purgatory they call Salt Lake Citi."

#ping#

The following entertainment portion of our citicast is brought to you by the Pharmers of the Future.

#ping#

If ever there was a waaaaay, that way is ours... sings a woman's voice over the citicast to a snappy, lighthearted tune.

That evening, Raymond turns from his day's work and steps to the kitchenette of his oblong, one-room living quarter. He hydrowaves dinner. After dinner, he drops his empty food container down the recycling chute. Sitting on his bed, across the room from the desk with the kitchenette in between, Raymond examines the pillbox. Anticipating a high, he takes the pink tablet, for dessert.

The citi's day lamps dim and switch to starlight. Night falls. A soft euphoria creeps in along the edges of his body. He feels disconnected from his life, like he is watching himself from a safe distance, hovering between waking and sleep.

That night, Raymond dreams of going to the bank and escaping with the jewel. As he dreams the scene, someone is watching through Raymond's own sensorium. Mr. Z, from a faraway place, along the electromagnetic network that binds together all citis, is monitoring the young amnesiac.

CHAPTER 2
THE BIRTH OF SALVADOR TOSC

One hundred and seventy six years before Raymond took Mr. Z's pill, civilization was, as it had been on other occasions, on the brink of momentous turns. The most pressing problems of our times were nearly resolved. Global warming was nearly resolved. The energy crisis was nearly resolved. Food and clean water shortages were nearly resolved. Overpopulation was nearly resolved. And not just temporary, mitigating solutions, either. No, this time, we humans, as a collective collaborative organism, were really going to redress the harms we had perpetrated on the earth.

Wonderful solutions arise because of terrible problems. This potent optimistic thrust of human cooperation was motivated by an undercurrent of treacherous circumstances. The carbon spike in our atmosphere made global warming worsen at an alarming rate. Weather patterns became more and more erratic, drying up once abundant farmlands while creating snowdrifts in deserts and droughts in swamps. Some physicists attributed the trouble to irregularities in the magnetic field of the earth. They were correct, in part, but no one explanation would suffice in our complex world. All the while, the holes in our atmosphere over the poles continued bleeding precious ozone off into the breathtaking void of deep space.

Scientists worked tirelessly at the cellular, molecular, and atomic level to create organisms that consumed and metabolized our most dangerous post-industrial by-products. Oil spills in the open ocean could be cleaned up with genetically engineered enzymes that ate crude oil and excreted fish food. Bioremediation and mycoremediation technologies created a whole host of these transformative enzymes. Some would eat the corn used to feed cows and excrete diesel fuel and ethanol to power the vehicles that were shipping the beef. If there was a hazardous fuel spill, scientists had an enzyme to eat the fuel and turn it back into safe organic matter and sweet smelling fresh air.

Farmers worked with scientists to create the highest yielding crops in history. And with enzymes to change the crops from one state to another, food could be used for an array of other purposes. Surplus corn, for example, could be converted into environmentally sound plastics.

Environmentalists made great progress in repopulating endangered species. Those species, like the majority of amphibians, that were becoming extinct despite humanity's best endeavors, were genetically catalogued with the hope of reintroducing them into nature later, via clones, when the ecosystem could sustain them.

Governments banded together, enacting sweeping reforms, like the Statehood Initiative, that eliminated our reliance on national political boundaries. Passports and citizenship were to become a thing of the past, because we all would be citizens of Earth. Humanity, it was said, was finally sophisticated enough to unite under one world government. Soon even war would be obsolete.

Corporations consolidated and spread, taking on the responsibilities of disintegrating local governments, constantly trading justice for expediency. Though the size and resources of the corporations enabled remarkable technological advances, they remained profit driven entities, keeping as much as possible for themselves. Where people once were entitled to basic needs, they increasingly had to pay for access. Those who could not afford them had to go without. Glaring disparities in wealth and privilege produced a militant fundamentalist population of marginalized revolutionaries that would stop at nothing to overthrow the established order. The people who would see society destroyed gathered a massive and dedicated following, creating an invisible government all to themselves that networked around the world. They declared war on the wealthy 5% of the population that controlled 99% of the world's resources. The system, in turn, deemed them terrorists and set to rooting out and exterminating them.

One day, a ransom note was issued to the world. A highly organized splinter group of terrorists acquired 24 nuclear bombs, one for each of the world's time zones. They placed them in a ring along the equator of the world, stowing bombs in anchored rafts out on the Atlantic, Pacific, and Indian oceans. Where the equator traversed land - northern South America, Central Africa, Sumatra, Indonesia, Sulawesi, New Zealand, and Papua New Guinea - they buried the bombs discreetly in the ground. If the governments of the world did not meet their demands within the allotted time, they would literally blow the world apart.

The terrorists broadcast a laundry list of demands, including the release of all political prisoners, massive funds for dissident groups, withdrawal of troops from occupied territories, and deposition (in some cases, execution) of prominent world leaders. Mining of rare semi-precious metals in South America and Africa by foreign interests, used to produce computer electronics, must cease. The list went on and on, enough work for a whole world of governments to do. "The 5% nation," their manifesto announced, "must give control of the world back to the people of the world – or it will be destroyed. The rest of us would rather die than continue to live under your oppressive rule." They gave the world one week to comply.

A wave of panic swept the globe. Never before had a threat galvanized the entire world into such frantic and cooperative action. Many governments began fulfilling as many demands as possible. Every able government and private agency investigated the placement of the explosives. They had no idea where the bombs were or how to find them. As the week ticked on, political prisoners were freed, countless sums of money and other aid exchanged hands, and many leaders who refused to negotiate with terrorists were violently overthrown. Some of the members of the splinter organization itself had a change of heart about destroying the world and began to diffuse the bombs themselves. Investigations, cooperation and world scale heroics eventually lead to the location and disarmament of nearly every nuclear device planted by the terrorist organization that held the planet hostage. In the end, for it felt like the end, 6 of the 24 nuclear bombs detonated, vaporizing most of Micronesia, the Marshall Islands, and a gargantuan quantity of Pacific Ocean waters from the King Seamount and the Central Pacific Basin.

This vaporized part of the earth was blasted up into the sky and bled out through the ever-widening holes in the atmosphere over Antarctica and the Northern hemisphere. So much of the Earth's Pacific Island chains and sea water poured out into deep space that it was the equivalent of Earth firing an asteroid out into space rather than being hit by one. Nearly the entire planet clouded over, ushering in a nuclear winter. Tests decades later established that, as a result of the nuclear catastrophe, the Earth had lost a significant enough portion of its total mass to constrict the planet's orbit. Consequently, the Earth was permanently resituated in space several thousandths of a degree closer to the Sun.

Climate change accelerated drastically. The Arctic regions began melting faster than ever. Coastal cities saw sea levels rising by the year. Skin cancer and retinal damage rates soared. Extinction of the smaller species at the root of our food chain skyrocketed. Bees and wasps disappeared entirely, decimating pollination rates. Flowering plants became a rare and coveted commodity. In an effort to avert the extinction of the human species or be driven to live underground, a remarkable and barely tested new technology called geoengineering was brought to bear on our atmosphere. Geoengineering was an effort to reduce the amount of heat from the Sun on planet Earth. Geoengineering called for measures like dumping iron molecules into the oceans to stimulate plankton blooms that would consume excess carbon dioxide, and launching floating carbon catchers into the sky to draw carbon dioxide out of the air. The carbon dioxide was then stored underground, like nuclear waste, to eliminate its greenhouse effect on the environment.

One geoengineering project, funded by a small group of billionaires who had little faith in representative government to affect meaningful change, was to install a reflective and cooling field into the earth's stratosphere. The world's top physicists were brought together to develop high altitude planes that flew in the ionosphere above both of the poles. From their lofty positions, the planes periodically sprayed quantities of microscopic sulfur and other custom engineered particles into the stratosphere below. The sulfur was supposed to reflect sunlight away from the earth, effectively turning the entire sky into a pair of polarized sunglasses.

A companion geoengineering project was cloud brightening. Clouds were seeded with salt water and other more complex compounds to make them brighter, so they would reflect more sunlight back into space. The ocean iron slurry, the carbon catchers, the stratospheric sulfur shield, and cloud brightening – all of these solutions were implemented in quick succession precipitated by the panic of the nuclear winter. All of these geoengineering technologies had one goal in mind, to reduce the overall temperature of our planet Earth.

These things worked in ways no one could anticipate or measure. The beautiful blue color of the sky that humans had known since the dawn of time was paled and tainted. Temperature differentials between night and day leveled out. Rainfall patterns shifted. The entire planet's heat distribution changed. The monsoon season, which naturally irrigated most of India and Asia, making food production abundant enough to feed billions, was shortened by over 50%, effectively ruining the entire subcontinent's ability to grow its own food.

After 40 years of blind desperate tinkering with Earth's naturally occurring ecosystem, things had gotten worse, and there was no way to pinpoint any particular cause.

Unnaturally heavy clouds began to form in the sky, precipitated by all of the foreign particles in the stratosphere; and they spread.

Every turn of human history is marked by the birth of a remarkable person. Humanity heralds the person as a genius, a master, or a prophet. Somehow, this one individual becomes a conduit for all of the innovation of their age. All of the progress and new ideas that are incubating in the society around them shine forth through the prism of the one genius mind. The genius imagination contained in that one human mind catapults the entire society forward on a wave of new ideas. They are a seed crystal in a supersaturated solution.

Like Aristotle, Copernicus, Newton and Einstein, Salvador Tosc was one of these luminaries, born into an era when it needed him most. Salvador was born as the unnatural cloud cover was thickening and spreading over the pale, sickly sky. Salvador could read before he was 2 years old. He loved stories about the distant past and the far-flung future. Stories about life at the dawn of time and about life at the edges of the galaxy fascinated Salvador. He wrote moving music and beautiful poetry as if idly doodling in a coloring book and was awarded his first university degree at the tender age of 8.

Before Salvador was 10 years old, the clouds had blanketed the entire planet. The clouds thickened and spread over islands, nations, and continents. Mists and tulle fogs lingered across marshes, plains and valleys. High noon started to look like evening; evening, like night. Rain ceased altogether, held in the sky permanently by the earth's coat of doctored clouds. By the time Salvador was 12 years old he had digested the latest physics and calculus of eminent scientists four times his age. By his 13th birthday he had correctly hypothesized the primary causes of the cloud cover.

Of all the things Salvador excelled at, cybernetics was his favorite field of study. He was fascinated by the artful, complex relationship between cause and effect. Cybernetics was often associated with robotics and artificial intelligence. He created robots containing elaborate cybernetic systems, making robots adaptable enough to begin replacing human functions. For the first time in history, a robot could adapt to reality. A holographic movie could read emotion, express emotion, and act in accordance with human feelings.

When Salvador was 14, he submitted a treatise to the Global Science Foundation proposing a solution to the pollination problem brought about by the extinction of bees and wasps. In his treatise he produced the specific design for tiny cybernetic flying droids that could pollinate plants much the same way that bees had done. The tiny droids could even recharge their energy supply through induction by temporarily landing on any piece of machinery which a charge ran through.

At age 16, Salvador wrote a celebrated analysis of geoengineering which explained much of the cloud plague that covered the world. He drew up plans for climate modeling that would open the doors for a new, advanced generation of geoengineering solutions that could be implemented with much more foresight than previously possible.

By age 17, Salvador Tosc was brought into the fold of the international scientific community. He continued to produce cybernetic systems and devices that helped reconstitute the ailing world. For example, he developed a source of energy that harvested and aggregated the minute electrical impulses produced during plant metabolism. This same energy could be used to power lamps that generated life-giving light for those plants, light that had been blocked out by the cloud plague. Because of Salvador's work, plants could produce not just their own food, as nature intended, but their own light. This was as close to perpetual motion as science had ever before been.

He sold his innovations to enthusiastic developers as long as they agreed to use the technologies as he designed them for the purposes he intended. Because he lacked a business sense, he did not become wealthy like his patrons were. This did not bother Salvador as long as the world was being even a little bit healed by his work. His great dream was to dispel the cloud cover for good and restore the natural atmospheric conditions of the planet. He spent his childhood poring over pictures and movies that showed him the gorgeous cerulean skies of days long gone, blue skies he himself had seen in his earliest childhood. Salvador's abiding passion was to see blue skies in his lifetime.

At age 19, Salvador made a best friend named Xavier, whom he would know for life. Xavier possessed charisma and business acumen on par with Salvador's scientific genius. Together they started their own technological development company, TJ & Tosc. In the following years, Xavier made sure that both he and Salvador became as wealthy as their patrons.

When he was 21, Salvador met a woman named Irene and they fell completely and irretrievably in love with each other. Irene became Salvador's muse, and his drive to restore the fabled blue skies was amplified, for he wanted to walk under the azure canopy of the heavens with his beloved. Their first child was a boy, named Germane. Of Salvador's three children, Germane was the only one who survived to adulthood. Germane had a son named Bishop and a daughter named Sylvia. Bishop, who did not live to be as old as his father, had one child, born in a village beyond the scope of the citis, named Raymond Tosc.

CHAPTER 3
CHAMELEON

Raymond opens his eyes. Noise again; the wake-up alarm. He has a cracking headache.

"Oh mah gawd..." he blinks and yawns. The phrase comes out as a sonorous mutter at the end of his yawn. "What time is it?" He thinks to himself, Is it Thursday? I think it's Thursday. He tries to close his eyes. Impossible; the pitched staccato beeping of his tiny apartment is ringing his ears. The apartment's computer voice pipes up.

Good morning, Raymond. It is @333 beats on the 118th day of the year. YOU HAVE URGENT MESSAGES!

The voice pauses, then becomes chipper.

The 200th State Celebration is coming up! Are you planning your Big Deuce holi-

"I'm up! I'm up! Okay!"

The beeping and the voice fall silent.

"Wait. Which day...?"

Raymond sits up in bed and slouches down again. His bed-tousled auburn hair is sticking up at gravity defying angles. His journal is face down, pages wrinkled, on the floor next to the bed. His eyes droop with sleep for a moment. He picks up the journal. The writing is messy, like Raymond was writing in the dark. He sees a series of hurried mathematical equations, notated with brief statements in the margins around a rough sketch of the citi center. He has marked the exact number of steps from the door of the bank to the safe deposit box, as well as many other meticulous details of the mission. The handwriting is definitely his own, though Raymond does not remember writing any of it.

GOOD DAY, RAYMOND, his apartment reminds him. *YOU HAVE UNOPENED URGENT MESSAGES.*

"I'm awake," he says to his apartment's clock. "Shut up." He looks at the clock. @334. Okay, I have time, he thinks, time for coffee before the bank run. Raymond looks at himself. He is still dressed in his day clothes. He is only wearing one shoe. I didn't change last night? Where the hell is my other shoe? He trudges, hunching and scratching himself, across the room, toward the kitchenette. He scratches his butt and orders –

"Coffee...."

Coffee in 1 beat, his kitchenette verifies. The timer begins ticking down.

The message slot is blinking. Raymond pisses into a tiny alcove bathroom. He yawns again. He looks at his clothes. Did I get drunk last night? He pats himself down. There is a softball-sized lump in his jacket pocket. His pocket is zippered shut, but an image glows vaguely on the periphery of his consciousness, like the first moments of dawn. It is the jewel. With his hand still over his pocket, Raymond's eyebrows draw together and down.

It can't be, he thinks. I haven't been to the bank yet. What the-?

RAYMOND, YOU HAVE UNOPENED URGENT MESSAGES, his apartment blares insistently.

"Okay! Okay! Shut up! Give me the messages."

Your coffee is ready!

Raymond sighs and takes the mug from the kitchenette dispenser. The coffee is lukewarm, flooded with additive caffeine, and does not taste very different from the tea beverage. The morning music continues, quieter. His messages play; two from Charmin. “Man, I hope you’re not home. Why aren’t you answering your comm?” And “Get the hell out and meet me at the exit rendezvous! Bring it with you!” Raymond has the anxious sinking sensation of being caught in a lie. He senses a drastic change in the situation, but is clueless as to what. He becomes uneasy. Is he late? The exit rendezvous is in Sailor’s Cove. Why did the plan change? Still wearing one shoe, he slips on another and bolts out the door.

Raymond arrives at Sailor’s Cove. It feels like there are a lot of cops out. Maybe I’m just paranoid about the job, he thinks. Someone taps him on the shoulder. Raymond flinches and turns. It is Charmin, dressed in a hooded gray body suit with the hood pulled back. He is tall and gangly, yet strong. When standing at his full height, he is a head taller than Raymond.

“Come on. Over here,” directs Charmin.

Raymond follows Charmin into an old building, built before the biosphere was installed. They hurry through the pre-dawn gloom.

“Why are we here?” asks Raymond. “What about the job? What’s with the jumpsuit?”

“Shut up and stay out of sight!” replies Charmin, leading Raymond up a stairwell to the roof of an old, pre-biosphere building. Once on the roof, Charmin trots across several roofs, hopping over the occasional narrow alley between. He slows down for Raymond. They make two turns. Charmin finds a dark airshaft. They make their way down by gripping plumbing pipes. Raymond accidentally grabs a hot water pipe.

“Ow!”

“Shh.”

They reach a foothold on windowsills three floors down and pause. The airshaft is lined with windows. Each window leads into a closet or bathroom of a different apartment.

“Now...what? First – Where did you go?” asks Charmin.

Raymond is confused and irritated by Charmin’s tone. He was up, early, making coffee.

“Home. What are we doing here?” Raymond retorts. “Why aren’t you at your post? What about the job?”

“You went home!? What’s the matter with you? We did the

job, Raymond! It's shot to hell!" Charmin peers up at the windows lining the airshaft. A bathroom light goes on a few floors up. A faint pallor of light illuminates their faces. They hear someone farting. "What were you doing at home?" he whispers.

"Sleeping." whispers Raymond.

"Sleeping!?"

"You said 'rest'! What do you mean we did the job?"

"Sleeping?!" Charmin looks wide-eyed at Raymond.

"You don't remember, do you?" Charmin asks, keeping the attention on Raymond.

The toilet above flushes. Raymond's stomach sinks. His bowels constrict. He feels like he needs to go to the toilet.

"You seemed so calm..." muses Charmin, nearly to himself. What was in Mr. Z's pill? Charmin wonders. No time for that now.

They hear the police knocking at an apartment near them. No one answers.

"He's not here," says one cop.

"It says he's here," replies the other cop.

"No heat readings either."

"Well, maybe higher up."

"It says he's here; maybe 20 meters."

"Yeah, in any direction. That bug's ancient."

"Dawgs will find them."

"Shut up." He hates feeling like the dawgs are smarter.

The cops move on to the next apartment. Raymond and Charmin breathe again. Raymond is getting scared, but Charmin is only irritated. Charmin has technology that obscures him from surveillance, but Raymond is not similarly warded.

"Listen," whispers Charmin, "what matters is: we did the job, you were there, and we have to get out of here. You were supposed to drop the jewel into a waste bin two blocks from the bank terminal, to hand it off to me, so you wouldn't be followed. You trotted right past the drop. Where is the loot?"

"We wha...?" Raymond thinks of the jewel in his jacket pocket, but the way Charmin is asking for it, he doesn't want to relinquish it. Raymond feels strangely possessive of the mysterious object. He has no idea how he even got the thing, or how it works. Raymond experiences a sense of conviction that he must keep it, and resolves not to give anything to Charmin until he can figure out what's going on.

"How do we get out of here?" asks Raymond. He looks around, to illustrate to Charmin that they are not in a convenient position to go anywhere. In response to this, Charmin produces two port clearances with a smug look on his face. He hands one to Raymond.

"One is for you," says Charmin. "Fresh name and everything."

"I can't...no."

"You can't know? What's wrong with you?! Do you want to get out of here, or what?"

Raymond, unaccustomed to conflict, stares at Charmin dumbly. He shrinks away from Charmin to a farther corner of the airshaft, out of quick reach. "I don't know," says Raymond.

"You chipped imbecile!" Charmin, frustrated, scrutinizes Raymond intensely. Raymond is avoiding eye contact, playing possum. An intuition flashes in Charmin's mind. "Wait a minute...You DO have it!" Charmin grabs at Raymond's wrist, but cannot get a good grip without losing his balance. Charmin does manage to wrest the travel pass from Raymond's grasp. It falls into the darkness below. Above, near the lip of the airshaft, there is a scraping and tapping sound, like rakes running. Charmin darts a glance upwards, towards the noise.

Shit, the dawgs! thinks Charmin. Time's up. Charmin casts the jumpsuit's hood over his head, activating the chameleon feature. The jumpsuit he is wearing seems to waver and dim. Raymond blinks, trying to focus on Charmin. Charmin slips into a darkened apartment. He looks like a vague shadow of a fat black cat flitting into the window. Charmin, now a dark, amorphous shape, closes the window behind him.

Raymond is alone in the airshaft, the citi's still dim artificial sky above him, a six-storey fall below him. The alloy paws of the dawgs scrape and tap. They trot to the lip of the airshaft and stop. Two sets of illuminated camera eyes peer down the airshaft. One of the lights from one of the eyes casts a fine red beam at Raymond. Raymond, trained to scan in, looks right into the red light of the dawg's eyes. He suddenly realizes what he's done and looks away. Fool! Luckily, he did not scan in. There is a *fwip* sound. Raymond feels a sting at the base of his neck. He tries to brush away the dawg's stinger but he cannot move his arms. His legs start to give out. He has a slow sensation of watching his body falling down the deep narrow shaft, bumping the wall along the way. Raymond's vision darkens. His body slowly peels away from the airshaft wall. He leans forward, imagining himself fall. The other dawg nets him and pulls him up the airshaft on a filament line.

Raymond comes to some moments later. Lying on his side, on the roof, he is tangled in wispy tenacious strands of multiplastic netting. Still he cannot move, but he can feel the stinger wearing off. One of the dawgs zip ties his wrists together. The other dawg zip ties his ankles. They wait, alert. Raymond hears the roof gravel crunching under human footsteps. Groggy, he tries to turn his head to see who is approaching. He sees the sheen of police uniforms. He hears their body armor rubbing and creaking. Shortly, the two cops who had been searching the building stand over Raymond.

"Well, if it isn't our little bank hacker," jeers Officer Booch. He unfolds a collapsible stretcher from his pack.

"Terrorist scum," says the other, and spits.

Officer Booch bends down and turns Raymond's face upward to scan his identity. Their routine apprehension is interrupted when a roaring, quaking explosion lights up the sleeping citi.

The building trembles. Raymond hears a far sound of screeching tearing metal and crashing glass. He cranes his neck feebly to look. He only sees the fire orange glow reflecting off the cops' black body armor. The cops snap a look at the enormous column of flame, a couple kilometers north, near the travel port. It tapers into rising plumes of smoke and dust. Sonorous waves of sound roll and bounce through the citi dome, like hammering a brass gong in a marble-tiled room. The dawgs freeze. Their lighting changes from police blue to emergency red. One of the dawgs disengages from the group and bounds away across the rooftops towards the explosion. The other dawg runs down the stairwell. It is making for the wagon on the street, leading the shortest possible route for its pedestrian followers. The cops' headsets crackle and a message comes through:

Emergency announcement! First response! All citi officers report to the travel port! Security Alert Seven! The Trilling Bridge is under attack!

CHAPTER 4
THE DESTRUCTION OF THE TRILLING BRIDGE

"C'mon. Let's throw him in the wagon and get out of here." says Booch. "We don't want section four to get there before us."

"Yeah...what the hell was that?"

"Damned if I know – probably more of this kind," he replies, kicking Raymond. They hoist Raymond in the stretcher and tote him down to the street like a funerary bier.

On the street, one dawg is waiting for the cops. When it sees them, it leaps into its roost and collapses, mounting itself flat against its side of the wagon. The cops hurriedly toss Raymond - stretcher, netting, and all - into their paddy wagon. Fear is swirling in Raymond's guts. He wants to grimace with hopelessness, but he cannot even move his facial muscles. The chemicals in the stingers interact with his chip-doctored nervous system.

Every day, citi dwellers eat fortified food, containing the nutrients necessary for survival. Part of the citi's food fortification includes chemicals not related to food, like caffeine for energy and nicotine for loyalty. The official explanation is that these supplements compensate for deficiencies in the laboratory-produced food. They also cover other proprietary chemicals of a confidential nature. These confidential, proprietary chemicals are in fact incomplete chemical compounds. Once eaten, the partial compounds reside latent in the citizens' bodies until activated by their counterparts, delivered either by stinger or airborne gas. If citi officials wish to investigate, interrogate, immobilize, or arrest a citizen, they merely need to introduce the other half of the appropriate compound into the citizen's bloodstream.

The citi's PA system blares, replicating the message the officers were previously given privately:

Attention citizens! This is an emergency announcement! The citi is under attack! All private citizens report to your domiciles. Turn off all unnecessary power! Await security attendance check! Attention citizens! This is an emergency announcement! The citi is under attack! All private citizens report to your domiciles. Turn off all unnecessary power! Await security attendance check!

"Shit! Now we're late!" says Officer Booch, bolting to the driver's seat.

The second cop looks into the wagon. He shines a light in Raymond's terrified, yet paralyzed, face. He shoots Raymond with a second stinger.

"Get some rest," he says with a sneer. "You're gonna need it."

He slams the wagon's metal door shut as Raymond blacks out.

The Trilling Bridge is the major citi hub for vehicular traffic and the exit point for Salt Lake Citi's data pipe. Built after the loss of satellite communications, it is part of a massive data pipeline that enables other biospheres on the North American continent to exchange information with each other and, subsequently, the rest of the world.

The police race to the Trilling Bridge accelerating eagerly, turning quickly, and braking suddenly. Raymond's inert body, slung to the stretcher, but otherwise unsecured in the compartment, is banged and jostled all the way there.

"Well, he hasn't escaped," jokes the second cop.

"Not on my watch," quips Booch in the driver's seat.

"Look out!"

A second explosion - much closer this time - blows another bridge truss. The ground shakes. Rubble pelts the paddy wagon. A two-meter length of rusty rebar, propelled by the blast, arcs through the air and embeds itself halfway into the paddy wagon's hood. It protrudes from the hood like a swizzle stick, wobbly with momentum from its flight.

"Holy shit!" exclaims Officer Booch. He swerves to a stop.

The air is choked with smoke and dust, orange with fire, trapped under the biosphere, with no sky into which to disperse. The bridge is teeming with activity, like an anthill stirred with a stick. Workers, medics, victims, and news teams scurry about in every direction, cross firing questions and commands at each other. The sound of auxiliary exhaust fans whirring to life fills the air, adding to the cacophony. Emergency vehicle lights flash and glow among the blazing bridge remains. The cops see their section banner fluttering several meters away. There is a news encampment between the paddy wagon and the section banner.

"Great," says the second cop, looking at the newscaster in front of a camera, blocking their way to their police group, "the vultures are getting faster."

The dawg dismounts from its wagon roost and bounds towards the damage, scanning for survivors. The cops jump out of their impaled wagon. They elbow past Carolyn, attentive to her monitor in the news camp.

"Clear out, this is a life saving operation," says Booch importantly.

"You look a little late to me, boys," she says. "Long lunch?"

They glare at her. She shows them that her recorder light is on and smiles. The cops hurry on. She looks over at the wagon they've left parked.

"Great!" she says. "Now they've blocked the shot!"

CHAPTER 5
KERWAC ABSCONDS WITH RAYMOND

At the citi food vault, one of the intruders responsible for the Trilling Bridge attack is clearing out the food stores. He looks around, surprised by the sparse rations.

"Just this?" mutters Kerwac, eyeing the interior of the citi food vault. "Where's the rest?" Kerwac is a tall, muscular, ex-military man in his late forties. He has short bristly silver blond hair, and a keen calculating gaze emanating from friendly grey eyes. After abandoning military life he took up with a village of outcasts and revolutionaries that live outside the biospheres, in the lands depressed by the plague. He and his companions eke out an existence despite the history of the plague. But because of food monopolization, they are forced to steal food from the citis. He thought he would find more food here in the citi vault, but the stores look depleted. Poor bastards, he thinks. He stuffs his pack with hearth subsidies – seed for crops and the vials of chemical additives needed to activate them. He also finds laboratory grade healthy seed.

One sack of corn - real corn - and a sack of beans.

This stuff is gold, thinks Kerwac. It doesn't even need the chemicals! He looks for his exit. He lost radio contact with the others when the second charge blew. The second explosion was not Kerwac's idea. Two blasts buys time, but it's more complicated. Well, they know what they're doing, thinks Kerwac. Stick to the plan. I get home with the seed and additives. They rescue the captives. The dome's open now, so I can theoretically walk out of here in this commotion. But they will seal that hole first and fast.

Kerwac creeps through the dusty fire lit grayness towards the charred gaping hole where a span of the Trilling Bridge used to be. The bridge still has fires burning, but they are smaller now. He feels proud, despite himself. He rounds a corner. To his right he sees a cop wagon. Adrenaline drips into his system. Kerwac reaches for a weapon. Then his adrenaline curdles. He sees that the cab of the wagon is empty.

Cops left it open, Kerwac thinks. Just the ticket! Lucky break!

He creeps low to the machine. No one else is near it. He can see a news team, busy with themselves, closer to the bridge. Beyond them, a police camp bustles. The wagon is covered with rubble and debris. The windshield has a spider web crack running through it. The hood is impaled with an iron bar, twice the thickness of his thumb. He pauses.

This thing looks like hell, Kerwac thinks. Cops could return at any moment. I hope this bar didn't hit the engine.

Still, Kerwac tosses his bundles into the cab. With a decoder from his pack, he activates the wagon. Nice! He revs up and speeds off.

With any luck, he thinks, they'll think I'm a first response unit. If not, well, this beats running. He tries his transmitter again, to hear from the team. "Condor - respond." Nothing. Dead air. Damn.

Kerwac steps on it and races past the recently relocated news camp. Carolyn recognizes the damaged wagon.

"So," she says, unable to see the driver, "those porky pigs found a rescue...Roll camera! Follow that wagon."

Kerwac crosses under an undamaged portion of the bridge and careens around a pylon. He squeals a sharp right turn and fires off east, in a service lane parallel to the bridge. Some section two cops see the wagon speeding by.

"Hey, Blue!" one of the cops hollers at Kerwac.

Kerwac studiously ignores him, racing on.

"What's section three doing on this end? This is our rescue zone."

"Could be a perp."

"More than we already got? We've got to get these in for reclaim."

"Dawgs will get him, then."

"Oh, shut up! Unit Two! Stop that wagon!"

The commander leads, firing immediately at Kerwac's escape vehicle. He is aiming at the driver, hoping to at least hit the fuel cell, or the treads. Another cop gets on the radio to central to report it. "A section three apprehension unit is out of its zone. Please inform."

Near the hole is more rubble. The wagon can handle it, though Kerwac must slow down. The last 25 meters are clear. The blasts knocked most debris farther out. A repair camp converges on the hole. A marching caution ribbon cordons off the repair site and the hole in the citi dome. Blazoned on it in meter high holographic red letters is a warning: *Plague Hazard * Plague Hazard * Plague Hazard.*

Kerwac stands on the accelerator again and dashes through the caution ribbon toward the gaping hole, his escape. Citi repair units, men in white body suits with breathing headdresses, have already laced the enormous hole with pre-sealing grid cable. Repairmen at the edges of the wound in the biosphere's side, some on cranes, begin spraying on sealing foam that will quickly expand and harden into a new, temporary wall.

Kerwac swerves around a crane that is spraying the top portion of the damage, so the sealant will meet in the middle. He clips the crane with his fender, sending the crane driver down like a cat in a falling tree. The crane crashes to the ground. The other workmen, startled and scared, run to tend to their fallen workmate. "Stinking cops!" Hollers the crane driver.

It is a tight squeeze between the pre-sealing cables. Kerwac does not slow down.

Will it fit? Please fit, he hopes. Please fit.

Screeeech. A cable snags on the dawg roost on the passenger side of the wagon, ripping it off. The cable twangs and snaps free of its anchor, tangled in the dismantled roost. Kerwac swerves and corrects. He is through. He speeds into the foggy grey landscape beyond, free of the citi dome, bereft of his team. The massive edifice enclosing Salt Lake Citi rears up behind him like a bald stone mountain. Driving on, the citi gradually falls away, filling the panorama between with fog.

CHAPTER 6
PURSUIT

As soon as Kerwac drives beyond the citi limits, beyond the biosphere, the two dawgs assigned to the wagon he has stolen pursue it for retrieval. They snap to attention. Their lighting changes from emergency red to caution yellow. Their roosts are in danger. They climb and skip over the bridge wreckage making a line to their wagon, running as fast as it drives. At the breach, the dawgs sail by the halted cops and newsies. The characteristic sound of tapping paws and pumping hydraulics fills the air. One of the dawgs stops when it finds its dismantled roost tangled in the pre-sealing cable. The other dawg zips out into the open landscape beyond the citi, hunting for its home.

Raymond – bleary, bound, and battered in the wagon's hold – is still unconscious. He dreams. In the dream, he is being chased. He is running, running, running. He wants to run faster, but his legs are heavy and difficult to lift. He hazards a look over his shoulder and glimpses an eager hunting dog, a sniffing, furry, bloodthirsty animal. It is a real dog with fur and real eyes, not camera eyes. He sees the pink lining of its alert, raised ears. It is not alone. He hears the other dogs yapping, snapping, and baying on his trail. He is running down citi streets looking for an escape, a doorway, a window – anything. He screams.

Kerwac hears a scream. He heard something bumping around back there. He didn't think it could scream. He brakes the wagon, hops out and walks around to the back. Kerwac swings open the paddy wagon door. Raymond is laying face down, the useless stretcher still strapped to his back. The bumpy ride has rolled him over a few times. Raymond is bound hand and foot, loosely tangled in multiplastic netting, like a spider has set him aside for later.

"By the sun..." murmurs Kerwac. "This guy's thrashed."

Kerwac reaches for his knife. Using the stretcher for leverage, he rolls Raymond over. He cuts the netting away from Raymond's face and neck. Raymond's left eye is swollen. He moans and rolls his head from side to side, trying to escape his nightmare.

Kerwac looks at the auburn haired young man, probably in his mid twenties.

"He looks like a kid," Kerwac says quietly, to himself. Kerwac thinks this is a casualty from the blast. He feels a quick pang of guilt, seeing the injuries so close, on a face. Then he realizes, if this kid was netted, the cops chased him. Maybe this is one of our rescue targets, hopes Kerwac. "You poor whelp...How did you wind up in the middle of all that?" Kerwac opens his canteen and gingerly pours a few drops of water over Raymond's parched and bleeding lips. Raymond sputters and opens his eyes. Once he tastes the water, he drinks greedily. Kerwac looks Raymond in the eyes, ensuring contact before speaking.

"Who are you?"

Raymond blinks slowly. "Where am I?"

"About 300 leagues west of the Battle Plateau...just outside of Salt Lake Citi."

"OUTside...wha...," Raymond falls silent. He closes his eyes, but doesn't want to sleep again. His headache is worse, clutching his skull with migrane talons. It's hard to think. It hurts to think. He still senses the slavering dogs just beyond his waking sight. He breathes two shallow breaths. He tries again to speak.

"I was arrested."

"I figured that, kid. Don't you remember anything? What were you doing before you got arrested?"

"Running..."

"Well, you can't be all that bad, if the citi police were after you. Who are you?"

After a pause,"My name is Raymond."

Kerwac stands up. Well, he thinks, Raymond sounds like one of the captives we are after, but inside a citi, a name could be anyone's. Kerwac walks to the hood of the wagon, where the rebar is sticking out. He removes a small, magnesium torch from his pack. With the torch he cuts off the bar above the hood of the wagon. He hefts the severed metal wand. He swings it twice. It'll do, Kerwac thinks.

This guy could be a cop, worries Raymond. Or worse, a psycho. "What are you doing that for?" he asks Kerwac nervously.

Kerwac walks over to Raymond. He stands over Raymond with the charred iron baton.

"Let me go," continues Raymond. "Why aren't you letting me go?" Raymond's voice is high and supplicating, with no command.

"Relax," says Kerwac. "We're probably being chased –"

fwip

A stinger whistles into the dialogue. It sticks with a small thwack into Kerwac's throat.

"There you are..." says Kerwac.

Kerwac pulls the stinger out of his neck and tosses it to the ground. He turns to meet the pursuing dawg, holding the bar horizontally in two hands. He braces for a charge. The dawg lunges. Kerwac whangs the bar right into the vertex of the dawg's mouth. He jams the bar in like a bit cinched torturously tight. The dawg bites down but its jaws are wedged open. Needle tipped incisors extend in its empty mouth, designed to deliver a poisonous bite. Kerwac twists the bar, reaches back and grabs his cutting torch. The dawg swipes at Kerwac's abdomen. Its alloy claw slices through Kerwac's body armor, raking his chest at the base of the sternum. Kerwac bows his body away from the dawg. He fires the cutting torch into the dawg's camera eyes, melting them and driving the flame blade in behind its face. He then purposefully slices across the poorly protected wiring harness on the dawg's throat. Smoke rises from its CPU. The dawg's lighting flickers then goes out. The bot twitches and falls with a clunk into an inert heap, Kerwac's bar in its jaw.

"What happened? What happened?" asks Raymond, who can only hear the commotion.

"I fried it."

"You ruined it!"

Kerwac raises an eyebrow at Raymond. He swings the wagon door closed in Raymond's face.

"Hey! Let me out of here!" comes Raymond's muffled voice from inside the wagon.

Much quieter, thinks Kerwac.

Raymond, frustrated, struggles with his bonds. He tries to kick his legs, to move his hands away from his body. "Aaargh!" he fumes in the paddy wagon.

Kerwac examines the wound on his own abdomen. Three slices in a rising diagonal. The blood, having first receded from shock, now returns to the wound to begin the meticulous process of repair. The cuts flow. He grabs the medkit from the wagon. Kerwac takes off his body armor and his shirt. He splays the bloody body armor on the ground and lies down on it. He blots the wound with a fat gauze pad. When he lifts the soaked gauze pad, a few special layers of skin scaffold fabric peel off and stay with the wound. He grabs the full spectrum skin foam from the medkit and sprays it on the gashes. Kerwac hisses a sharp intake of breath. Lying there, he fumbles for the biggest patch in the medkit. He peels the back off of a large semiliquid adhesive sheet. He lays it taut over the bubbling synthesizing foam. He stands, puts his ripped shirt back on, and finds new body armor in a utility compartment of the wagon. He still hears Raymond's fitful struggles in the paddy wagon.

"I can help you!" implores Raymond. "Please!"

This kid's too much, thinks Kerwac. Kerwac drinks water from his canteen. He climbs into the cab. He revs the wagon and rolls on, east. Eventually, he flips on the intercom monitor in the cab to get a view of Raymond back in the hold. A small light goes on above Raymond. Raymond stops writhing and huffing. Now they can hear each other.

"So, kid, how can you help?"

"When you destroy one, several follow. You should have subdued it!"

"It came for blood, Ray. How do you subdue that?"

"It didn't come for blood. It came to retrieve this wagon."

"That thing's just a dumb bot," says Kerwac.

"Maybe, but it's still a mechanoid with AI capacity. Dumb can be fooled! Please! Let me out of here! I can help! There will be more of them soon!"

Kerwac watches Raymond on the monitor. The kid's irritating, yes, but Kerwac feels no danger from him.

Back at Salt Lake Citi, Lattice, Corp. regional office:

"Mr. Cannes, sir."

"mmYes?"

"This is Simmons, in HR. We've lost an employee in your division."

"Well, then get me another one."

"No, sir. He didn't expire. He left without processing."

Mr. Cannes pauses. A rogue. He may have data. First, the guard leaving his post at the Spire, the bridge attack, and now this. "Which employee?" he asks, guessing the answer.

"Raymond Thurston, sir. Number tr0293jld94."

That program manager we cleared the other day, thinks Cannes. "I see. Patch his ID chip to my terminal. I want to see the tracking blip. Get me the citi police on the line."

"Right away, sir."

At the Salt Lake Citi police headquarters:

"A section 3 first response unit has dismantled both of its security bots. One bot signal lost outside; the other orphaned at the breach. Terrorist suspect."

The commander is on the line with the Lattice, Corp., office: "Consider it done," he confirms. He hangs up, then addresses his command. "Dispatch a pack. Retrieve the wagon. Bring the perpetrator back for reclamation."

"Yes, sir." The dispatcher taps the command into his

console. Below, in the HQ garage, a dozen dawgs light up yellow and file out of the citi through the police port. They emerge outside the biosphere from an underground tunnel. Once outside the dome, the dawgs spread into a chevron and run with quick, full strides after the hijacked police wagon and the suspected terrorist driving it.

The wagon bumps along the landscape and jostles Raymond. The camera light winks at him, indicating Kerwac can see him from the driver's seat. I'm still tied up like an animal, Raymond fumes to himself, and I've got some nut carting me through plague lands to god knows where. And Charmin! That rat faced son of a bitch left me there! Sold me out! "Rrrrg!" Raymond strains against his bonds. The zip ties tighten. He grinds his teeth.

The wagon slows to a stop. Kerwac hops out. Raymond follows the sounds from his dark cell. The wagon door swings open. Dim grey daylight pours into Raymond's cell. He squints up at Kerwac, who is carrying a knife. He holds it where Raymond can see it. Raymond's courage shrinks.

"How do you know all this stuff? About the dawgs," asks Kerwac. Raymond's eyes are on the knife. His mouth is dry. "Speak up, kid."

"I ... was a programmer."

"You were? What are you now?"

"A runaway thief, like you," Raymond parries.

Kerwac smiles briefly. He figures his intuition is right. This is one of the rescues that the rest of his team was after. He slips the knife under the multiplastic netting. He slices away from Raymond's body, cutting the stretcher straps and the netting. Now, only the zip ties on his ankles and wrists restrain Raymond. He sits up and turns toward Kerwac, getting his first good look at him.

Kerwac is older than Raymond, at least 20 years older, by the looks of it, and possibly more, given the good shape he's in. His skin is tanned. He is broader, taller, and more graceful than anyone Raymond ever met in Salt Lake Citi. He could block Raymond out of view in a line up by standing in front of him.

Raymond holds up his bound wrists expectantly, "Now...?"

"Wait—why did the bridge blow off schedule like that?"

"I don't know anything about the bridge," replies Raymond.

A glimmer of comprehension illuminates Kerwac's face. "You mean you lived in that citi? You're not from Appalachia?"

"Appalachia?"

"Do you know Alain? Or Winston? Colin Chris?"

Raymond squints with confusion. "What are those?"

"Oh great!" Kerwac throws his hands into the air. "I nabbed a hapless citizen!"

"I'm not hapless!" Raymond exclaims indignantly. "I robbed a bank! I was trying to escape."

"What'd you nab?"

"A jewel...I think."

"You think? Where is it?"

Raymond feels the same sudden defensiveness he felt in the airshaft with Charmin. He knows the lump in his jacket pocket is the gem, and he doesn't want this guy to have it either. "I don't know," he answers. "It's all kind of fuzzy."

Kerwac thinks about this. He says, "You may yet be one of the people we were looking for. You're about the right age. If you lived there, you were chipped. Taking your chip out will help."

"It sounds like the same language," says Raymond, "but you're speaking gibberish."

Kerwac grabs Raymond's hands, but does not unbind them. He feels around Raymond's wrists. He presses each of Raymond's thumb pads, but feels nothing.

"What are you doing?" demands Raymond. He yanks his hands out of Kerwac's grip. Kerwac, irritated and stronger, grapples Raymond and drags him out of the wagon. He tosses Raymond face down on the real earth. Raymond tries to roll over and resist. Kerwac plants his knee on Raymond's back. He presses around on the back of Raymond's neck.

"Let me go, you sicko!"

"You don't know shit, kid." Kerwac finds what he is looking for, a small dense capsule-shaped bump under Raymond's skin. "Ah! There it is. Hold still."

"What are you doing? Get off me!"

"You're chipped, dope. Now hold still or this will hurt a lot."

Kerwac digs the tip of his knife into the back of Raymond's neck. He quickly makes a short, deep incision under a layer of skin. "Aaa!" hollers Raymond, tensing up. He struggles, but now Kerwac is straddling Raymond, securing him with both knees. Raymond's face is in the dirt. When he inhales he starts coughing. "Hold still!" commands Kerwac, digging into the wound with grabbers from the medkit. Raymond clenches his jaw and grimaces, in a panic.

"Got it!" Kerwac exclaims, finally securing the identity chip in the grabbers. He pulls the chip out of Raymond's neck, cuts his bonds, and stands up off of him.

When Raymond's chip comes out, he suddenly feels unknotted. He rolls over and looks up at Kerwac. His vision blurs, fades back in, and then darkens completely. Raymond suddenly feels sad. He feels a heavy, pitiable loss.

"What have I done?" he says to himself, on the verge of tears.

Raymond holds his open hands in front of his face, but his blinded eyes see nothing. His anxiety disappears in a puff of memory. He sees, in the theater of his mind, a canopy of rustling trees at night. He was almost 15 years old, still running away south on a balmy September night. This was the first time Raymond was ever on his own. He remembers farther back, to the night he fled at his mother's behest from his childhood home, before a deadly attack at dawn. He remembers the urgency in his mother's face and the distinct sense of danger that stirred in his gut. The memory of his mother's face, though her name is still lost to him, fills Raymond with a watery swell of emotions that overwhelm him; a blend of sorrow and nostalgia mixed with the frustration of incomplete recall.

Another flashing memory in a cluster of trees, a windbreak planted by people. Walking slowly, reaching the top of a hill. The breeze picks up, with a whooshing rising chorus in the tree boughs above. He pauses on the apex of the hill and gazes down on a village. Lights twinkle in the valley below. A plume of smoke from a cooking fire trails out of a vent in the roof of a long cabin in the center of the village. He knows it is home, but he questions if he's ever been there. His heart lifts at the thought of familiar people but sinks because he cannot remember their names or faces. This clear hilltop memory stayed alive in the recesses of his mind. The obscured past calls out to him with the promise of fulfillment, but the chip's amnesia devours his memory field.

Kerwac watches Raymond for a moment, intrigued beyond his impulse to act. He's only seen a handful of people immediately after a chip removal.

"Can you hear me?" Kerwac tries to interrupt Raymond's intense train of thought. Raymond draws up his knees and rests his head down upon them. Kerwac presses gauze against the incision at the back of Raymond's neck. "Press that there," he instructs.

Raymond emerges from the memory as if from a dream. Light returns to Raymond's field of vision. He starts, suddenly noticing Kerwac again. No longer blinded, he looks up at Kerwac, pleading in his face. "What have I done?"

"I'm not sure, kid." Kerwac puts a hand on Raymond's shoulder. "Can you hear me?" he speaks louder, assessing Raymond's presence. "Listen, kid. Can you hear me?"

"Don't call me 'kid.'"

"Good. Get up." He shows Raymond the tiny, bloodstained, adamantine transmitter capsule that had been in his body. "You were chipped. Get it?" Kerwac holds the capsule up for Raymond to see. "See these tiny filaments sticking out of each end?"

"Yeah. They look like antennae."

"They're nanotrodes. Like antennae, I guess. This is a neural implant; a tracking device. They are used to bypass your own cerebrum, to alter you with the least amount of surgical memory work." Kerwac tosses the chip into the wagon's holding cell. It tinks against the side like a tooth tossed into an empty pot. "That is why more dawgs will come."

Kerwac hops in the wagon and steers it into a sharp left turn, headed northward. He tosses his pack, his loot, the medkit, body armor for Raymond, and any food out of the wagon, including some vending machine snacks the cops had not opened. He uses the collapsed stretcher and the tattered netting to press the accelerator of the wagon. It coasts forward. He slides out of the driver's seat, hanging on the side of the wagon. Reaching in, he gives the stretcher rig one hard, wedging nudge against the accelerator. The wagon lurches forward, speeding ahead. Kerwac is thrown from the vehicle. He rolls once to break his fall and rights himself onto both feet. The wagon tears off north along the plain, cutting a wake into the tulle fog under the impenetrable cloudy sky. He watches to make sure it keeps going. The fog closes. He walks back to the spot where Raymond sits clutching the bandage on his neck.

"I think you're alright," Kerwac tells Raymond. "Your mind is going to be...unsettled for a while. I don't know how to describe it to you. Just focus on the present, and the past will resurface. Can you walk?" Kerwac extends his hand. Raymond accepts the help up.

"Yeah...sure."

Kerwac looks at his old, weather-beaten compass. It is wavering, which is usual, but it still hovers near north, which is labeled "S" on this old pre-switch compass. He orients them east. "Now we stay this way. Carry what you can."

They begin the march east across the foggy, windswept field. The blustery air feels charged with storm. The ground is parched. Dark gray clouds roil restlessly in the sky above them.

"What's your name?" asks Raymond, hoisting his share of the load.

They look at each other. Kerwack sees Raymond's bruised face, remembering the ride he took in the back of that wagon, imagining what had gotten him arrested. When's the last time he ate? And there he is, tossing on a laden pack, ready for a march. Kid has mettle.

"Kerwac," he replies extending his hand. The two men shake hands. "Good to meet you, Raymond."

"Hello, Kerwac."

CHAPTER 7
THE HALL OF ANCESTORS

In the year 2140, just over a century before Kerwac and Raymond began their trudge across the Battle Plateau, Salvador, Irene, and Xavier were living productive and prosperous lives. The Toscs raised a happy family. Salvador's friendship with Xavier strengthened and tempered as their enterprise grew. Xavier marketed Salvador's inventions worldwide, ensuring their financial security on the world stage and the proper applications of Salvador's technologies. Salvador invented fog catchers and various water redistribution technologies to compensate for the drought caused by the cloudy yet rainless sky. Ever Salvador labored to discover how to break the clouds, and bring rain.

When Salvador was 31, the cloud plague grew into a deeper problem. Salvador's technology was able to insulate humanity from the ecological disasters, allowing the human race to thrive despite the degenerated food stocks, drought, and endless cloud cover. Some attributed it to the long lack of sunlight. Other's blamed the high concentration of genetically modified foods in our diets. Still others said it was because our society had decayed so thoroughly that it had nothing left to do but die. No matter the cause, the depression came.

As sophisticated as technology had become, the one thing people couldn't save themselves from was their own hearts. An epidemic of clinical depression claimed humanity. It kindled simultaneously in the hearts of millions of people and spread faster than a rumor. There was no way to measure the magnitude of the epidemic, because the scientists and demographic researchers we depended upon did not have the will to live, let alone work. Entire households, neighborhoods, and towns shut down. No one went to work, no one spoke, no one had sex – many even stopped eating for they could see no purpose in staying alive. There was a short rise in violent crime, but even the criminals of the world lost their motivation to exploit. Police could not be mobilized because the individuals who worked in law enforcement couldn't bring themselves to even put on their uniforms. Suicides soared for a time, but even the suicidal could not stand to willfully destroy their own bodies. People stopped getting out of bed, even to go to the bathroom. They welcomed death in their sleep from malnutrition, depression, and infected bedsores.

Watching the plague claim humanity broke Salvador's heart. He delved deep inside himself to stay motivated, to work to open up the sky and let the sun shine through. Then Irene fell ill with depression. Whatever Salvador tried, she responded less and less. Months turned into a year, and the year went by. She spent most of her days in bed, unless Salvador took her by the hands and walked her through their garden.

By Irene's bedside sat an aging bouquet of flowers. Salvador entered the room, carrying an arrangement of irises, sunflowers, and peonies. Her skin was drawn. She'd lost so much weight that her ribs shown through her skin. The sight made Salvador feel even closer to her. For the first time in his life he sensed the feeling that their bodies were only vessels, animated by a spirit that endures. She was decaying, just as he himself would decay eventually. Faced with losing her body, the feeling that their spirits were attuned filled him with a somber hope, because the bond between them denied decay. But still, he couldn't wrestle with the thought of living without her. For the first time, Salvador sensed his own fleeting mortality. It was to be the last time Salvador and Irene spoke together.

"Oh, darling," she said, with a plaintive ring of fatigue in her voice. "No more flowers, they're too expensive."

Salvador looked at the bouquet, appreciating the rich coloration, the complimentary affect of the violet and yellow petals. "Don't think about that, honey," he said, replacing the wilted bouquet with his new offering. "They're uplifting. Besides, they're from Xavier."

Irene looked at her husband helplessly. She knew he was coming in to bring her cheer, but she had lost the feel of cheer. She only vaguely remembered that it used to be part of her life. Her anxiety at being estranged from cheer fed her depression. "Yes, it's nice," she agreed feebly, weighed down by wishing her emotions worked. She felt guilty, seeing Salvador's smiling face, tension behind his smile, fueled by his determination to lift her depression. She knew him well enough to understand that he was frustrated, angry despite himself at her emotional distance. She felt like she was failing him by not overcoming her depression, and this depressed her more.

Salvador moved about the room for a while, putting the old flowers out of sight, straightening Irene's sheets, turning on her UV lamp, changing her saline drip. When he could not be sure that she was drinking enough water, he had insisted on the saline drip to keep Irene hydrated despite her diminishing will.

"I can't understand why you keep turning this lamp off."

"It's too bright."

He smoothed her hair, gently stroked her temple, and affectionately tucked an errant lock of her hair behind her ear.

"Germane painted this for you," he said, showing her their son's handiwork, a watercolor of what appeared to be their terrarium, with pollination drones buzzing around the plants. "And the twins have decided they want to make a movie," he added, smiling, "but I think they just like playing with the director's clapboard we gave them."

Though it was a cute image, she did not show any amusement at the prospect of their youngest children fancying themselves filmmakers. She thought of Germane, so absorbed in paints. What is this mind we have brought to bear on the world? Germane, so young yet already with his own independent destiny. Salvador sat at her bedside and took her hand. It felt so light. He knew she was thinking of Germane. "Would you like to take a little walk?" he asked sweetly. "We've got some new plants in the terrarium."

She did not reply. She enjoyed nothing, felt no urge but to stay covered in bed. She grazed her fingers across the back of his hand, a single emotionless caress done for his sake. He was so close, right next to her, his love warm and real, but she felt like she was under cold water, veiled by inertia. Somewhere inside of her she felt a dim, dying spark of desire to squeeze his hand and smile, but it was impossible. The distance that impulse had to travel from her mind, through the torpor of her heart and nervous system to her hand, was insurmountable. Her feelings were not as obedient as Salvador's. Somehow he seemed to withstand the depression. Her affliction had not spread to him.

"I'm so sorry, my love..." she murmured, a tired refrain by now.

"No need for that, baby. Don't be sorry. You've done no wrong."

"I can't lift myself up," she admitted miserably.

"What can I do?" he asked pleadingly.

But she only stared numbly at his hands. Her own hands looked ugly to her, by comparison. She could not answer. Her thoughts could not reach her lips. Save me from the darkness, her thoughts begged, but no words came. Salty tears welled up in her eyes and ran down her stony face. Save me from the darkness, my Salvador. The tears dripped onto his holding hands.

"Let it out," he urged. "Let it out! Fight! Let it out!" He took her in his arms, and held her snug, rocking her gently. "We'll be alright. We'll see through this." In the back of his mind, Salvador hoped that her tears were some kind of release. It was more emotion than she'd shown in weeks. As he squeezed her, she felt frail and cried harder, unconvinced by his rote optimism, the thought never leaving her mind: I can't lift myself up, my love. Save me from the darkness.

She drifted off to sleep in his arms. Salvador laid her down in bed, covered her lovingly, and returned to the company of their children, to tell Germane how much his mother appreciated the painting. Like a candle burnt to a nub, Irene died in her sleep that night, finally breathing her last quiet, sputtering puff.

After her death, Salvador sought quiet contemplation with an engine of grief in his heart. Sometimes he spoke to his children, because he knew they contained congenital experiences of Irene, which he wanted to capture. But eventually, Salvador broke contact with the real world. In turn, Xavier broke Salvador's code and began selling store housed innovations with no contractual obligation on application. Salvador didn't care, he barely noticed. He could only think of Irene's spirit, expired from her body. What happened to that energy which had animated her? Did it survive anywhere in nature? Was there any way to find it? To record her spirit? With every aching pang of misery, he thought deeper and deeper into the woman who was Irene, the pattern of behaviors that constituted Irene in his memory. At least he could think of her.

For the first year, Xavier left him alone, calling it grieving, but seven years later, Salvador was still living isolated with his work, and Irene. Eventually, Salvador's contemplations of Irene translated themselves into inscription, and formulas. The written thoughts, in turn, yearned for material representation, for circuits and nodes, and Salvador followed, alone with the ghost of Irene residing in his memory.

Sequestered away, he began work on a machine called the Hall of Ancestors. Salvador imagined the Hall of Ancestors as a spacious computer catacomb using neural scanning and cybernetic technologies. Salvador worked non-stop to build a machine that could record the synaptic firing patterns of a total human nervous system. If some curious individual wanted to know what happened in an old war, they could ask the record of their veteran great-grandfather, rather than read about him or watch vids. He believed in the preservation of the human spirit through memory, and wanted to contribute to the perfection of that endeavor.

To Salvador, a nervous system scanner was just the beginning. He wanted to eventually commit a living map of a human being to the electromagnetic data field of the Earth, all accessible by computer. It was a long road, and Salvador resigned the rest of his life to this labor. He was motivated by his loss of Irene. The loss was so big it never stopped being frightening, even after the grief softened. Salvador did not let himself live free of Irene. He believed it would be unfaithful to let her go, no matter the hurt. So he worked as hard as he could at something seemingly impossible, to distract himself from the hole in his heart, to fantasize it could be repaired by a machine.

In an effort to save their floundering enterprise, Xavier orchestrated a deal to sell TJ & Tosc to a corporation called Lattice, Inc., headquartered across the Atlantic, on the now privately owned Rock of Gibraltar. Part of the deal was that Xavier would sit on the board at Gibraltar as one of their executors, in perpetuity. Lattice had a plan to rescue humanity from the clutches of the depression epidemic. That plan entailed having full access to Salvador's catalogue of inventions, so they bought it all. Salvador could continue working on the Hall of Ancestors, under the auspices of Lattice, Inc.

The plan from Gibraltar was to build biospheres, citis of the future. By integrating technology from the atomic level right on up to the municipal level, the Gibraltar based Lattice Corporation, with Xavier's aid and Salvador's technology, produced fully contained sustainable citis. By meticulously manipulating matter and idea, they were able to dictate the form of an entirely artificial environment that could produce all of its own fuel and recycle all of its own waste. It was a technological endeavor that Xavier and the rest of the Lattice board traced back to the ancient art of gardening, but on a godly scale. The new citis would have verdant gardens, UV parks, clean streets, blue skies, and starry nights. The technology was available to produce all of these things indoors, with sufficient space.

The biosphere citis had been in the planning stages for some time, but not even Xavier could get Salvador on board to power biospheres with his cybernetic genius. Salvador abhorred the idea of being entirely sealed off from the cycle of true Nature. He wanted to restore the sky, not live under an artificial one. With the death of Irene, and Salvador's consequent personal degeneration, Xavier was able to move the plan forward.

Over the years, construction began on biospheres while Salvador toiled away at the Hall of Ancestors, with Xavier as his only contact with the outside world. By the time Salvador was 41, he had developed something called neural interruption technology. This was the keystone to the neural recording that would make the Hall of Ancestors possible.

Salvador's heart had healed enough that he began to take an interest in the goings on of the world outside his laboratory. When he learned what Xavier was doing in Gibraltar, Salvador resisted the building of the biospheres. He saw them as a cancerous growth of technology entirely isolated from the natural ecosystem. Salvador also learned of some unjust and nefarious side plans built into the biosphere initiative, namely the production of an identity chip based on what Salvador considered a perversion of his Hall of Ancestors dream. The identity chip plan and others were powered by technology that he never would have approved if he weren't so lost in his mourning. But by then it was too late, the big wheel of progress was turning and Salvador was crushed beneath it.

Salvador had threatened to capitalize on his individual worldwide recognition to expose the executors of Gibraltar and their biosphere plan. He tried in his way to sabotage the project, and nearly succeeded. But he was murdered before he emerged from the obscurity of his long mourning for Irene, and the biosphere initiative moved on according to plan. The world bemoaned the loss of one of history's most brilliant scientists and humanists, Salvador Tosc. It was reported that Salvador died alone, finally succumbing to the grief of losing the love of his life.

Of course, as with any epidemic there were survivors. And these survivors were promised salvation inside the biospheres. They could live under a better-than-life sunlit blue sky, designed according to the imagery of the past. They could stargaze at night and watch the constellations rotate through the seasons on the vast underside of the citi's dome. They could walk through flowering gardens and feel the welcome wet sprinkle of rain on their faces from the irrigation systems. Sun, rain, flowers, and stars could all be had again. Food would be nutritious and abundant. Every one would have a job and a place to live. Life expectancy was projected to increase significantly.

People signed up in droves. But biosphere citizenship came with a few caveats. The most significant and most underplayed requirement was the installation of a chip in each new citizen's body. This chip, it was said, would facilitate identification and help in resource distribution. It would act as a cutting edge comm and electronic wallet, so everyone could use the phones for free and no one would have to carry money any more. What's more, every citizen was required to wear one. It was a network technology, said Lattice, and worked optimally when all nodes of the network were activated. There was more to it, of course, but the executors at Gibraltar did not see any need to make that common knowledge.

Salt Lake Citi is part of the biosphere network. It is entirely sustainable. It has enough vegetation to produce breathable air for the population range it was built for. 100% of waste is recycled into parks, gardens, and products for citizens. There are elaborate food production facilities. The only commodity that needs to leave and enter the citis is information, traveling over long-range data pipes like giant computer highways. The data pipes became essential after the cloud plague blocked out any major electromagnetic transmissions over airwaves and satellites.

Ninety-four years after Salvador's murder, the biosphere citis are the mainstay of human civilization. Robotics and automation have improved with the times. The citis have evolved in kind, codifying new standards of human quality of life according to models of corporate expediency. Shortcomings in nutritive needs are met by adding chemicals like vitamins and caffeine to the citi's food. Other chemicals added to the citi's food are more esoteric and secret. Those biochemical solutions, coupled with the neural interruption technology in the identity chips solved many population management problems for the Lattice executors before they even occurred. The identity chip, so harmlessly marketed as an electronic wallet in the early stages of biosphere life, is used to doctor people's emotions and memories to prevent people from sinking back into the depression. It is also used clandestinely to control subversive thought and efficiently manage the population from an administrative level.

CHAPTER 8
OF FOOD AND IDENTITY

At Salt Lake Citi police headquarters:

A cop is on the monitor, watching the blip that is the suspect in the wagon. He's been stopped a while, thinks the cop. The blip kicks back into motion. Only this time it has turned. The cop updates. "Fugitive has turned north."

The pack of dawgs runs in a chevron across the foggy grey and yellow plain, sparsely dotted with scraggy grass and low brush. Responding to the change in the coordinates of Raymond's chip, they sweep to the left, bearing north to cut off the fugitive wagon.

Raymond and Kerwac march for hours, trudging through the grassland, rustling in the squally air. Raymond is tired and slows them down.

"It's been dim for a while. When does it get light out?" asks Raymond.

"It is light out," replies Kerwac.

Raymond looks around him with a worried expression on his face. Kerwac says no more. They walk on. After some time, they come upon an abandoned granary.

"Don't we need a shelter?" asks Raymond, casting his gaze toward the rusty silo.

"We don't need a shelter."

"It might rain," says Raymond, peering at the sky.

Kerwac emits a salty chuckle, "It's not going to rain."

They pass a rusty old silo and the prospects of food and rest pique Raymond's interest.

"There might be food in there."

"No food we can eat."

"Then let's sleep in there."

"We're not sleeping in there."

"Why not?"

"We must go much further today."

They walk on, under a cloudy sky of clay gray. Far and high, dull thunder murmurs across the American plains. Kerwac knows they are about a week east of the Rockies, as a human walks, and moving away from them every minute. He is not quite sure how far north or south they are. It will be dark soon, but they do not need to find a camp yet. There is plenty of ground to cover.

"What is that stuff?" asks Raymond, pointing at a field of tall green plants.

"That's canola...and...that's corn."

"That's corn? Those are HUGE!"

"You've never seen cornstalks?"

"Corn stalks? I eat corn with dinner."

Kerwac raises his eyebrows at Raymond. He strides towards the cornfield. "C'mere. Check this out." Raymond follows. Kerwac places his hand on one of the tall, green plants. "This is corn." Kerwac plucks an ear of corn from a cornstalk at the edge of the field. "This is corn, too. An ear of corn." He pinches the end of the ear of corn and peels back a sheaf of cornhusk. He hands it to Raymond. Raymond peers at the cornhusk, fascinated. He rubs the supple cornsilk hairs between his thumb and forefinger. The soft, attenuated yellow plant hairs seem to glimmer in the graying light.

"Woaw," mumbles Raymond. He reaches up and plucks an

ear of corn off of an adjacent cornstalk and shucks the whole ear himself, playing with the corn silk like tinsel. He runs his fingers along the taut ordered rows of corn embedded in the cob. Smooth soothing compact bumps.

Kerwac looks around. The cornstalks are taller than him and fill their whole field of vision. It grows like grass, but in tall stalks crowded against each other for what seems like miles. "This corn is droid farmed. Except that it's totally artificial, this corn is growing wild. No rows, nothing."

"It's so organized," says Raymond, still inspecting the corn kernels on the ear in his hand. "Is this how we designed them?"

"No," chuckles Kerwac, warmed by Raymond's fascination with the corn. "That is simply how they grow. You can't see what is designed into them."

"Well let's take some! They're fresh! We are going to need food."

"This is not what it seems. Long ago, this was a Monsanto field. Could be anyone's now - whoever fights for it. If anyone harvests this stuff, they probably use it for manufacturing. This is corn that must be chemically bound to other foods to become nutritive. Eating it before it goes to plant is useless. In fact, it drains the body. It will run through your body without getting digested. It will yield no calories of energy, no carbohydrates, no fats or minerals or amino acids. The energy it will take to digest this hollow food will eventually cost your body more than the food gives you. The energy you expend on the digesting process, without yielding any nutrients, makes you even hungrier after you eat. It is locked. Nothing will absorb until this corn is harvested and goes to the treatment plants.

"But," continues Kerwac suddenly acerbic, "it is also versatile. It can be turned into plastic, by just sending it to a different plant. That's the corn you eat, Raymond. We cannot digest these. We should go now."

Raymond bites into the raw corncob and chews with gusto. It's tougher than any corn he can remember eating. Raymond frowns. He makes a face like he is getting used to something that seemed initially unpleasant. Kerwac shakes his head and smiles at his foolish companion. Raymond continues defiantly munching the corn until the cob is stripped. It tastes a little sweeter now. It takes forever to chew. Corn juice runs down the corners of his mouth. If he's right, thinks Raymond, at least I got some water.

They hear a humming in the air. A dark, moving cloud emerges on the horizon.

"Let's go. Run," commands Kerwac.

Raymond's mouth goes slack as he spies the cloud, darker than all the rest. The humming noise gets louder.

"Is that a thundercloud?" asks Raymond.

Kerwac grabs Raymond's arm. "They're locusts, fool! Farming droids! Run!"

The locusts, small insect-like, airborne robots, are each about the size of a football. They have six thin, segmented legs for alighting on plants. They have hollow, tapered, cylindrical bodies that are encased by their wings when stationary. The wings, when active, such as now, spin like helicopter propellers. At the bottom of each droid's cylindrical body, opposite the spinning wings, is a small mechanical mouth with a chemical olfactory sensor to help navigate the cornstalks.

The droids swarm around a central unit, a tractor hive that rolls along the ground. It is a mobile mini-silo and roost for the locust droids. Now close enough, the swarm descends on the cornfield. Each locust lands on a cornstalk. Some hover like hummingbirds over their plant. Using their legs to hold on and dig in, they eat everything that's not green; corn silk, kernels, and cob. They burrow into the ear of corn from the top. The mechanical mouths grind the usable corn product into meal. The green, leftover sheaves of cornhusks spread open like banana peels. Once a locust's container body is full, it zips to the nearby tractor hive to deposit its meal. It then returns to the cornfield to continue feeding. In this manner, the swarm strips the entire field in a matter of minutes. By the time the tractor hive reaches the edge of the current cornfield it is almost time to move on. The mobile mini-silo never needs to stop its slow roll across the plains.

Kerwac and Raymond run as long as they can away from the harvesters in the cornfield. Kerwac is not afraid for his life, but he does not want any droids sniffing out the stolen seed they are carrying. If that gets eaten, he may as well not return home. After a few kilometers, Kerwac slows down; mostly for Raymond's sake, and they watch the locust cloud moving on, north, to the next cornfield. The men continue east.

Night approaches. Kerwac and Raymond set up camp for the evening. Raymond comes back from burying his feces. He sits down gingerly. "Oh mah god...it tickled awful. It was all corn. Hardly any crap at all."

Kerwac laughs. "Hungry?" he asks. He tosses Raymond food from his rations; dried apple, nuts, and some goat jerky. Kerwac tosses more foliage, dry twigs and underbrush on the small emerging campfire. Yellow and orange tongues of flame lick the brush and branches and rise.

"Thanks," says Raymond. They munch in silence for some time, watching the alluring fire dance and waver. They stare into the fire, contemplating it like time travel, glowing and flickering with the same qualities that mesmerized early humans. Now, Raymond and Kerwac, sitting alone in the dark, relying on one of man's most ancient technologies, the campfire, stare into the growing blaze, transfixed and reflective. Raymond tosses a cornhusk into the campfire, watching it curl and burn. He asks Kerwac, "How do you know so much about the cornfields?"

"I was a mech pilot," replies Kerwac.

"Woah."

"It's not so glamorous. I spent a lot of my time in base, in virtual cockpits."

"I said 'woah' because I was a mech programmer."

"Woah."

"I worked on their cybernetic feedback loops."

"Huh?"

"Their learning abilities, basically. Like how they know they're hurt. And how to prioritize damages, or navigate an irregular rocky landscape."

"Whatever you say. They're tanks with arms."

"But they're built with so much more potential!" interrupts Raymond. "Sorry, Kerwac – How did being a mech pilot teach you about corn?"

"I saw things. I ran away."

"AWOL," says Raymond.

"Precisely."

"Why? Why run from a career war job?"

"I didn't run from war, Raymond. No one can. We're all in a war now. I chose my battle."

"But a war mech pilot; what a cushy job. You just drive machines all day. You're playing vids!" Raymond says. He smiles at Kerwac.

Kerwac looks at Raymond like something smells bad. "I guess you could look at it that way. Piloting mechs was only part of my job. We are still warriors. There is still war. There is always war."

"But war is cheap now! The New Geneva Convention gave us humanless warfare. That's what the remote control mechs and the Battle Plateau are for! War is safe. War kills less people than car accidents."

"You don't know shit, kid."

"Modern war kills less people than car accidents! The unarmed are not permitted to engage in warfare," recites Raymond by rote. "Besides, the Waiting Death got most of them."

"You aren't wearing that chip anymore. Can the Pravda. Yes, there was a plague of depression. We did not all die," says Kerwac with disgust. "Most of the people that did not die signed up for biosphere life, thinking the illusion of common purpose, new drugs, fortified food, and UV parks would save them. The biospheres took in, on a false hope, nearly all of the critically and terminally infected. Rather than curing the depression, they enabled it, just keeping the depressed comfortable, securing docile urban working class laborers. The biospheres were a calculated quarantine of the most critically depressed plague survivors."

"No," retorts Raymond automatically. "I've heard this conspiracy theory drek before." His unchipped mind is reordering itself as he argues with Kerwac.

"You worked on the mechs," says Kerwac. "Do you know the ERVs in the citi?"

"Yes, the ambulances."

"In the citi they're ambulances, sure. In the battlefields we use the ERVs on the enemy. In the corps, we use the same vehicles to scoop up villages of undamaged humans in outside lands. Like the corn out here, the people are being harvested."

"Then, who is kidnapping people? The citis?" Raymond is remembering facts he used to think were lies.

"No. The private corporate militaries are kidnapping people, under the guise of prisoners-of-war. I do not know where they end up. That's when I left. I think the POWs get shipped off to citis, to replenish dwindling citi populations. The biospheres are slipping. Citis don't work as well as they claim. Sure, they've minimized the loss of life during wartime. But now wartime is all the time. We've traded large sudden death tolls separated by large spans of time for a smaller, but eternal, death toll taken every single day."

Raymond stares into the primordial fire, calculating Kerwac's point.

"Who do you think wins, Raymond?"

"Death wins."

"Yes. Mine was one of those war jobs and I'm through with it."

Gazing into the warm, crackling, light giving flames, Raymond feels for a strange moment that he is not watching the fire, rather that the fire is watching him. He imagines fire watching all of mankind, ever since the dawn of civilization on to this gloaming twilight of a fading empire.

CHAPTER 9
DAWGFIGHT

The black of night lightens to the lead gray of early morning.

"Rise and shine, tiger!" says Kerwac. "The wagon must be caught by now. They'll know we're still running."

Raymond blinks. He looks up at the heavy, granite sky. An endless undulating blanket of clouds rolls eastward. "Still cloudy," notes Raymond.

"Always cloudy," replies Kerwac. Kerwac is up and ready.

Raymond and Kerwac nibble some nuts and jerky for breakfast. They sip water.

"I'm still so sleepy," marvels Raymond. "I wish we had coffee."

"It's the caffeine withdrawal," says Kerwac. Those citis add caffeine to almost everything you eat. You would be hard pressed to drink enough coffee to match the caffeine intake your body is accustomed to. You were likely on a gram a day."

"The sky looks like yesterday. It's got to rain today."

"It will not rain."

"How are you so sure?"

"It does not rain anymore, Raymond."

Raymond finds this hard to believe. “How do you get water out here, then, with no rain?”

“Conservation, desalination, fog catchers, and various plants.”

“It must rain some time with all those clouds.”

“It hasn’t rained my entire life,” says Kerwac. “The sky has always looked like that.”

“Not always.”

“Oh?”

"Yeah, what about the sun?"

“What about the sun? Have you ever seen the sun?”

“Well...no. But we have the citi UV parks. We don’t need it so much.”

“The UV parks? You might as well use a birthday candle to light a coliseum.”

Breakfast ends. They march. In less than half an hour, Raymond is exhausted. His sedentary life has made him unfit. He craves coffee. His pale cheeks redden with exertion. He huffs and puffs. He hangs his head. He labors under the weight of the pack and parcels.

“Keep it up, cadet!” goads Kerwac.

Raymond grumbles and marches. Kerwac slows the pace a bit, but keeps a scout’s lead. There are more cornfields. They go on and on. The overcast light holds steady for uncounted hours of plodding.

“You can go faster than that, squirt!”

“Shut up!”

“There you go, youngster. Keep your blood raised.”

“Stop calling me that!” Raymond, sweating and hunched, marches faster. His jaw is set. His glistening brow is furrowed. He gains on Kerwac.

“What’s that, sonny?”

Raymond heaves breaths. He throws his achy legs forward faster. He catches up with Kerwac and shoves him.

“Shut up!” exclaims Raymond. “Stop calling me those stupid names!”

The shove stumbles Kerwac a few steps ahead. He rights his balance. He turns around, smiling. “What's wrong, Mr. New Geneva? Your ears can’t take it. You think you’re tired, but you’re just lazy. Now we have to keep marching, kid, or we will die out here, not just get achy.”

❧ ❧ ❧

Thirty-six hours later, they are still marching east.

"Geez...it's like this plain goes on forever," notes Raymond. He is bored of the scenery and still craving coffee.

"It's great, alright."

"Hey Kerwac, what is that?"

Kerwac follows Raymond's gaze. Small dark shapes emerge on the horizon, through the billows of fog, hardly visible, not moving. They walk towards the shapes. Kerwac's eyebrows rise in recognition. "The Battle Plateau!" he cries. He starts jogging forward. Raymond tries to keep up.

"Mechs," says Raymond to himself. He jogs along. He is losing ground to Kerwac. Eventually, the small dark shapes become large dark shapes. Some have wheels, some have treads, some are low to the ground, and some are tall.

They reach the field of robots. Most of the war machines are burnt and mangled, frozen in the last stages of battle with each other. One down, one victorious, as another one took out the victor. Piles of destroyed equipment have been thrown together by other mechanoids to make shields and barriers. The ground is mostly dirt. Any grass left on this grassland is yellowed and smashed flat. With the eerie stillness of a wax museum, the billowing foggy air whirls among the limbs of the giant war machines. Most of them are obviously destroyed. Panels are ripped off. Computer guts are exposed. Chassis are blasted and charred.

Kerwac is examining the mechs. "There's gotta be something we can –HA!" He spies one. Kerwac runs over to an upright mechanoid. "Look! An EMP must've hit here."

"How can you tell?"

"You are just full of questions, aren't you?" Raymond feels like shutting up. Kerwac gazes across the parched field. "There are tanks everywhere but these few are not damaged. Just...down." Kerwac's face lights up. "Lucky break! I've been hoping for something like this! C'mon!"

It is a humanoid mech, standing upright. It has a rotund body and squat, heavy legs. Its long arms end with grappling four-finger hands hanging down past its knee joints. The robot is 7 meters tall, three and a half times taller than

Kerwac. Kerwac walks a circle around the colossus, searching for any sign of the damage that shut it down. Its armor is unscathed. Kerwac is visibly excited. His eyes light up. He claps his hands once and rubs his palms together.

"This thing has been fired by an EMP! No structural damage. By the sun! I've been hoping for an EMP repair! This is our chance. Reformat the memory and it's on! To think, all tanks used to be built on treads, rolling along. Well, we got an ambulator. I think these are better fighters than the rollers. Not quite as fast on the plains, though."

"What about the power supply? Wouldn't the EMP swipe that?"

"This is a 3000 class," explains Kerwac, slapping his open palm onto the robot's shin panel. "These are golden oldies. The power supply is an atomic cell. EMPs cannot affect their atom batteries. Before we use it, we have to remove its tracking system; its whole military uplink." Kerwac begins climbing the robot like a rock wall.

"Wait! Do we have an OS to start it?" asks Raymond from the ground. He cranes his neck to get a view of Kerwac climbing. "Keep the uplink until we download an OS. We can get full functionality."

Kerwac reaches the giant's shoulders and opens a panel at the back of the mechanoid's head. He puts its power online. The mech's console lights illuminate, but much like only turning on the parking lights of a car, it remains inert. Its huge blue lens eyes are still dark.

"Sounds risky. Trackable. But, then again," continues Kerwac, half to himself, remembering life in base, "the chances of anyone on the grid thinking much of an old mech rebooting are pretty low. They may dispatch droids to salvage it." Kerwac activates the uplink. The mech begins downloading its operating system from the shortwave military net. The progress bar reads eleven hours to go. "Hmph! Eleven hours!" Kerwac crosses his arms. They wait, watching.

Back at Salt Lake Citi, office of Mr. Cannes:
"Wagon has been apprehended, sir. No perp aboard."
"What about the tracking chip?"
"Got it right here."

"Hm...a damn trickster. Get the wagon back here for inspection. Keep dawgs after the fugitive."

Back on the Battle Plateau, Kerwac is grumpy. He scratches the bristly whiskers on his chin. "Hmph! Ten hours, forty-five minutes! Those dawgs could show up any minute and we're just sitting here."

Raymond, on the ground at the mech's feet, sits down on Kerwac's pack. He stares between the robot's ankles at the melancholic landscape beyond. The earth has been pounded to a flat hardpan crust by the years of mechanoid warfare and weapons testing.

Another of Raymond's memories surfaces from his recently unfettered mind.

Kerwac calls Raymond out of this reverie. "Raymond! Raymond! Hey kid!"

Raymond winces and looks up at Kerwac on the mech's shoulders. "What?!" Raymond is still thinking of his memory. That was a beach, he thinks. There's no beach in Salt Lake. Ah, that woman! I know her! Who was she?

"You're a programmer," says Kerwac. "This download is still a blip on the military net, no matter how small. Got any ideas?"

"I'm thinking," replies Raymond. He stares out across the plain through arch formed by the robot's legs. The tulle fog swirls and periodically obscures the barren landscape. A project, a project for the hunter dawgs Raymond had worked on. He begins to speak quietly to himself. "I have something...the learning dog." Raymond's idea comes. He speaks louder, "I have something! I wrote a program once! They didn't like it when I showed it to them at work – said it was outside the scope. I just worked on it on my own."

"It'll wake this mech up?"

"Probably."

"What are you waiting for!?"

Raymond unlashes the computer deck from his rucksack. He tosses a loop of data cable up to Kerwac. "Here," Raymond instructs, "jack me into its neck. Cancel that download." He plugs his end of the data cable into the laptop and boots up.

Kerwac cancels the download. He finds the comm panel and removes the uplink. “Fire her up again, and we got ourselves a mech!”

Kerwac stands watch on top of the mech, looking out west for any signs of pursuit. Raymond works. He taps and drums on the deck. He is still in the clothes he wore when he rushed out of the apartment. How long ago was it? Four days? Five days? A week? How long is a day out here? He fishes into his jacket pockets. Now, am I going to have to rewrite this thing from scratch or did I bring my flash drive? His left pocket is empty.

His right hand, in the other pocket, closes on the data gem. Raymond pauses. Memories begin to surface; memories of Charmin and the heist. A dark swirl of avoidance rises up inside him. He does not want to take it out of his pocket. That jewel drive, the safety deposit box heist, whatever happened. He does not want to think about it now. It feels like part of another world. There is no time. Raymond continues to rewrite his pet program from scratch to the deck. He makes some modifications. For the next hour they hear nothing but the rustle of the blustery air and Raymond’s fingers drumming the computer deck.

Kerwac, on his watch, does a double take. He peers into the mist. “How’s it going, Raymond?”

“Close...”

“I hope you are almost done. Something is moving out there.”

“Oh great. Don’t tell me.”

“Um, some things, that is.”

Please enter pet’s name for initialization sequence.

“Close...just gotta name it,” says Raymond. He chews on his lip. He looks up away from the computer.

“They’re coming this way,” warns Kerwac.

“Okay, okay.”

R-O-D-N-E-Y, enters Raymond.

Please confirm pet’s name

R-O-D-N-E-Y, confirms Raymond.

Name accepted

The mech’s powerful blue eyes flash on. All of its systems engage in quick succession. It raises its arms forward. It paws at the air like a zombie about to march. Kerwac, standing lookout on the mech's shoulder, is startled. Instead of stepping forward, it bends over gradually with arms outstretched until its enormous hands touch the ground. As the mech bends, Kerwac maneuvers down and jumps off. It stands at attention on all fours. Though its hands and feet are flat on the ground, because of its long arms, it looks less like a dog and more like a monkey. Raymond stands in front of the robot. It bends its forelegs and brings its face close to him. He places his open palm over the giant luminous blue lens of the mech's right eye.

"Hi Rodney. I am Raymond."

The mech scans Raymond's palm and remembers its first human.

Hi Raymond. I am Rodney, it recites. Even on all fours, the machine is over twice the height of the humans.

Kerwac checks the horizon. He can make out the shapes now. "Dawgs! Raymond, what is this thing?"

"It's a dog." Raymond is smiling, cataloguing a retrieved memory from his obscured childhood. "I've never seen a real dog, so I got into them when I was young. After seeing all those vids and reading all those books as a kid, I wished I had one. I got the idea during a municipal project, upgrades for the citi dawgs, but didn't know why. They canned it at work. Told me to stay inside the scope. So I kept it. Wrote my own pet dog. I just covered the basics so it could use this mechanoid's chassis."

"Look when he chooses to get loquacious!" says Kerwac playfully to himself. He is delighted to suddenly have a weapon, an ace in the hole. The dawgs are now close enough to count. "Hey dog! Blast those bots!" Kerwac barks at the mech.

"Call him by his name. He'll learn better. Besides, he doesn't have guns."

"Yes, he does! Look at those things!"

"Those aren't integrated into the mech. I only gave him a basic OS. No time for gun drivers."

"They won't fire?"

"No."

Kerwac looks disappointed. "Fine," he says, "give me the laptop, I'll drive it."

"You won't have to." Raymond turns to address Rodney directly. "Rodney, defend Raymond. Stop those intruders."

Rodney defend Raymond, confirms the mech. Rodney lurches forward on all fours.

There are 10 hunter dawgs of the original 12 pack running eastward scanning for humans. They pick up minute activity near an ambulatory mechanoid two kilometers ahead. Zeroing in on Raymond and Kerwac, they charge. Rodney strides past Raymond toward the approaching dawgs. The ground near Rodney rumbles. The dawgs' hydraulics are pumping. Their alloy paws leave claw marks in the earth as they run. Rodney closes with the pack of dawgs. The dawgs shoot stingers at Rodney. They bounce off like arrows to a steel wall. He rears up onto his hind legs like a horse. He takes instantaneous aim and slams his forelegs down into the group of charging dawgs, smashing one under each of his massive front hands. The eight remaining dawgs swarm Rodney. They bite, to no avail. They climb his legs. They get onto his back. They are making for his head.

Rodney rears up high again. Instead of slamming his crushing feet to the ground, he lifts his arms high into the air. He falls backward like a felled redwood, crushing another two dawgs under his weight. The four dawgs that scramble free try to get on top of the supine Rodney like Lilliputians on Gulliver. One of them now has a twisted leg. Rodney grabs the damaged dawg off of his abdomen and tosses it into the air. It soars in a high, fast parabolic arc, rising and shrinking into the overcast sky, then cruises back down. The dawg hits the ground with a slam and a tumble. It freezes for a moment, rebooting from the shock. Its crushed front leg is hanging useless.

Kerwac nudges Raymond. "Now's our chance! Knock it over to its lame side. Keep its teeth away from you. Expose its throat." He charges the stalled dawg. Raymond follows. They slam into the dawg's side. The resistance of its weight is jarring. It barely starts tipping over. Kerwac flares his mini torch again. He slices the busted joint of the dawg's shoulder, severing its crushed leg. It falls over onto its face. Kerwac wedges the scrap leg into the dawg's maw, but the dawg is faster. It twists and cranes its neck. Despite Kerwac's effort, the dawg bites Raymond. Only its incisors reach, but that will do.

Raymond cries out in pain. The dawg holds Raymond just above the ankle, below the calf. Its needle teeth extend, piercing Raymond's skin like coffin nails into a loaf of soft cheese. Raymond screams again. The injection begins. Kerwac takes advantage of the dawg's exposed throat and slices through the under protected wiring harness. Too late. Kerwac pries apart the fried dawg's maw enough to free Raymond's leg before the self-destruct begins.

"Raymond! Are you alright?" Kerwac yanks the medkit off their pile.

"Aaa, gawd! I'm bit!" Raymond grips his injured leg. He rocks back and forth in the dirt. He is taking shallow, hissing breaths.

Rodney destroys the last of the dawgs. Their remains smoulder on the ground.

Kerwac swabs the puncture wounds in Raymond's leg with neutralizer. Most of the stuff is already in Raymond's blood, figures Kerwac, but he does it anyway.

"Ow!"

"Keep breathing! Hold still. I'm going to give you a shot."

"Not another one!"

"This is different!" There isn't much to do, thinks Kerwac. The bite has been taken. Kerwac injects a full spectrum mega-vitamin into Raymond; into the thigh above the bite. "This will bolster your immune system for a while...Let's hope it's enough." Kerwac bandages Raymond's leg and stands him up. "Can you walk?" Raymond limps forward a step, leaning heavily on Kerwac.

Rodney hunkers down near Raymond. The potent light of his blue lens eyes dims. He bends his forelegs to get closer to Raymond.

Rodney failed. Master injured.

"Good boy, Rodney," Raymond replies. "You did good, Rodney. That's a good boy." Rodney's lighting brightens. He stands up tall again on all fours. "Help us, Rodney. I need you to carry us." Rodney lowers again. He stands still, awaiting instructions. Kerwac secures their packs, loot, computer, and medkit onto Rodney's back. Kerwac and Raymond laboriously climb up onto Rodney. Raymond sits on their gear and props his leg up. "Take us east, Rodney," commands Raymond.

Rodney turns due east and sets out. “That’s a good boy,” says Raymond between drawn breaths. Raymond and Kerwac rock back and forth on top of their ride. Rodney takes long, hulking, 4-legged strides, a colossal robotic gorilla traversing the blasted American plain.

CHAPTER 10
RAYMOND'S FEVER, CHARMIN'S EMPLOYER

"Kerwac...I don't feel so good."

"You're bit. It'll get worse before it gets better. Sit tight, Ray. We need a few days. At this rate we should be there in a few days. This is a lot faster."

Faster, replies Rodney. He speeds up. The rocking intensifies. Up by Rodney's shoulders, at the opposite end of the long strides, they hold on, wedged against their packs, and get used to it.

"Where are we going?" asks Raymond. A tiny shiver runs through Raymond's body. He feels a cold like iron in his limbs. A thought, unbidden, floats to the surface of his consciousness: This is fever.

Kerwac is silent for a moment. The sky is darkening again. Rodney's eyes cast blue beams of light that cut into the ashy gloaming. He follows Rodney's trajectory with his own eyes. He peers eastward towards the interminable gray horizon. "Home," he finally replies. "We're going home."

Kerwac convinces Raymond to work, though he is unwell. He boots up the computer deck and places it next to Raymond. "Rodney is quite a charm, but we're going to need his weapons. I need you to write those gun drivers, Raymond. When those dawgs don't return home..."

"Yea...Yeah...you're right," Raymond concurs weakly. Another shiver rattles his body. His teeth chatter. Raymond hugs himself. He is achy. "I feel so sick."

"I need you to do this. I need your help, Raymond."

Help Raymond, insists Rodney. His eyelights shine ahead. Raymond heaves the little computer deck onto his lap, sneezes, and begins working. The work goes slower as Raymond gets sicker. Raymond wraps the medkit's reflective emergency blanket around his shoulders in a vain attempt to keep warm. By the end of the day, he can no longer work. His teeth chatter from the initial chill of his fever. His throat is sore and his glands are swollen. It hurts his parched throat terribly to swallow. His muscles are permeated with a dull ache.

"How are you doing, Raymond?"

"Cold...cold..." Raymond lies as still as Rodney's lumbering gait will allow. He hugs the blanket around himself. Late that night, before passing out on the still ground, Raymond instructs Kerwac to upload the newly scripted weapons drivers from the deck to Rodney's onboard system.

Rodney armed

By the morning of the next day Raymond's fever is full blown. He can barely stand the heat. He casts off his blanket. He fumbles with the straps of his body armor. "Too hot...too hot..."

Kerwac recovers Raymond. "Hang in there, Ray. Stay insulated." He knows Raymond needs to sweat out the fever, but he does not have enough water to keep Raymond hydrated. It doesn't look good. Two days left of fever sweating before we reach home and we're sharing one water ration. Kerwac fishes around in his pack and finds a vial of a sticky elixir. He puts the bitter brew to Raymond's lips. "Here, drink this. We're almost out of water. This will slow your metabolism so we can reach the settlements." Raymond sputters and spits, but eventually drinks the medicine.

❦ ❦ ❦

Back at Salt Lake Citi:

Charmin's comm rings. Checking, he sees that it is his employer, Mr. Z. Before Charmin lived in Salt Lake, before even his outside life in settlements, he was a military man; a good one, at that. He worked black ops for a mercenary company that did Mideast and Asian contracts for Lattice Bioworks. He had an excellent record. Several years back, because of this excellent record, Charmin was tapped for true private work. A client by the name of Mr. Z needed his own personal operative, and Charmin fit the bill. Though Mr. Z does not reveal his identity to Charmin, the pay is staggering. Charmin is given full command of his missions, he never has to wear an identity chip, and Mr. Z's resources seem inexhaustible. Charmin took the job, no questions asked.

Charmin enjoyed living in citis unchipped; real prime work. He had access to state of the art military industrial technology that none of the chipped citizens even knew existed. He was immune to surveillance. Long ago, working here in Salt Lake, Charmin learned about a unique, advanced generation optical processor. Plugged into the right equipment, this jewel could outrun any computer in the world. That was about the time, almost 5 years ago now, that Mr. Z relocated Charmin to an outsider settlement in the Appalachian mountain range to keep an eye on young Raymond Tosc. "I want monthly reports on the kid," Mr. Z had said. After five years in Appalachia, Mr. Z instructed Charmin to recruit Raymond to steal the jewel back in Salt Lake Citi. For the most part miserable work, but he met Noriko out there.

It took years to fit into that settlement, befriending the teenage Raymond, who was a genius at codes and programs, and then longer to groom Raymond for a raid on the citi, to steal the data jewel that Mr. Z had located. During those years, Charmin's heart raced ever towards beautiful Noriko. All the while, she only had eyes for Raymond.

Then Raymond got caught on his first attempted data jewel heist, four years ago. For the last four years, Charmin has stayed in Salt Lake Citi, baby-sitting chipped, amnesiac

Raymond until he could be persuaded, coaxed and convinced to rewrite the bank hack software and go on another raid for the jewel. Raymond had the coding skill for the job. Z paid a lot of money to make sure that Raymond performed the jewel heist. "It must be Raymond," commanded Mr. Z.

Charmin's comm keeps ringing. He is not looking forward to answering this call, since he dumped Raymond. He still has to finish that data jewel job which Raymond botched. Security is so high right now, though, that it is a real thorn in his side. No matter, Mr. Z always seems to find clearance for his man Charmin. In fact, he was hoping to leave Salt Lake for another citi. Maybe this is that call. Charmin flips on his comm.

"Hello, boss."

"I expected to hear from you sooner, Charmin."

"Just tying up some loose ends."

"Like failing your mission?"

Charmin flushes beet red. "No, sir. I just lost our operative. He never got the prize. I am going back for it myself."

"Too late. The prize has left Salt Lake. Did you make sure our operative took a neuralizer?"

"I think so, sir. He seemed really out of it when I saw him. He couldn't remember what happened. I don't understand why you insisted on sending Ray in again. He's a great coder, but he's a novice."

"If I want your opinion," replies Mr. Z, "I'll give you one."

Charmin clenches his jaw.

"He couldn't remember, you say," notes Mr. Z, "Hmm. Couldn't remember what?"

"The heist, any of it. Said he was sleeping. He thought we hadn't done the job yet. Weird. He was captured."

"Captured? I'm thoroughly disappointed, Charmin."

"He was addled, slowing me down. He would have gotten us both arrested."

"No matter. And you are not certain he took a neuralizer. What do I pay you for?"

"No, sir. But by the way he was acting, I'd say it was very likely he took one."

"Double whammy, Charmin. I should have stuck with your predecessor. Consider it an unpaid training exercise."

Angered by this treatment, Charmin not for the first time entertains the idea of quitting, letting this shady, voice-disguised benefactor do his own dirty work. Quitting would be difficult. It would have to be done secretly and Charmin would have to be able to get beyond Mr. Z's reach. Charmin was not sure he could elude Mr. Z. Besides, the pay was unbeatable. He threatened to quit once, years before. Mr. Z calmly informed Charmin that Charmin would work for him until the end. Unless, that is, Charmin preferred to be swiped, chipped, and dropped into a citi doing some mindless task or another for the next few decades. For now, Charmin winces at his ignominious loss of pay, responding, "Of course, Z. Where to next, then?"

Mr. Z continues, "Return immediately to your Appalachian post and await instructions. A fresh port clearance will arrive shortly." Mr. Z signs off. Charmin is left alone with the blank comm.

"Fuck," he says, "back to Appalachia." Charmin hates living outside the citis; the crappy beds, pissing in jars, drinking from desalinators and fog catchers, living off dry rations and goat. At least I will get to see Noriko again, he thinks. He misses Noriko, her fine face and stout character. Because Noriko had never been chipped, Charmin believed she was special, better. And now that there is no one between them, who knows...

CHAPTER 11
HOMECOMING

The jewel in Raymond's pocket recognizes their kinship and reaches into his dreams.

Raymond dreamt as his fever burnt on, incubating the currents of his mind into images of otherworldly vividness. Raymond was floating calm and invisible in a darkness like outer space. A face extended in smooth, beautiful parsecs far beyond his sight. The face seemed to curve. It curved onto itself into a smooth massive planet.

"You are a Tosc," the face said.

"Raymond! Raymond! Wake up! C'mon, Raymond." Kerwac gently shakes Raymond. "You're holding your breath. Raymond, breathe! There, that's better."

Rodney moves along, as fast as he can go without bucking his passengers. During the dim silence of morning, they cross the wide, dry Mississippi River, through what used to be Cairo, Illinois. Kerwac recognizes Cairo by reading the highway markers on an old bridge, Interstate 57. Though there is no need for a bridge now. Riding Rodney across the parched riverbed, crushing the dry grass, they watch the desiccated delta. The blue lamplight of Rodney's eyes flits over remnants of old porches and dilapidated river houses. Kerwac sees a group of people, maybe squatters, maybe a band of travelers passing through, maybe knuckleheads kicked out of their settlement looking for trouble, sitting out on the porches of two adjacent houses. When they hear the rumbling tread of Rondey's stride, they scatter and duck into different seemingly abandoned shelters. Kerwac does not want to learn the intentions of these wayfarers. He is glad they were rightfully afraid of Rodney, thinking the mechanoid was a member of citi forces. Earlier this morning, two naps ago, Kerwac interrupted Raymond's delirium to give him a drink. That was the end of the water. Kerwac is staring beyond the path Rodney's azure eyebeams cut into the graylit countryside.

We should be close by now, Kerwac thinks. He sees a range of large, dark humps near the horizon. The hills! We are close, he thinks. We're going to make it. Kerwac deeply exhales a long held breath of his own. "Hang in there, Ray!" Raymond is oblivious to Kerwac. Kerwac still speaks to him. "We're almost there, kid. We'll get you all taken care of." Kerwac studies the hills. He looks for two stacked rock formations that mark a passage through the foothills and peaks at the southern end of the Appalachian ridge. Nestled in those foothills, on the ocean side, is Kerwac's home. He finds the columns, two stacked pillars of stone that mark a path over the hills. He stands, beaming at the familiarity, and directs Rodney toward the columns.

"Gimmie the bow."

"You can't even string this bow."

"Yes, I can!" replies the younger boy indignantly.

"Zane, Bleeker – shut up," says Ora. "There's something out there."

Ora points west from their vantage point on Lookout Rock. The two younger hunters follow Ora's direction. Ora does not come on hunts as often anymore, since she began studying medicine with Noriko, so the young boys are exceptionally attentive to her because they have missed her in their woodland play.

"It looks like a gorilla," says Bleeker, the youngest. He is a little too young to be on a hunt, but they were only looking for rabbits before Ora found this visitor.

"It moves like a robot," notes Zane.

"It's a mech," confirms Ora, peering into the distance. "Maybe come to collect folk."

"We've got to warn everyone!" says Zane.

"Yes, but there's no time. Look at it." Ora says this calmly, instructively. She does not betray the same sense of urgency as Zane, though this is serious. She is clearly speaking more directly to Zane than to Bleeker, though both boys are listening. Ora does this partially because Zane is her little brother, but also because he is old enough to learn strategy, while Bleeker is just along to become acculturated to hunts. With Sam and Cyrus off actually catching rabbits, Ora seized the opportunity to take the younger hunters on a field trip to Lookout Rock. Ordinarily Ora would not do such a seemingly indulgent thing when they should be out hunting for the plow teams' dinners. But Ora had to go to Lookout Rock today, her intuition insisted.

"It's moving fast," notes Zane. "It will reach the village before we do."

"Yes," confirms Ora.

"What do we do?" asks Bleeker.

"We stop it," Ora answers.

Ora has a coil of thin, shining rope slung diagonally across her shoulder like a bandoleer. It is a fine silvery rope, hardly the thickness of her finger. The outside of the rope is a synthetic insular sheaf. The inner weave of the rope is metal. Thousands of conductive filaments of metal are coiled together inside the sheath. The rope is as strong as bridge cable, yet weighs barely more than old jute rope. If used properly the rope carries a charge. She grabs this rope now and speaks to her companions, focusing mostly on Zane.

"This rope touched end-to-end and charged will disperse an electromagnetic pulse," explains Ora. "The EMP will stop that thing dead. I'll go set this lasso for the mech. Zane, you and Bleeker hurry back to town for help."

"Please, let me set the lasso, Ora!" Zane requested. Ora looks at her little 12-year-old brother, still seeing the small child in his face. Ora sighs with wistful affection to see how fast Zane has changed in the last year. Zane wants to be grown up so fervently, she thinks, he might just get there sooner than he expects. Ora has a hard time denying her little brother anything, which Zane takes advantage of as often as possible.

"Okay, Zane you stay, I'll show you how to use the lasso –"

"I know how to use it," Zane assures her, hoping she'll be surprised.

"– and Bleeker," Ora continues, "you run and warn everyone, tell them to come to the columns! Find Sam and Cyrus if you can, but don't slow down!"

Bleeker is delighted to have this mission to himself and it shows clearly on his face. His eyes widen a little and he stands up straight.

"O-kay!" crows Bleeker enthusiastically, and runs off at full speed toward the village, calling for Sam and Cyrus along the way.

Down at the columns, a short while later:

Bleeker finds Sam and Cyrus first. When he tells them a mech is coming they bolt straight to the columns to get a better look. They arrive just as Zane is laying the EMP trap. Huffing with excitement and purpose, Bleeker continues on toward the village.

"It's definitely coming towards us now," confirms Cyrus. He is on watch, perched on the foothill side of the northern column, hidden from the approaching intruder's sight. Everyone can feel the ground shaking now, as it walks.

"Looks a few beats away," says Sam, from atop the southern column.

Zane already laid the metallic rope in a rough circle between the columns, touching its ends together. The rope is wired to a button remote that discharges the rope's capacitor. It is essentially like firing a camera's flash bulb, but the "flash" is an invisible electromagnetic wave that can disable any electronic device and erase its memory. A correctly fired EMP will shut down all electronic functions it comes in contact with.

"Then you two better get away," Zane calls up to Sam and Cyrus. "Don't let it see you. I'll man the trap." Sam and Cyrus climb down and disappear before the mech gets close enough to read their heat signatures.

They wait. Eventually, the huge mech slows down for the passage through the hills. It passes between the columns at a slow glide. Zane hears the gears and joints of the dusty robot creaking as its heavy footfalls shake the ground beneath his feet.

“Now!” Zane punches the button that fires the lasso.

The electromagnetic pulse freezes Rodney in mid stride. All of his systems shut down immediately. It is as if all four of his limbs are suddenly held in place. Rodney’s blue eyes extinguish. He is suddenly as inert as Kerwac and Raymond found him. On Rodney’s back, the sudden stop tosses Kerwac forward onto Raymond. The packs flanking Raymond are jostled. One rolls off of Rodney and sails to the ground below. The kids leap from their hiding places. Ora, still at her spot on Lookout Rock, smiles. From her vantage point, she sees who and what are on top of the hunched mech. By the sun, she thinks gratefully, he’s back! She hurries her way down to the columns. The rest of her hunting party is already down there.

“Ha Ha!” calls Sam.

“YES!” cries Zane, jumping for joy, his fist in the air.

“We got ‘im!” says Cyrus.

The youths rejoice at the feet of their quarry.

“Who’s pack is this?” notices Cyrus. “Hey! Someone’s up there!”

“Cyrus?” says Kerwac, peering down over Rodney's shoulder.

“Kerwac?”

“What the-?”

“It’s Kerwac! Kerwac’s home! They’re home!”

The children become frantic with celebration. Kerwac is like an uncle to them. He left weeks ago on a seed and rescue mission and the whole settlement has been waiting for the return of the party. The plowing had begun today; Kerwac was overdue. The reason Ora was on Lookout Rock at all was because her intuition insisted there was something to see. She did not have the affront to think her intuition accurately predicted Kerwac’s return, but her heart hoped it would be him. She knew they’d need medical attention so Ora hurried down to join the hunting party and see Kerwac.

“Kerwac!” They begin climbing up Rodney’s still legs to see their Kerwac.

"No! Stop! There's someone with flu up here. Stay down there!"

"Who's got flu?" asks Sam. "Where is everyone else?"

Kerwac went on his mission to Salt Lake Citi with a team of three companions. All but himself were lost in the citi, though he came away from there with Raymond. If his fellows were not captured outright, they would be singled out in the citi soon enough for not wearing chips. Then it is only a matter of time before they are assimilated, like Raymond had been. Kerwac swallows hard. He has not thought of his team since losing them in Salt Lake Citi. He had been on the run ever since. Kerwac feels a sinking sensation, he feels suddenly tapped out and tired. Knowing he is so close to home makes him begin to rest prematurely and, right there on Rodney's back, he begins to slip into reflection, to remember himself and hurt for his lost friends and feel sorrow for not serving them better, for losing them.

"Kerwac?" asks Sam again.

"Raymond has flu," says Kerwac, trying to ignore her second question because it is all he could think about.

"Raymond?" asks Sam in disbelief. "You mean RAYMOND Raymond?"

"Raymond...Raymond..." mutters Zane. A glimmer of comprehension illuminates Zane's face, memories of a childhood that was not yet far away.

"I'll explain everything later. For now, do not come up. Go home and get help."

Sam and Zane look at each other. They look back at Kerwac. "Yes, sir!" they exclaim in unison. They take off towards the fields.

"Grab the Doc! Bring Noriko." Kerwac calls after them.

"Yes, sir! Noriko!" they reply from a running distance.

Ora arrives from Lookout Rock.

"Look, Ora!" says Cyrus. "It's Kerwac!"

"Isn't it grand?" says Ora, barely able to contain her smile. She unslings her belt pouches and begins to unpack the medicine inside.

In the foggy late morning, some distance away, small groups of people till fields near the foothills of a mountain. The water is ready now. There is no seed yet. Nevertheless, everyone has decided to begin work today, in faith of the absent team's return. They may be late, everyone agreed, but the plan is good. We will plow. They will come.

In this field, two men are laboring over a plow, slowly carving shallow trenches into the earth. An adorable cinnamon colored mutt attends them. The dog runs circles around the men, trying to help. She sniffs the freshly turned earth behind the plow. She digs her own little holes. The shorter of the two men, who is also younger, stops to dry his perspiring brow. He catches his sweat in a small flask, by drawing the rim of the open flask across his brow and temples. He pets the excited dog.

"Good girl, Gracie," he says, scratching her behind the ear. Gracie wags her tail happily. The taller, older man takes this opportunity to lean on the plow and take a short rest. The young man turns his attention from Gracie to his plowing companion.

"Alain, where are the kids this morning?" asks the young man.

"Out hunting, I'll wager," replies Alain.

"Who's with them?"

"I don't know, Colin Chris. Probably Ora. See who's not around."

Colin Chris stows the sweat flask, to empty it into the desalinator later. He grabs the plow again. "I wish those kids would stick around and help," he comments.

Zane and Sam burst out of the woods, running across the field toward Alain and Colin Chris. The kids are running at full speed, waving their arms to get the adults' attention.

"Kerwac!" they keep yelling excitedly, "Kerwac's back!"

By the time the doc, Ora's teacher, arrives, Ora has already replaced Kerwac and Raymond's bandages. She has also given Raymond a fever suppressant. Ora hands the detailed care over to Noriko, her instructor. Noriko is trembling with excitement and handling Raymond with utmost attention. He went unconscious after Zane zapped Rodney and stayed that way through the commotion of transporting him to the infirmary. The town is abuzz. Nearly half of the thirty-two person settlement drops what they are doing and rushes out to help. Most watch. They marvel at Kerwac's new toy; at riding a mech home.

"Thank that kid," says Kerwac about Raymond. "I wouldn't have made it without him."

"It's Ray!" marvels Alain. "God, what's happened to him?"

"Where is everyone else?" asks Winston.

"I'll tell it once, in the long hall," replies Kerwac.

Kerwac calls a gathering in the long hall. Twenty of the settlement's thirty-two residents attend. Everyone wants to know, but is afraid to ask – did you get any food? He reports the results of his mission and the details of his escape. Wails of sorrow rise up from the group.

"Ray rescued, with flu!"

"Three men lost!"

"Lost! Lost!"

"Less than half the amount of expected seed!" says Alain, the father of Ora and Zane.

"We must decide what to do," adds Townsend, Bleeker's father. We will reconvene after a memorial fair for our beloved lost. Let Raymond heal. Then all may be decided with cool heads and complete facts."

They take great care of Raymond. He is washed in fresh water, waste or not, as honor for delivering the seed. His clothes are changed. His old things are saved untouched. He is treated with medicines – poison neutralizer, herbs, roots, and aspirin made from the area willow bark. Raymond finally opens his eyes. He emerges from his stupor soaked in sweat. His dawg bite is patched. Two women are by his bed. The older woman addresses the younger one.

"Thanks for your help, Ora. I'll take it from here." Ora nods. She gets up quietly and walks out. The other woman, the doc, pads his forehead with a damp towel. She smiles at Raymond. She has a delightful face with attentive brown eyes. Her eyes are set wide, accentuating the elegant bridge of her nose. He looks at her and feels calm.

"You've got a smile that breaks chains," he says weakly, vaguely recalling her face from the depths of his gradually returning memory, a memory of a beach at night that flickered through his mind back on the Battle Plateau before he figured out how to activate Rodney. But who? He does not know her name. Disoriented, Raymond closes his eyes again and sinks back into his pillow.

She smiles, barely able to contain herself. She kisses Raymond on the forehead and squeezes his hand. “You’re up! Thirsty?” She hands him a mug of cool water. He gulps all the water down. She refills the mug. He drains it again. “You should be, honey. We changed your clothes three times from the sweat.”

“Hungry,” he mutters.

“Good. I hoped you’d be. It means you are getting well. The caffeine and supplement withdrawal will take more time, but you are looking better.” She gives Raymond a bowl of boiled potatoes, salted and softened with a fork. Raymond eats slowly. He is unaccustomed to his motions, after days in fever. She watches Raymond intently while he eats.

Kerwac told Noriko that Raymond had been chipped. He showed her the cut at the back of Raymond’s neck from the chip removal. Noriko knows there is no telling what state Raymond’s memory is in. For this reason she restrains herself as best she can from flinging her arms around Raymond and smothering him with kisses. She has patched all his wounds. She pats down some of Raymond’s damp, bed tousled auburn hair. Oh Ray, she thinks, such riverbed brown eyes and handsome, raised cheekbones. He leans forward when Noriko touches him, enjoying her warmth, as a plant turning toward sunlight.

“Where’s Kerwac?” asks Raymond. “Is he alright?”

She smiles tensely, like she is waiting for something. “He is waiting to speak with you.”

“Where am I?” he asks.

She looks around. “The infirmary. Don’t you remember?”

“No.” replies Raymond. “Was I awake earlier?”

Judging by her facial expression, he is sorry to give her that answer.

“I guess you could say that,” Noriko answers, crestfallen.

“What do you mean?” asks Raymond, sorry to see her look so disappointed. He wishes he could do something about it.

“Nothing, you’ll find out soon enough,” replies Noriko, conjuring up a radiant smile. If he does not remember my name, she thinks, I must not force it, not so soon. “For now, you must rest. To answer your earlier question, we are somewhere near old Georgia, in the shadow of the Appalachians."

"Still outside?" he asks. His eyes widen.

"Yes, of course." Her answers sound more automatic.

"Wow. How many people live here?"

"There are eleven houses in our settlement, totaling thirty-two people, including Old Michael down by the seashore. Well, thirty-three now."

"Old Michael?"

"The oldest one here."

"How do you survive out here?"

"We take care of each other."

Noriko looks at him sympathetically. She smiles and reaches out to touch his cheek. "You still think like you're in the citi," she says quietly. Her happiness is pleading for release, but as she looks at Raymond she thinks perhaps they did more to his memory than can be healed. Perhaps he no longer knows her.

She smiles, nuzzling into his gaze, searching Raymond's face for all of the things she spent years missing about him. His eyes follow the reach of her slender arms. She rests her precise, caressing hands palm up in her lap, in a gesture of openness and anticipation. All of the minutiae of Noriko's movements, the lilt in her voice, her evident comfort around him, condense on Raymond's heart out of the mist of his amnesia.

"I know you ..." Raymond says. He feels a rush of sympathy for Noriko, like he has known her for years. He feels the complete and instantaneous compassion that outdwellers recognize as love. "The beach ... the bonfire ... we kissed ..."

"Which time?" Noriko asks playfully, her eyes glistening with tears of joy; joy for seeing her Raymond again, and tears for the time they have lost. She throws her arms around him. "Oh Raymond! I missed you! I missed you to the sun and back; oh my darling!"

"Noriko...Noriko!"

Raymond holds Noriko, filled with pleasure and disbelief. He pauses, looking at the roundness of her chin. He notices the subtle shades of color in the strands of her hair, deep honey blondes softening the tree bark browns. He tries, he tries hard to remember more of that night at the bonfire, that ephemeral scrap of memory. He tries to remember what happened after they eventually got up and walked back to join the bonfire party, for they surely must have. But that secluded kiss, on the beach that night, with a bonfire in the distance, a bonfire surrounded by friends, was the only moment he could recall. In that instant, that diamond flash in his memory, he and Noriko remained suspended, breathing in the scent of each other's breath, which they had come to know as home. That kiss had worked like language, for he understood her better because of it.

And now as he holds her, his nose buried in her hair, the smell of her is the same. The same as on the beach in the memory, and his heart floods with the memory of love. For all the things he could not remember, this love remains. They hold each other apart to take a good look. The years had changed them, inevitably. Raymond notices the few fine traceries that are only beginning to form on Noriko's face, subtle memory marks creased into her countenance by the laughter they had shared and the tears she had cried for him.

"How long has it been?" asks Raymond.

"I don't care." says Noriko with glee, not inclined to stop and count years. "You're back! Baby, you're back!" She hugs Raymond again and cries joyous tears of relief, with the galvanizing charge of seeing her living Raymond's expressions again, smiling again, with love for her in his face.

Raymond says nothing. He is elated to see this woman of his dreams, to remember something of his life before Salt Lake Citi. Yet he cannot confess to her that he remembers only a single moment with her, at a bonfire. It seems a meaningless distinction now. Even if he had never met her before, he would still love her. An atomic mote of her spirit had survived, glowing inside his heart, during his chipped exile in the heartless efficiency of the citi. And now with the sight of her, the touch of her, the swan octave waver in her voice as she cried with joy, it kindled inside him. They kiss, and he remembers every contour of her mouth. Though his past is pockmarked with voids of recall, this memory of Noriko has endured, reemerging sweet and splendid. As he draws back from the kiss, his face splits into an exalted smile. He is reunited with his love.

PART II:
THE TURNING TIDE

CHAPTER 12
RAYMOND AND KERWAC IN APPALACHIA

Kerwac visits Raymond, in bed at the infirmary.

"That was a hot one. Welcome back, kid."

Raymond flips off Kerwac with raised eyebrows and a patronizing smile, for calling him 'kid' again. Kerwac laughs.

"How are you feeling?" Kerwac asks.

"Like a husk of that corn," answers Raymond. They grin, sharing the memory of the locust droid swarm, pleasant now by virtue of being past.

"People here are curious about you," continues Kerwac.

Raymond sits up. Kerwac places a hand on his shoulder. "Not now. Rest well. Eat up."

"I've had a lot of rest," insists Raymond. Raymond stands up, then swoons. He balances against Kerwac, breathing deeply, a film of sweat beading on his forehead.

"Better yet," says Kerwac, wryly, "have a look around."

"Wait," says Noriko, "Put some dry clothes on." She stops Raymond at the door with a bundle of clothes. The fabric is supple, but durable. He tugs the shirt.

"Is this denim?" he asks.

"It's a bamboo and hemp fiber blend," replies Noriko. "We grow and weave it here."

"Thank you, Noriko," he says, looking into her eyes, smiling.

Dressed in his new attire, Raymond meets Kerwac out in front of the infirmary.

"How about a walk?" asks Kerwac.

"I could use a walk."

The tree leaves rustle in the wind. The trees look so old and tired, compared to the trees in the citi UV parks. The air is heavy and humid. At the end of the short lane, they walk a wide path that leads through the town toward the east. Scraggly high, yellowed grass, a sight all too common on Raymond's march with Kerwac, lines the banks of the lane. The tinny sound of hammering echoes off the foothills. They pass a group of people decorating onion paper lanterns. They nod and smile in exchanged salutation, welcoming Kerwac home, and greeting Raymond warmly, but with an air of anticipation, which Raymond does not understand. For Raymond, it is still hard to tell what time of day it is.

"It's still foggy," notes Raymond.

"Don't be surprised. You expected it to be different closer to the ocean?"

Raymond walks toward a row of houses. Most are made of different and irregular materials, but sturdy enough homes. Mostly wood, lots of plastic and fiberglass panels, too. Even some sheet metal salvaged from vehicles and robots. Raymond sees another building nearby. It is not along the row with the thatched houses. It is a bit larger and has antennae on its roof.

"What is that place?"

"The library, and the radio station. We have a short wave radio. Any long-range wireless is useless because of the thick cloud cover and the electromagnetic disturbance. Though, we can use it to keep in touch with other settlers along the coast."

"Where is everybody?"

"Most are at the long hall, preparing for the fair." Kerwac points to the right, between the homes lined up along their walk. Just beyond them there is a large long cabin several times bigger than any of the other structures. Raymond recognizes this as the building from his memory when Kerwac took his chip out. He was looking at this building, this long hall, from the top of a hill.

"A fair?"

"A memorial fair for those who did not return...the rest of my team." Kerwac is done speaking about this subject. They walk on slowly, in silence.

"What about the plague? How do you survive out here?"

"One day at a time. But questions like that are best answered with the group. We have many different people here, with many forms of knowledge." Kerwac turns right. He walks past a short row of houses. Raymond follows. They stroll toward the long hall in the center of the village. A plume of smoke from a cooking fire trails through a vent in the roof of the long hall. This is the place, thinks Raymond. I remember this long cabin. He speaks up to Kerwac. "This is the place I remembered when you took my chip out. But I remembered it from far away, from the top of a hill, at night."

"Ah, yes. I could not really tell what was going on with you then. But I'm not surprised that this is something you remembered."

Everyone is either at home or at the long hall, or walking back and forth between their homes and the long hall, arms laden, preparing for the fair. Kerwac gives Raymond a tour. People are making lanterns, banners, or portraits. Some are writing music or poetry. Townsend and Zane are practicing an old folk song that Zane wants to perform at the fair. Raymond meets the butcher and the baker. He is introduced to the goat that will become dinner on the day of the fair. He is at first startled, almost revolted by the hairy, animal smell of the livestock, the manure, the hay, but its potency reminds him of times when he had woken up early to feed goats, his eyes heavy with sleep, and the morning chill creeping under his blanket. People are bustling around cooking food. Someone tosses a handful of chopped onions into a pan of heated oil over an open flame. The food sizzles. A delicious, homey scent wafts through the air. Ahhh. Raymond breathes deep. He watches people, the smell and smudge of turned soil on their work clothes, returning from the fields for a meal. He walks around, breathing the fresh ionized air from being so near the shore. He thinks of the beach and wishes to see it, to watch the waves. The air feels so different here, even with the clouds blocking the sun. That smell! It's a lighter air than the citi and the people of the citi would never even know. He realizes that life is better outside of the citis. They're living proof that we can live outside of the citis and make it work, thinks Raymond. Some people take a break from their work to see him, as he has been gone for years. They say "Hello, Raymond," or "Welcome," or "Feeling better?" or "Build up your strength," or "Nice pajamas." Kerwac and Raymond exit the other end of the long hall. They make a circuit through the village.

"We should get back," says Kerwac. "Noriko has prepared some food for you. She asked me not to keep you out too long today."

"But I have so many questions."

"We have as many for you. In the citi, they surgically tampered with your identity. I imagine you are still in for a few surprises. Take it easy. Focus on the present. All will be addressed in its time."

CHAPTER 13
THE MEMORIAL FAIR

The memorial fair comes. The celebration is daylong. There are foods, dancing, streamers, ancestor alters, games, and bonfires on the shore at night. There are lighted paper lanterns everywhere, illuminating the village and the paths through the woods to the shore. Raymond is struck by the atmospheric lighting of the handmade lanterns, fueled with vegetable oil. "So, that's what everyone was making..." he says to himself. Noriko accompanies Raymond.

"Where's Kerwac?" he asks. "I've barely seen him."

"He is in the cave," says Noriko.

"Where's the cave?"

"Inside himself. Notice how we don't see him around? See how he walks when we do see him around? He is not quite here. He has much to think about; much to feel. He'll be back. We protect him in the meantime. Keep him safe. Keep him fed and loved while he travels deep inside himself – alone."

"That's depression, isn't it? The plague isn't cured is it? I thought it might be cured, or at least over, out here."

"Depression still happens. In balance, it has its purpose – its necessity. It's like any vaccine. You take a little, a weak dose, to develop a resistance to the lethal strains. Depression doesn't happen for nothing. It is the soul's way of saying, 'Something is wrong and needs to change.' The challenge lies on you to find out what. Deeper still, to implement the change when you know what it must be. Depression takes its toll on humanity as a collective soul. Rather than feel all of the emotions, people are conditioned to evade certain emotions. Particularly depression. But, depression offers an opportunity for self examination and change that is excruciating, yet a key to freedom."

"That's a lot to think about, Noriko."

"Here, we condition ourselves to understand our emotions - not evade them, like in the citis."

From sunset into early night, Raymond meets all eleven houses. He is introduced briefly to the kids. At a huge meal, Raymond sits and eats with a small group entertaining an infant, tickling its feet, making funny faces, and playing peek-a-boo. One couple, the infant's parents, steals kisses together while watching the baby get tickled. Noriko takes Raymond's hand and introduces him to the couple, interrupting their smooching.

"Hey, get a room, you two," she jests. "I've got someone here you may want to see."

"Hello, Raymond! It's good to see you," says the woman. She smiles at Raymond fondly, like an old friend. "Katrina," she adds, naming herself as an afterthought.

Raymond feels shy. "Hello, Katrina," he replies. She remembers me, thinks Raymond. From the movements of her eyes, the familiarity of her demeanor, he is sure she remembers him.

"Hi, Ray," says her husband. "Welcome back. I'm Winston."

"Hello Winston. It's good to meet you."

Winston takes the infant in his arms, smiling.

"Who is this little baby?" asks Raymond.

"This is our Oro," says Winston.

"Oro," repeats Raymond. "What does that mean?"

"He is named after Ora. His name is also Spanish for 'gold,' like his hair, and 'corn' like the food we rely on."

"Who is Ora?" asks Raymond.

"Why, she's Noriko's protégé," chimes in Katrina. "Surely you've met her."

Raymond remembers the young, green-eyed girl at his bedside with Noriko when he first woke up; the young woman that Noriko sent away.

Noriko speaks. "There are few children and, now..." Noriko pauses. Her face falls, somber and pensive. She remembers the people who never came home from Kerwac's mission. She remembers Charmin, who was lost on the same mission as Raymond, over four years ago. She closes her eyes and swallows slowly. "Now, even fewer men. The birth rate plummeted far below zero during the plague years. Some, bless them," adds Noriko, "like Katrina and Winston here, are still having babies. Most do not."

"Our village," enjoins Katrina, somewhat boastfully, "has the highest reported birth rate on the Appalachian coast."

Baby Oro starts crying with hunger. Winston hands him over to Katrina. Katrina takes the baby. She scoops her pendulous lactating breast out of her shirt and begins feeding Oro. The infant latches onto the nipple and falls silent, suckling contentedly. Katrina addresses Raymond. "It's difficult to manage the feelings sometimes. It is easy to get depressed. Things get dark, yes, but we take care of each other. We have to keep on," she says.

Raymond's unchipped and repairing mind vomits an impulse. Raymond, looking at parents, feels disdain and disgust at the idea of parenthood. This is how it felt in the citi, he recalls in a mercurial flash of memory. The BSA would have a field day with this homeless outdweller living in squalor, begging and stealing to feed a mewling whelp, another unlicensed pregnancy drawing resources away from the honest hard working citizens. But in that same instant, Raymond's disgust is countered by shame at his ignorant judgement. Katrina is a mother, a matriarch with healing powers, a revered and beloved member of the community, for having the strength and patience to rear a child.

A band strikes up. A tambourine shakes. Cyrus bangs his

drum for attention. The villagers fall silent and turn their attention to the noise. Folks trickle into the long hall from outside. Settlers approach from walks on the beach. They congregate towards the fire.

In the center of the long hall are the kids. They are gathered near the fire preparing to play music. The orange glow of firelight shines on their faces. Cyrus plays his drum. Bleeker, a tambourine. Sam, a ukulele. Ora, an ocarina. Zane is not playing an instrument. He has a look of anticipation, for he is about to sing. He has been told it is the nervousness of caring about something. He has been taught that he must love himself through his fear and he is nervous about getting up in front of the the whole town. But he loves to sing. He practiced for days with Townsend. And it was an old song. He picked an old song, so all would know it.

As the melody of his friends' playing finds its momentum, Zane closes his eyes and opens his mouth. Zane sings a song for the lost, a folk song called "Reverie":

We swing
Falling backwards
The chain goes slack
I swing back
The chain snaps back
Oh the landing
Ascending again
A reverie
A reverie
Remember a playground
Come swing with me
Oh the landing
Ascending again
The chain goes slack
I want to leap off and fly
I want to fly so high
That, falling, I never land
I swing back
The chain snaps back
In my throat, I feel my heart
Oh the landing

Ascending again
A reverie
A reverie
Remember a playground
Come swing with me
Oh beloved, having lost you to time
We are left here to swing twixt reveries.

Jubilation! Everyone applauds! Everyone is so proud! "Wasn't he wonderful?" "What a beautiful voice!" "Those kids just played their hearts out!" There is dancing, drinking and storytelling. Old Micheal and Ora put on a puppet show. Barley wine, mead, and potato vodka flow. Some people return to the food table to fill in the corners. The goat had been given a long soak in brine, then roasted in a pit by Colin Chris, Townsend, and a reluctant Alain who had not wanted to stay up all night for the roasting, until Colin Chris and Townsend convinced him with wine.

Katrina, Winston, Noriko and Raymond's group resumes passing Oro around, delighting in his infantile expressions. Noriko notices that Raymond does not hold or touch the baby. Two men and a cinnamon brown dog join their group. One of the men is tall, with close-cropped black hair. His dark temples are salted with a generous patch of gray. The shorter man has an earnest face, with amused blue eyes. He looks around him with a subtle curl of smile on his lips. They had been plowing and planting all day, and there were still fields to go. Tonight is a welcome respite from somewhat arduous labor. Their spirits are light. They introduce themselves as Alain and Colin Chris. "And this mutt here is Gracie," adds Colin Chris.

Alain and Colin Chris look at each other and verify that they are sensing the same thing. They can tell that Raymond is withdrawn. Being the more experienced, Alain understands that Raymond must be feeling a bit overwhelmed by all of the attention. After spending years isolated in the citi, he has not been left alone since he arrived here, and his discomfort is starting to show. Alain and Colin Chris, with a knack for communicating with each other silently, address Raymond kindly.

"You know, Raymond, I've heard from Kerwac how you arrived here, how you activated that mech."

"Yes, Rodney," says Raymond, a little absently.

"Do you suppose," asks Alain, "you could have another look at that mech?"

"Sure," says Raymond.

"Excellent," says Alain. "I'll let Zane take you out there tomorrow. He's bound to try to get out of field work again."

"Do you think it still works?" asks Colin Chris.

"Rodney's a little beat up," responds Raymond reluctantly, "but he'll probably work. He'll need a lot of repairs."

"We've got tools," says Alain.

"We've even got a few parts," says Colin Chris.

Raymond doesn't answer. He is feeling tired and overstimulated. The celebration is wearing thin on him and he is beginning to yearn for solitude. Alain understands his silence as a response. No need to press, he thinks.

"So Raymond, you look like you're feeling better. How's your appetite?"

"I've got an appetite for another one of those kabobs," says Raymond, making a polite effort to change the subject. "Goat, you said? I never thought I'd eat goat – and like it." He gets up and walks away.

They smile and leave him be. Alain and Colin Chris take turns holding Oro. Gracie sniffs around for a dropped morsel or a plate to lick. Conversations go on without Raymond. He grabs a goat kabob near the fire, returns, sits near the group, and silently munches. He listens attentively. People remember lost loves. They retell old stories, handed down, of life before the biospheres, before chemical control of the food supply; of a life when people could plant a seed in the ground and simply eat the fruit that grew. A few people eventually tell jokes; Winston first, followed by Noriko. A light laughter begins bubbling up from the group, gaining mirth and momentum, as the jokes remind people of better jokes. Raymond feels outside. He cannot relate to the fertility and depth of these people's emotions.

Day comes. The plow work begins anew. Zane explains to Raymond that he talked his dad into letting him take Raymond on another tour before getting to work.

"...and we live in all these houses. That's my house. Bleeker's house is at the other side of the long hall. Sam's is on the south end. Cyrus is next door to her. But that's it," says Zane. "Ora mostly studies with Noriko these days. It gets boring. Everyone is usually doing work, like the plowing today. Or making clothes, or storing corn, or treating bamboo, or hunting."

"Hunting?" asks Raymond. "What do you hunt? How do animals find enough water to survive out here?"

"Well, they're all small animals, squirrels and rabbits and stuff. They steal water from our fog catchers, or lick the morning dew out of hollows in the grass. That's how we find them. I never see big animals around here, except for the goats we raise."

"Where are all your friends?" asks Raymond.

Zane pauses. He looks down at his feet. "They're out in the foothills."

"Out with Rodney?"

"Rodney?" says Zane. He repeats the name, digesting the idea that the mech already had a name. Zane had already thought of a couple good names for the mech. "Rodney...Well, Kerwac mentioned you knew things about Rodney. If you don't mind, everyone's so curious about him..."

"Where is he?"

"At the columns. That way," says Zane, pointing toward the western foothills.

"Wait," says Raymond, "Let's grab the computer deck from the infirmary. That laptop has a backup on it."

Zane takes Raymond to the foothills, back to Rodney. The others are there. Cyrus is sitting up on Rodney's shoulders, level with the tops of the columns. Sam is sitting under Rodney. She is playing cards with Bleeker. They are using the top of Rodney's extended right front foot as a playing table. Bleeker is sitting, with the cards, on top of Rodney's foot, across from Sam. Cyrus spots Zane and Raymond approaching. He bangs a notice to Sam and Bleeker.

"Here they come," declares Cyrus

Sam puts down her cards.

"I win!" announces Bleeker.

"We didn't even finish, Bleeker," says Sam.

"Yeah, but I have more points."

"And I have less cards. Let's call it a draw."

"Draw," affirms Bleeker happily. He hops down off Rodney's foot.

Zane arrives, leading Raymond. Everyone says hello.

"Can you help us?" asks Bleeker. "Our giant's busted."

"Is that so? What happened?" says Raymond, playing along.

"We zapped him," reminds Cyrus. "Don't you remember?"

"Not quite," he replies.

Zane and Raymond climb up Rodney. Cyrus moves over to make room. Raymond opens the panel at the back of Rodney's neck while Zane boots up the laptop. Raymond explains as they work,

"Software in a machine, much like a person in a body, develops a memory of its routines in the body itself. Residual power in the machine retains certain routines. Because of your EMP trap, Rodney has been reset. None of those routines survived in his body. This backup would give him his brain back."

Sam and Cyrus help Bleeker climb up onto Rodney's back. Bleeker is excitable. He has been itching to climb the giant since they caught it. Sam climbs up also. All of them are crowded onto Rodney's back, huddled to watch over Raymond's shoulders. Raymond jacks the laptop deck into the Rodney's control panel. He opens the copy he made of Rodney's pet software. He begins drumming and tapping on the deck, rewriting parts of the program. He narrates his train of thought to the kids.

"The main problem is his AI hardware looks damaged, including his guidance system. He can't tell when he has stopped moving. So even if you tell him to stop, and he thinks he's stopped, he keeps walking. But we can repair that later, if we can restore him."

"He'll have to power down every time he stops walking, won't he?" figures Zane.

"Exactly. What we really need is a new guidance system for him. Until then, we can operate him on manual mode." Raymond reloads a Rodney from the computer deck backup.

"Alright," Raymond says. "Everybody, hold on."

Please enter pet's name for initialization sequence.

R-O-D-N-E-Y, enters Raymond.

Please confirm pet's name

R-O-D-N-E-Y, confirms Raymond.

Name accepted

Rodney's blue eyes flash on. His systems re-engage in quick succession. Raymond leans forward from his seat near Rodney's neck and places the palm of his hand on Rodney's eye. Rodney scans Raymond's hand, assigning a master.

"Hi Rodney, I am Raymond,"

Hi Raymond, I am Rodney,

"Rodney, be sure not to drop any of us," says Raymond.

Do not drop any person, confirms Rodney.

"Good boy," says Raymond. "Now let's go for a walk."

Rodney lurches forward, completing the stride he was frozen in. Rodney walks between the columns and into the foothills. The kids roar with delight.

"We caught a giant!" brags Bleeker to the sky.

"Yii-haaa!" hollers Cyrus, banging his drum.

Sitting at the computer deck, Raymond steers. Rodney is not functional enough to learn any other identities or obey verbal directional cues, but he can be moved around. Zane watches, rapt and smiling. The path into the hills forks shortly. The south trail leads to the settlement. The north trail leads to the crop fields.

"Which way?" asks Raymond.

"Left! Go left," commands Zane, selecting the north trail. He has an idea. They follow the north trail.

"This is awesome," muses Sam, watching the land go by from the hulking giant's shoulders. "But why are we going this way? Don't we want to take him to everyone at the long hall?"

"Not yet," replies Zane.

Raymond shows Zane how to steer. "Use these keys for direction. Use these keys for speed. Easy." Raymond smiles. He moves aside and lets Zane steer.

"How do we make him jump?" asks Zane.

"We need to repair him before he can jump," says Raymond.

"Aww."

Zane uses Rodney to climb over some hills that they normally circumvent, ignoring the footpaths. He speeds Rodney up.

"Woaw!" yells Zane, thrilled. "This is so much faster!"

"Not too fast," cautions Raymond, "we don't want to drop anyone."

Out at the cornfields Alain and Colin Chris are pulling a plow again together. Others are plowing the other side of the field. Winston is working the potato field elsewhere.

"Do you feel that?" asks Alain.

"Yes, and I hear something. What is that?" declares Colin Chris, pointing at a hill over Alain's shoulder.

Rodney, with the cheering kids on his back, comes into view over the lip of the hill. Some people are scared. A few drop their tools and bolt before they know what's going on.

"It's an attack!"

"Mechs!"

"They've come for us!"

Alain looks up at the source of the commotion. "Well, would you look at that? They woke that mech up." He cups his hands around his mouth and hollers at his spooked neighbors, "Come back, you jitterbugs! It's just the kids!"

Zane slows Rodney down. "How do I stop him?" Zane asks.

"Well, for now, just punch his off key," says Raymond. "He'll power down, but it will stop him. So hold on everybody!"

Zane slows Rodney down before stopping him at the edge of the field. Rodney's passengers are jerked forward a bit by the sudden stop. Rodney's blue eyes flash off.

"So what are we doing out here, Zane?" Sam asks.

Zane smiles. "Remember, you said we should help the plow teams? We're gonna help."

Zane climbs down to Alain and gives his dad a hug. They begin speaking. Zane gesticulates toward the field, his arms outstretched. He points at Rodney. Raymond and the kids climb down off Rodney. They follow Zane into the field.

"Hello, Raymond," says Alain. "Getting a little play time in?" He smiles at Raymond's accomplices.

Raymond smiles sheepishly. "They're showing me around."

"So what do you think, Dad?" asks Zane, referring to whatever they had been speaking about before the others caught up.

"I think it's a damn fine idea, Zane," responds Alain, who already had the idea during the fair, but let it ride for a while, figuring it was good for Zane.

"What's that?" asks Raymond.

"Zane here got the bright idea to use Rodney as our plow beast."

"He could pull all these plows in a minute!" explains Zane excitedly. "We just have to set them up right and tie them to Rodney."

"That's a fine idea, Zane," reaffirms Alain. "A damn fine idea."

The plow teams regroup. They line their plows up and brace them to each other. The kids use the EMP rope, now inert, to sling the plow line to Rodney, near his neck like a bridle. Zane sits on Rodney's back and steers. Bleeker throws a tantrum until he is allowed to ride up top with Zane. Rodney plows the fields in short order, carving half a dozen long, straight furrows into the ground at a time. The farmers are unable to keep up simply planting seeds in Rodney's wake. Zane and Rodney are finished with all of the fields before the farmers have seeded the first one. Everyone plants seeds. Older farmers, like Alain, tutor those with less experience.

"For corn, the ideal depth is 4 to 5 centimeters. The beans, even less. When we irrigate, the drying water can form a crust of soil. If we plant any deeper, the seed will not have the energy to break the crust."

The children, the farmers, and Raymond travel along the plowed rows; seeding and irrigating back and forth like a typewriter carriage. The seeds are planted long before dark. Zane is the hero of the day.

There is a bonfire at the beach that night; a bonfire at the whalebones. Some years ago a whale had beached there. After scavengers had picked it, the giant skeleton had been cleaned and sealed, then reassembled into a play area. A slide for kids, some bone benches for adults, and a fire pit. Orange firelight and black shadows play along the weathered, white bones.

There is a buoyant air of thankfulness in the village.

"By the sun," says Colin Chris, sitting next to Raymond by the fire, "You lot saved a dozen people three days work." He raises his drink to Raymond and the kids.

Raymond smiles and sips his drink. "It was Zane's idea, really. I just helped get Rodney running again."

"Just as well. We couldn't have done it without you, Raymond."

"Thanks, Colin Chris. I was wondering, have you seen Kerwac?"

"Not much. He was having coffee at Old Michael's this morning. We said hello. He and Ora were speaking together. I think he's in the cave; rewriting the stock phrases of his internal monologue."

"Oh, the cave..." says Raymond, recalling what Noriko said about the cave. "What are you talking about? Rewriting the what?" asks Raymond.

"Everyone talks to themselves, inside their heads, right?" replies Colin Chris. "Sometimes a person gets depressed, where most of the things they say to themselves become mean and unloving. Consequently, to heal, the depressed person must learn, and actually rehearse, kind, loving language to use on themselves. Kerwac's been through a lot. He lost his team. Although, I don't think he understands how important it is that he's rescued you. That might cheer him up. But he arrived here after you were gone."

"How long have I been gone?" asks Raymond.

Colin Chris sticks out the tip of his tongue and calculates for a moment. "Oh," he answers, "over four years, closer to five, really."

"Five years! I was here five years ago? By the sun, I barely remember anything." Raymond knew it had been "years," from the way Noriko spoke, but he did not know how many.

"I'm sorry," says Colin Chris. "You can't get it back, I'll bet," he adds realistically.

"You mentioned Kerwac at Old Michael's? Where's that?"

"Old Michael is the oldest man in town. He lives on his own, in a café he built, just down the beach a little way, past the bamboo grove," Colin Chris says, pointing southeast toward the shore. "When he has enough fuel for a good hot fire, he even does some glass blowing. You should visit him. Have some coffee at Old Michael's." Colin Chris changes the subject, "You know, your bot reminds me of a big gorilla. Do you remember King Kong?"

"No. Who's King Kong?" Raymond replies, distracted. Coffee sounds good to Raymond. His caffeine withdrawal is still nagging his spirit. He tries to imagine Old Michael, maybe a hunched old granddad in a hut on the beach.

"Yeah, who's King Kong, Colin Chris?" asks Bleeker, eavesdropping.

"He was a giant gorilla. He was an ancient ape the size of a skyscraper." The kids listen in. "He was captured long ago in a deep, dark jungle, and brought captive to old New York."

"Ooo. Old New York..."

"Well, we've got a King Kong, too!" says Cyrus. Cyrus jumps up. He marches around the fire, banging his drum. Zane, Sam, and Bleeker follow Cyrus' lead. Ora remains seated next to Alain, her father. The kids' bodies cast large flickering shadows around the bonfire. They roar and beat their chests. They chant around the fire, in a call-and-response fashion.

"Gather 'round the family tree!"
"Gather 'round the family tree!"
"Rodney King Kay-Oh-N-Gee!"
"Rodney King Kay-Oh-N-Gee!"
"Rodney Kong!"
"Rodney Kong!"

CHAPTER 14
SALVADOR CONTACTS RAYMOND

Three days pass. During these days, a meeting of the settlement is planned. The long hall is prepared for another gathering, a council of the village. Noriko, while treating Raymond's wounds, noted the large gem in his dusty jacket pocket. She put Raymond's clothes and his objects in a safe place until he was well. Noriko did mention the gem to Ora during lessons one day. Ora told the kids a story that evening about a powerful computer jewel lost on a quest years ago, when they were too young to remember. The kids bring it up to their parents and guardians at meal times, and the adults who remember those days know that Raymond's return implies the fate of this jewel. In this way, word of the gem's arrival with Raymond spreads quietly but inexorably. Raymond's return is bigger news than he understands.

Raymond takes a liking to Zane and is gratified by his curiosity. Zane, who is almost thirteen, has vague memories of Raymond from his early childhood. He remembers riding on Raymond's shoulders when he was a toddler, especially the first day Raymond remarked that Zane had grown too big to ride on his shoulders any more. Also, Zane wants to learn as much about Rodney as possible. It is the kernel of their new friendship. Raymond finds it easier to get up in the morning because the interested and eager Zane is waiting. Raymond begins repairing Rodney, mostly to teach Zane. The damage is extensive. It is a slow and laborious process.

Fixing Rodney pleases Alain, who sees a powerful use for a functional, military mech. With a mech to defend them, the settlement is much less at the mercy of a citi-based invasion. Rodney could patrol a wide perimeter all day and all night, every day and every night.

The morning of the council, Raymond visits Old Michael. Taking a break from Rondey and Zane in the late afternoon, Raymond walks down to the shore. He turns south, according to Colin Chris's directions. He walks for about a half hour. He passes the whalebones, then the bamboo grove. Soon after, he sees the silhouette of a structure on the shore ahead. It looks like a canopy. Raymond sees the canopy is woven of reeds and corn husks, planted on a collection of stakes. As Raymond nears the canopy, he sees a figure reading in a hammock near the edge of the canopy.

The figure swings out of the hammock. It is a shirtless, white haired old man in Bermuda shorts. He stands at the edge of the awning, facing the gray ocean. He continues reading. His book is popped open in his upturned left palm. He wedges the book open with his thumb. Raymond is closer to the shelter now. There are small wooden tables and chairs set about the place. The old man has nut-brown skin. His arms and shoulder blades are covered with downy white hairs. He closes the book, tosses it into the hammock, and turns to face Raymond. Raymond steps under the canopy into the café. The canopy rustles in the breeze. Raymond and Old Michael shake hands. The old man is smiling, clearly pleased to see him.

"Good day. I'm Michael."

"'Morning. I'm Raymond. Pleased to meet you."

The old man smiles. His eyes are clear and wide.

"Fine spot you've got here," says Raymond, easing into a chair.

"Thank you. Coffee?"

"Coffee sounds great," replies Raymond.

Old Michael tosses a palm full of roasted coffee beans into a mortar and pestle. He begins crushing the beans. The pulchritudinous, nutty scent is intoxicating to Raymond.

"It seems like you don't spend much time in the village," says Raymond.

"Now that I'm old, I find that I've been around. I like to spend my time here," he says, looking around at the café and the ocean. "I have friends who visit."

Raymond sips the fresh coffee. It is fantastic. It wafts a rich, warm, round aroma with a hint of spice.

"Damn, this is the best coffee I've ever had," says Raymond.

"And I didn't even have to say it," replies Old Michael. "Where have you been having coffee?"

Raymond does not answer, but he thinks briefly about the coffee dispenser in his Salt Lake Citi apartment. He stares forward for a moment, then returns.

Raymond asks Old Michael, "How do you make this coffee?"

Old Michael laughs gently. "Come by when you have some time and I'll teach you."

Raymond sips coffee. He savors the fragrant, earthy aroma of the hot brew. He stares at the sea under a dim cloudy sky, the eternal break of the waves. Wisps of mist flutter by like tumbleweed. He listens to the roar of the ocean and stares at the sea. Even though the world looks dreary and desolate compared to the pictures and models in the citi, he feels a touch of the beauty around him. He is seated on the edge of a sinking continent, gazing off at the vast ocean, which dominates the horizon. He remembers the astounding size and scope of the earth, the splendid organization of life and natural forces of which he is but a mote of humanity. Eventually, Old Michael speaks.

"You looked pretty bad when you arrived. How are you feeling today?"

"Much better. I still get fits of laziness and sleepiness. Noriko says it is withdrawal from the citi's chemical supplements, the caffeine and stuff in the food."

"Yes," says Old Michael. "That will wear off soon enough."

"Not soon enough for me."

“Do you miss the citi?” Old Michael asks.

“Sort of,” says Raymond, thinking about his answer, “but only because I remember it against my will. It’s not my home anymore.”

“What is?”

“I’m not sure. Noriko feels like home.”

“That’s a good start.”

Raymond’s coffee has cooled a bit now. “So what’s with this council?” he asks. “What are we going to talk about?”

“Whenever a significant enough amount of new information is added to our community here,” explains Old Michael, “the group is naturally compelled to discuss it. Basically, they will talk and ask questions about the new information until everyone feels like they have benefited from it. This time, the new information is you.” Old Michael speaks an afterthought knowingly, “And anything you brought with you.”

Anything I brought with me, thinks Raymond. What’s that supposed to mean? Raymond thinks again of the jewel, feeling suddenly defensive. He recognizes the sensation this time and it makes him curious. Just what is that thing? he wonders. It’s caused a heap of trouble. I want to take a good look at that jewel before everyone else does. Maybe I can figure something out before all these people get involved. I’m not going to walk into that council totally blind, if I can help it.

Raymond downs the rest of his coffee and gazes at the horizon, imagining the next continent across the water, trying to leave his seat at the café, trying to escape the questions. He gets up and walks out toward the water. Old Michael follows him a few paces behind. They sit down on the sand and watch the break. For a time, Old Michael is the only one speaking. Raymond’s attention drifts between the sound of the roaring ocean and Old Michael’s description of the early days of the settlement. He listens half heartedly, alternately yearning for solitude and glad for the knowing company of Old Michael. Presently, Old Michael notices that Ray is not listening.

“Raymond? Ray?” Old Michael discontinues Raymond’s reverie. He places his hand on Raymond’s shoulder. “Come back. Are you alright?”

“Yes, thanks. I was remembering something about the citi.”

“Something against your will?” asks Old Michael.

"No, not quite. I think I need to go." Raymond stands up to leave. Raymond's own thoughts have made him antsy. He does not want to sit with them anymore. He wants to go look at the jewel. It feels like that jewel has been steering him since Salt Lake Citi, and he is still no closer to understanding its nature. His curiosity is stirring up a modicum of anxiousness about the jewel.

"It's clear you have a lot on your mind. Whatever it is, you need to feel, to mine through your feelings. You may find memories."

"You're probably right, but that's enough for now."

"Don't fret. Change does not come as fast as thought. After you think of the change you want to see, you must also do it."

"I will. Thank you for the coffee."

"Sure, any time. Come by again."

On his way back to the infirmary, Raymond runs into Noriko on the beach. They walk together a while, towards the settlement. They reach a cluster of empty homes farthest from the entrance to the long hall. Of the sixteen houses surrounding the long hall, five of them are now deserted.

"Why are these empty?" asks Raymond.

"There are so few of us, we don't fit in those houses any more. Colin Chris used to live there with his dog, Gracie, but it got lonely. He moved in with Alain after Ora and Zane's mother died."

Noriko walks Raymond over to an empty house. "We could move into one of these," she suggests, her voice brightening.

Raymond's mind is still on the defensive with thoughts of the jewel. His eagerness to catch up to the events that drew him out of the citi are foremost in his mind. Though he has nothing against Noriko's suggestion, it feels too demanding. To hide from this conversation, Raymond thinks hard about nothing. He does not speak. Noriko, warmed by the thought of them living together, takes his hand, not realizing his apprehension. Raymond pulls his hand from hers.

"I should not be here," says Raymond, finally. "It's just so desolate. There are no people around. I just don't know if I can stay here."

"Where would you go?" she asks. "Would you go back?"

Raymond does not answer. Her questions make him feel defensive. Noriko senses his thoughts, his withdrawal. Despite herself, she pushes him, becoming irritated that he might have sympathy for the citis.

"Those citis formed like cancers on the earth," says Noriko.

"They keep so many people alive, though. Their system."

"You call that living?"

"You call this living?" he gestures toward the settlement.

Her eyebrows lower defensively. "What do you call it?" she asks.

"Exile, in a dozen shanties in the woods, scraping a meal off the ground."

Noriko bites her lip before replying, "You'd go back?"

Raymond does not answer.

"Here, we love one another," she continues, vehemently. "We build families here. We live with the earth, not just tread upon it. We hope to remake the world that all their war science destroyed. We don't hide in a bell jar pretending that was progress."

She looks even more endearing speaking so passionately.

"I don't care what happens to the cities," he replies. "I don't care about their domes, their mechs, their rotten locked food - of course I wouldn't go back. I'm sorry I insulted this place, honey. I knew I was wrong the moment I said it. I think I just need some time to get back to myself, to remember what is good about life out here. Can you give me that? Before we start decorating one of these houses?"

She nods willingly. A slow smile begins at the corners of her mouth. He takes her hand again and squeezes it warmly. He gently places his palm on her elegant cheek, and softly brushes her cheekbone with the pad of his thumb.

"When I look at you, I see a thing more beautiful, more memorable than any luxury promised by the citi, more moving than anything I've ever seen. I look at you and I know that you are what's good about life. You're my Remi Zero, shorty!" He swats her on the ass and says, "Now get back to them sheets!"

They break into laughter. Noriko affects a mischievous face, looking at Raymond suggestively. She jumps up and wraps her legs around him. Not fast enough, Raymond falls catching her. She straddles him in the dirt on the lane and kisses him.

"You need to get going," giggles Noriko. "See you tonight," she adds.

"I love you," he replies, with a smile.

"I love you, darlin'," she says.

Raymond walks toward the infirmary. Noriko does not follow him. She continues her walk among the empty houses. There is still about half an hour before people start gathering for council.

Back at the infirmary, Raymond is alone. Would I go back? The question returns to his mind. He sits down alone. Raymond remembers his home office; the climate control, his memory foam bed on one end of an oblong room, his workstation on the other end, and the kitchenette/bathroom in between. He remembers the last time he was in his apartment. The morning Charmin left the messages. This thought makes Raymond anxious, remembering what he's been avoiding - his last day in the citi. His thoughts jumble.

I remember waking up dressed, he thinks. I had that weird dream about going to the bank. By the sun! I didn't sleep at all, did I? I blacked out. Raymond has had blackouts before, booze soaked nights where he forgets hours at a time of his escapades. Once he woke up in his room with his trousers on the doorstep, his wallet empty, a red welt on his forehead, and a comm number written on his hand. But this night was different, even than those. He remembers the pill. What did I take?

Raymond opens the small cubby where Noriko stored the clothes he was wearing when he arrived in Appalachia, feverish on Rodney's back. He lifts his dusty, tattered jacket from the pile of clothes. He unzips the pockets. He removes the jewel, places it on the table, and has a seat.

"So it's a computer brain," he muses. It resembles half of a faceted diamond coconut. The center of the flat side has a blue pad of a malleable substance.

"It's some kind of processor putty, probably where it connects," he says to himself. "Heh, it looks like a frozen snow globe." He presses his first two fingers into the blue pad of processor putty. It yields. His fingers sink in. Something in the putty pricks Raymond's finger, drawing a drop of blood.

"Ow!" exclaims Raymond, more surprised then hurt. When he pulls his fingers away, the putty returns to its original shape. There is a tiny smudge of blood on it. The jewel glows dimly. Some residual power, thinks Raymond. A tiny holographic sign projects from the jewel, a few centimeters in the air above it.

DNA scan successful. ID verified. Access granted to rakan prototype.

Rakan, he thinks? Access to what? There are no ports, jacks, nothing. I don't see any wireless apparatus in it, he thinks. He picks up the glinting half globe. Again he squishes the blue putty pad with his first two fingers. He squints and tenses, anticipating another prick to his finger. Again it stays squished until he stops pressing, where upon it reverts to its flat oval shape. Nothing else happens this time.

"I'll bet it needs to be connected to a computer, or at least a power source." He looks into the cropped bottom of the crystalline hemisphere. It looks like processor putty, but it remembers its shape perfectly. He examines the base of the blue putty, to see how it is attached. The seam is clean and perfect. It's not some adhesive. It might be welded. Putty welded to diamond? I doubt it is diamond. It's probably a synthetic. The attached side of the putty is firmer, almost hard. Again, Raymond speaks aloud to himself. "It's like they meld right together. Cool." Raymond is lost in thought. He glances at the crystal.

"Rakan," he mutters, repeating aloud the name the crystal gave him. At "rakan," a message in the jewel is activated. The gem emits tiny pins of light that converge a few centimeters above it. The tiny beams of light speed up, dancing and weaving into each other. They form a small holographic image, ten centimeters across. Raymond hunches close to see the picture. The picture begins to move. It is a very low-resolution video. A round, ruddy faced man in an olive green suit is shown addressing a group gathered around a large, elliptical, polished table. The man is mostly bald, with a crown of wispy brown hair. He is selling something. He is illustrating an example. Raymond listens intently to the tinny audio track:

"The third generation biospheres will each contain a central computer bank with a dedicated processor. To create this super processor, we will build an optical model for each of our human senses, integrated into a computer brain. These computer brains will also build the machinery for the Hall of Ancestors. We will trace the processes and biochemical pathways that lead from the meat that is our body to the substance that is our mind, eventually creating a supercomputer capable of powering an entire city. Identity will be housed in something that is not just biological. This model of the human processing ability will exponentially increase our computer processing power."

One of the assembly interrupts: "Mr. Ledbetter,"

"Call me Xavier."

"So be it. Xavier, this sounds like one of those wild old white men's ideas. You come asking for all we have. It is likely you promise more than you can give." The dissenter is greeted with murmurs of assent and scattered applause.

Xavier pauses. He looks at one of the men at the table. He is a black haired man in a white lab coat, the only lab coat at the table, in fact. This man, Xavier's friend, nods encouragingly. Xavier looks down at the notes in front of him. Somehow, Raymond can hear Xavier's thoughts, or otherwise understand them. Don't blow this, thinks Xavier. We need their money. Stick to the talking points, Xavier reminds himself. He musters his liar's courage. Appeal to their greed and vanity. Xavier takes a breath and continues.

"So imagine those old white men saying this to you now: 'We're talking about World Government, gentlemen; a world government of commerce, based on a world network of secure citis. The energy interests of the world have taken on, though some say usurped, the responsibilities of inefficient and outdated representative governments. Think of the economic security! Think of the control of production! Of course we're going to need Arab leaders to manage the Arabic constituencies of the world. It's better if we pick them ourselves. This is certainly how the Saudis feel about the Americans also, is it not? 'We're going to need white men in our pockets to deal with the white masses. We might as well pick them ourselves.' It works out well.

"The first citis to successfully biosphere will be a handful of the United Arab Emirates. This will safeguard a lot of money that is being spent back and forth between other nodes like America, England, and China. Money is impossible without a healthy human populace. Our experiment has proved fruitful. This is a vast and far-reaching global endeavor."

Xavier nods to a group of Asian investors at one end of the assembly. He continues, "Thanks goes also to Communist China's quantitative precision in population management. These technologies are synthesized in Lattice's initiative; fully realized! Consequently we can create more effective workgroups based on compatible psychological profiles. With our vertically integrated distribution networks, the depression is entirely treatable inside of our domes. Our biospheres are more than merely safe! They are nothing short of genius! By biosphering you ensure public health and the security of your commerce networks." Xavier is building momentum, standing up taller. "You, the illustrious financiers of our international market economy, are here at a critical juncture in history. We now have the technology to install one world government.

"Nations are done! Welcome to the future! Our network governs the world. What we offer, gentlemen, is a share of the foundation!"

"Woa- foundation?" says Raymond. "What the -?"

"Raymond?" Noriko ducks her head into his partition. Raymond turns to Noriko. She smiles at him. "It's time, honey. Come to the long hall. Bring everything you have questions about. I'll wait out front."

The long hall has a large hearth for fires in the center. In the roof above the hearth there is a sky light for ventilation, a large rectangular aperture with no pane of glass. Along the walls are protruding partitions, breaking the perimeter of the long hall into small bays that each house uses in its own fashion. In this regard, the building resembles a large stable. Some store cooking supplies and sundries here. Others keep their building supplies, or dried food, or textile projects stowed in various bays.

Other settlers have already begun arriving. They greet each other and group together. The settlers gradually gather in a broad ring around the hearth in the middle of the long hall. Some step out briefly to make sure the rest of their house is on the way. The kids arrive and are corralled into one of the partitioned bays along the wall. Noriko and Raymond make their way to the center, near the hearth. They sit cross-legged on the ground next to Kerwac, who smiles wanly and nods in greeting, but does not speak. Alain is there, too. Colin Chris builds a fire on the hearth. Ora is sitting farther back, near the kids' bay, keeping an eye on the youngsters. Eventually, everyone is present, milling together, finding seats to watch, or taking positions to speak. Just as a gathering flock of birds somehow knows when to take off, the humans eventually are ready to begin, though no one is clearly the leader. The assembly falls silent.

Alain stands up. He counts 32 people. Everyone, save for Old Michael, as usual, is here. He raises his hands and looks around, smiling, before he speaks.

"We are so happy to welcome you home, Raymond. You were captured in Salt Lake Citi nearly five years ago trying to steal the computer jewel. That is why you and Charmin went to Salt Lake Citi in the first place. Charmin learned about the secreted crystal drive. It is purported to contain enough information and processing power to rescue any citizen we wish; to hack any citi for food. You two made a plan to sneak into Salt Lake and steal it. Neither of you returned. After that, we gave up on the dream of the jewel drive. A few of years later, Kerwac arrived with all of his military contraband. With his knowledge and equipment, we decided to try again to find you and Charmin. Kerwac left with three others. He returned with you, and no one else."

Kerwac bows his head, loath to recall his failure.

"You did not fail us, Kerwac," interjects Townsend, who has been quiet for some time. "Your help has brought us Raymond, and the fabled gem."

At Alain's utterances of the name "Charmin," a keystone is placed in the broken arch of Raymond's memory. Raymond remembers Charmin. More clearly than he remembers the bank, he remembers Charmin. Tall, lanky, smart mouthed

Charmin at the food court, asking him *"Nervous, Huh? Take one of these before bed tonight."* Raymond did not sleep that night. He took one of the pills.

"Charmin, here...?" Raymond says quietly.

Alain sees Raymond drifting in thought. "Yes," Alain says. "Do you remember, Raymond? Charmin lived here," he confirms. "You were friends."

"We were friends? Here?" asks Raymond, incredulous.

"How did you get out of the citi, Raymond?" probes Alain. The group falls silent.

"I did not sleep," speaks Raymond. His memory of that night, which briefly resurfaced at Old Michael's, blossoms now in his mind. "I took a pill. A pill I got from Charmin. I washed it down with whiskey. I wrote in my journal.

"That morning," continues Raymond, "I ate, took the shuttle downtown, and went to Central Bank. I squinted at the bright morning lamplight reflecting off of the doors. I scanned in. At the teller machine, I mashed processor putty into the ATM data port. The putty contained the hacking virus with the mainframe code in it. A guard checked me out because that damn putty was taking forever to hack the system. Three people at the ATM next to me finished their business and left. The guard saw me look at him. I must have looked strung out, drunk. He started watching me. I went through a sliding glass door to the safe deposit box room.

"Like Charmin said, the virus did the rest. The box I wanted opened right up, I took out the gem and pocketed it. Trembling, I walked quickly to the door. It didn't scan me. It didn't swing open. I stuck out my arm, opened the door and walked out. The alarm didn't sound. Cameras were frozen. The security bots didn't budge. The stun darts didn't fire. The guard's radio didn't work. I was out of there. But that damn guard. I can't believe they needed human employees in that place at all, with the security so tight."

"It's a sign of class and wealth," mutters Kerwac, "employing humans for security."

Raymond nods and resumes. "That guard saw me. He suspected something. He followed. I walked easily out of the bank. I heard the door behind me. He followed. I sped up. He sped up. I shouldn't have hurried. But I knew he knew. I turned around. He said, 'Excuse me! Sir! Stop!' He had his hand on his weapon. I ran. He chased me.

"I crossed the thoroughfare and ran up to the skyway. It was crowded with citizens. They flowed out of the subway wells and honeycombed high-rise reservoirs into the orderly channels of the skyway. The guard followed me. It was thronged with people, walking above vehicle traffic. The walkways ran off into tributaries and trickles of catwalks and crosswalks, collecting in pools at bookstores, coffee shops, net portals, clothing boutiques, and libraries. He chased me through a shopping corridor. Then I saw scaffolding on the skyway. They were repairing a pylon supporting the next skyway.

"I scrambled up the scaffolding, climbing around to the outfacing side of the pylon. The traffic zoomed by, hundreds of meters below. On the other side of the scaffold-encrusted pylon, the guard had reached the bottom and started climbing up toward me. I climbed faster and maneuvered sideways, to get out of his view. I wanted to lose him. If I could make it to the next skyway before he sees me, I'd be clear. That guard was fit. He caught up to me. But I was at the top by then, the underside of the next skyway..."

Raymond stops speaking. He is staring forward, into the memory, as if it would be imprinted on the back of his eyelids if he closed them. He is wearing a thousand yard stare.

"Go on, hon," says Noriko, touching his arm.

"There was a ledge above my head about half a meter out. I had to climb out onto the overhang and around its far edge. There were two rungs at eye level, leading to the edge. The traffic below looked dreadfully small. I leaned out and grabbed the first rung. My feet couldn't stay on the scaffolding anymore. My legs hung in the air, a storey above the edge of the skyway level below, and two hundred meters above the roadway. If I didn't fall and crack my head open on the edge of the skyway, I would fall past it into the rumbling, zooming traffic below. The guard refused to lose me. I was so close." Raymond has a pained look on his face. He clenches his fist and repeats, "I was so close! I swung my body a bit to reach the next rung. He grabbed my ankle. I tried to kick loose. He held tighter...then he slipped...but he didn't fall."

Raymond remembers everything. He shudders. The blocked memory snaps loose. It careens through his mind, with a flood of details in its wake. He stops speaking. The council waits a moment. Then Colin Chris asks,

"He didn't fall?"

Raymond returns from the memory. He shakes his head. He looks at Colin Chris.

"He lost his grip on the scaffolding, but he had my ankle. He clutched my ankle with both hands. Hanging there, his weight wrenched me down.

"'Get off me!' I hollered, 'You'll kill us both!'

"'Help me!' he yelled. 'Swing me back!'

"I couldn't swing! I barely had a grip. I looked at him. He wasn't chasing me anymore. He wanted to live. I saw his badge. I knew that he was the only one who noticed me. He knew I was guilty. That bank's surveillance was jammed, but he was right behind me. I remember it perfectly."

"I was scared, but...detached. I heeled his hand with my free foot. He cried out, getting angry. He didn't let go. He tried to shake me loose; take me with him. I used my free foot to kick the shoe off of my trapped foot. My shoe came off. It disappeared, falling to the ground far below. His grip on my ankle slipped, but he held on. His grip was like a vice, he was so scared. I kicked him hard in the face. I aimed the flat of my shod heel at his forehead. I kicked down on his face as hard as I could, fully extending my leg. He fell. I regripped the bar. I heard his screaming disappear into the traffic below." Raymond's voice wavers as he finishes his tale. "I climbed to the next level and ran. I cried, running home. I drank the rest of my whiskey and passed out until the alarm woke me..." Raymond trails off. He keeps seeing the guard's mortified, desperate face, gripping his ankle. "I kicked him in the face and he fell. He is dead, and I killed him."

A black balloon of guilt inflates in Raymond's heart. He remembers the kick. "We were going to fall...Oh my god! Oh my god!" Raymond begins to tear up. His relief rivals his pain. He is angry again. Remembering to keep water, he uses his fingertips to wipe the tears into his mouth. Somehow, this makes him cry harder. He falls to his knees, trying to drink his tears.

"That poor man," says Noriko.

A murmur of unrest moves through the people gathered in the long hall. The assembled villagers speak among themselves.

"By the sun!"

"That's monstrous!"

"But, what could he do?"

"Wait-what happened?"

"Ray killed a guard!"

"Right on!"

"Impossible."

"He just remembered it!"

Some have short arguments with each other about Raymond. Many feel a little afraid. Raymond looks miserable, and he is a killer. He might get depressed. He might get contagious.

Alain and Townsend stand at the center together, near the fire, and raise their hands. Their immense shadows are cast up on the walls. The crowd falls silent.

"Good riddance," says Alain about the guard. "Don't you understand? You got the jewel, Raymond. We have the power to hack a citi! We can find our friends and family! We can release them! That guard is an acceptable cost."

This kind of talk riles a few people up. Townsend thinks it wise not to raise tensions.

"Much information has been laid before us today," Townsend says. "We will break for a meal. Then we will reconvene to decide what to do. Bring ideas!" The council adjourns. People begin to mill out of the long hall. They are polite but nervous near Raymond. He already looks depressed. Fearing he may get contagious, they keep their distance for the time being.

CHAPTER 15
CHARMIN RETURNS

Back at the infirmary, Raymond and Noriko have just eaten a light repast. Sitting silently together, Noriko notices Raymond's pained brow, takes his hand with a nurturing smile, and walks him to their bed. As they kiss, her breath and her tongue cast away his dark thoughts of guilt and pull him out of his own mind. They undress each other, driven by instinct and a tender attentiveness to each other's now naked bodies. They make love on a cresting wave of passions. Noriko's energy amplifies, her body rising to Raymond's, pushing back and forth with him, as she joyously relinquishes all the empty years of yearning for her Raymond. Raymond's deep aroused breaths overtake his moribund thoughts as he plunges into Noriko, as close to her body as he can possibly get. The pleasure of the sex reaches into a deep emotional level of his heart, reminding him that despite all of his flaws, he is ever loved.

They lie in bed and hold each other, glistening with sweat, waiting for the council to reconvene. Their love feels like a temple around them, formed by their bare bodies wrapped around each other. Noriko is absentmindedly caressing the scar at the back of Raymond's neck.

"My dad was from a citi," Noriko finally speaks. "He met my mother here. She died when I was three. They thought it was cancer, or kidney disease. Everybody says something different. Plague took my father ten years later. It kills people in their own way. He died drinking. He drank every day, most of the day. He used to hide booze around the house, bottles of whiskey in the toilet tank, or under the bed. He thought we didn't know. Oh Papa! My lovely Papa! I couldn't stop him by reasoning with him or fighting with him or pleading with him. I started to miss him while he was alive. He wasn't a mean drunk. He didn't brawl or try to hurt me. He'd get sad and quiet. I'd ask him, 'What are you thinking about, papa?' Sometimes he would respond. Usually, he would apologize or cry. I forgave him."

She inhales a quick deep breath. She is staring far, far away, miles past the walls of the large infirmary tent. Her teeth and lips are parted by the memory of a pain she has felt since she watched the plague claim him. A pain she has conquered many times before, but never stays defeated. She exhales.

"I forgave him," she repeats, quietly.

"It's okay, baby," consoles Raymond. He holds her as she cries. "Let it out, my love."

Noriko cries. Raymond holds her silently. She feels better. When she is able to speak again, she looks directly at Raymond.

"Raymond, I don't know who deserves to die. The way you tell it, you killed someone because they would have killed you. If he had caught you, or made you fall, I never would have gotten you back. That guard was part of a bigger purpose, honey. Please forgive yourself. You must, if you want to survive the plague."

They kiss and hold each other. Raymond excuses himself to go to the outhouse.

❧ ❧ ❧

During the siesta break, at the northern edge of the settlement, beyond sight of the long hall, Charmin arrives alone in a stolen citi shuttle. He parks by the goat corral. He is wearing the chameleon suit, hood pulled back, deactivating it. It is the same suit he wore when he gave Raymond the slip. It is a full body suit with boots, gloves, and a hood. The suit is made of tight elastic coils of flexweave fabric looped together like filigree chain mail. It absorbs and radiates millions of colors. He takes off the jumpsuit and stows it in the shuttle.

Well, he thinks, back to the backwoods. He looks around the village. Despite himself, he is comforted by the familiarity and the quiet. He walks to the center of town. The long hall is deserted. People must be at their houses, he figures, or the shore. Charmin makes for the infirmary to see Noriko.

Noriko is tidying up after she and Raymond's supper. Raymond is still at the outhouse. It'll be time soon, to get back to the long hall. Charmin steps in.

"Charmin?" says Noriko, in disbelief. "You're free? How did you get out? It's been years! By the sun!" She hugs him.

"Yes," he says. He breathes in the familiar scent of her hair. He remembers how sweet it was to want her from so close...

Noriko lets go of Charmin and looks at him, ecstatic, "Are you hurt? Tell me what happened. Tell me everything."

"I stole a chameleon suit and hid near–"

"You've returned just in time!" Noriko interrupts, she is too excited. Her lover was brought home, and now their old friend has returned, too.

"Oh? How so?"

"Alain is going to be so glad to see you! You're never going to believe this – Raymond escaped too."

Charmin looks surprised. "Raymond? Escaped? Raymond is here?"

"Yes!" Noriko is beaming. "Kerwac brought him out!"

"Kerwac?"

"You haven't met him yet. He arrived here while you were gone. He's a military man, like you."

Raymond returns from the outhouse. He had a spontaneous, solitary cry after his bowels moved. He enters the infirmary, feeling thoroughly relieved, buoyant and optimistic. He sees Noriko speaking excitedly to Charmin.

"What are you doing here?" Raymond asks. His confused mind vomits questions, questions about the last time he saw Charmin, questions about this moment. "I thought you were – " "Who–?" "What did you–" He finally chooses one "How did you find me?"

"That's a fine hello," replies Charmin. "Find you? I lived here, too, Ray. What happened to you?"

"Leave him alone, Charmin," Noriko says. The emotional scene of Raymond's story in the council is still fresh in her mind. Looking at Raymond, Noriko feels an empathetic sense of fear coming from him, like he is afraid of Charmin, but angry. She had expected them to be glad to see each other, but now she adopts a defensive posture toward Charmin, moving close to Raymond and crossing her arms.

"You know this guy?" Raymond asks Noriko, disbelieving.

"You did too, honey," she says tenderly.

"I want to speak with you Raymond, about that day. Can you remember what happened at the bank that day? Why did you panic? What went wrong?" asks Charmin. He wants to control the conversation away from memories of himself. Charmin does not want Raymond to recall the airshaft. He focuses on Central Bank.

Raymond answers, "That guard chased me! That's what went wrong."

"That guard was supposed to leave before you. We had a command planted for him, but his radio was out! You started the job late. He wasn't chasing you."

"Not right away, maybe not when you were watching, but he chased me."

Charmin tries to explain, "It got mixed up. He walked out behind you, but he was not following you."

"Damn right he followed me!" Raymond is angry again. "You said it was all set up. You greasy sneak. What was in that pill? You set me up!"

"I didn't set you up. Do you even remember what happened?"

"You little rat," Raymond murmurs. When he begins speaking again, his voice gradually increases in volume, ending in a hollar. "Don't pull that shit. You left me there!"

"I – I – " Charmin pauses, summoning his liar's courage.

"I left you? You froze! There were dawgs! What good are we both caught? I had to get away to try to save you. I followed those cops, Raymond."

Raymond looks at Charmin silently, confused by Charmin's sudden appearance, and familiarity with Noriko. He is dissatisfied with Charmin's plausible explanation for what he felt was a malicious act. Noriko looks at Raymond sympathetically. Raymond is confused; that pill, that chip, Charmin's schemes – though he can share his murderous guilt and regret with Charmin, who set him up, it is no relief. In the theater of his mind, he sees that bank guard's desperate face falling away from him. Then he sees Charmin, in the airshaft, wearing the chameleon suit, just before he disappeared into that apartment building. *"Dawgs have you, weasel,"* Charmin had said. Raymond's eyes snap back open. Kerwac wasn't supposed to find me in Salt Lake, realizes Raymond. Charmin thought he'd left me there for good.

"Raymond...?" Noriko probes, hoping he is remembering more.

"What was in that pill you gave me?" Raymond asks, his face stony.

"What pill?" interjects Noriko, her turn to be confused. She makes a suspicious face at Charmin and asks again, "What pill?"

"The night before the heist in Salt Lake," continues Raymond, doggedly advancing toward Charmin. "What was in that pill?"

"That pill was a tranquilizer," Charmin lies. He hurries to misdirect the conversation away from any clues, which might lead to his allegiance with Mr. Z. "You were drunk," says Charmin. "You smelled like a saloon. You looked at me like a stupid idiot in that airshaft."

Raymond's mind feels clearer than it has in a long time. He feels angry, but he barely recognizes the sensation. He knows Charmin is lying, and it makes Raymond braver.

"But after I took that pill," insists Raymond, "everything got messed up."

Charmin himself does not know what was in the pill, but he has been working long enough to have seen pills like that.

"I don't know what was in it," he answers, "but I think it

was a deneuralizer. A nervous system script to get you through the heist."

"What kind of deneuralizer?" asks Noriko, interrupting again, steam rising in her voice.

"I don't know," confesses Charmin, bowing his head. Admitting this, thinks Charmin, will be enough to satisfy them. I can afford to sacrifice my reputation in this squatter camp, to keep Mr. Z a secret, to keep my job.

"Where did you get it?" Raymond asks, pointedly.

"I stole it," lies Charmin. He does not speak the truth, that the pill was supplied by a secretive, wealthy recluse who hired him to watch Raymond for the last 9 years.

"You gave him a deneuralizer," Noriko's voice hits a vehement, chastising pitch, "and you didn't even know what kind?!"

"He'll be alright," says Charmin.

"You! You're not alright!" Noriko is incensed at the thought of Raymond in any more danger, especially from someone she thought was so dear. "You could have killed him! Why would you do that?"

"Me? Raymond's a drug addict. Back in Salt Lake, he was taking any pills I could find him. I gave him that pill because I wanted him to get some rest before the heist. Don't shovel this on me!"

Raymond is not convinced.

Charmin looks at his feet. He can't tell the real reason, that he was hired to do it. Charmin's face is drawn. Time for a little bit of truth, he thinks. He burns the emotional bridge, for cover.

"Why?" replies Charmin. "Because I wanted to return here to you, alone. Without him."

"You covetous scarecrow!" Noriko yells. "You sold out Raymond to steal me?!" She takes a breath, regains her composure, and chooses not to hate. The next words march out of her mouth on a tightrope: "You could never have me, Charmin. You are an envious, two-faced fool to think you could destroy your friend to steal love." In an instant, Noriko's medically trained mind conjurs optimism, a learned emotional defense. "I'm still glad you're home, safe from that citi."

Well, that worked, thinks Charmin.

Raymond sees the way Charmin looks at Noriko. He wonders, What was between them? Tiny hot bubbles of rage form in his heart and start fizzing like soda pop. A defensive ripple of anger rises up from his gut. His stoic face disguises his rage. Taking advantage of surprise, Raymond punches Charmin low and hard in the abdomen, right on the bladder. Charmin doubles over, and pisses his pants a little bit. Raymond is tempted to attack Charmin without reservation, to kick Charmin in the face while he's bent over; to unleash his rage on this slippery false friend that nearly cost him his life. But the recently revealed memory of killing the bank guard cools his rage with a sickening guilt. He has already killed, and cannot bear the thought of more.

"A low blow for a low man," says Raymond, looking down at Charmin clutching his midsection. Raymond walks slowly out of the infirmary, head high.

"Baby, come back!" calls Noriko, but she knows better than to follow him now.

Raymond walks on, toward the shore. Charmin straightens up slowly. He has a small wet patch on the front of his trousers. "Sucker punch me? I will reach down your throat and rip–"

"Shut up, Charmin. Don't you touch him."

Charmin stands down. "Feel better now, buddy?" he calls after Raymond, sarcastically kind. Charmin gazes at Noriko. In his heart, he feels the same old torturous, intoxicating swirl of sympathy and desire for her. He touches her arm.

"Noriko, I'm sorry."

"Get out, Charmin."

"But, I –"

"Get out."

Charmin goes to Alain's house. Colin Chris and Ora are also there. They are having a bite to eat and digesting the news about Raymond. Ora plays tug-of-war with Gracie, using the dog's rag doll chew toy. At the sight of Charmin, Alain's face lights up. Colin Chris hugs Charmin enthusiastically, clapping him on the back.

"It is good to have you back, Charmin," says Alain. "This is truly fortuitous! The original team is returned."

Ora smiles politely at Charmin. She welcomes him home. She does not stand up nor embrace him. She senses an unnamed desire in him, a vortex of lust that she prefers to keep at a distance.

Alain sits face to face with Charmin, his smiling face animated with excitement. “We have big news,” he begins, “We have the gem. Ray brought it.”

“The gem is here?” says Charmin, playing dumb. “Ray brought it?”

“Well, he has not shown it to everyone yet,” explains Ora, “but Noriko has seen it, among his things. Everyone knows, like Christmas. When the council reconvenes after siesta, we will see it.”

“The mission is complete,” says Alain happily. “These years have not been wasted. If that gem contains even a portion of what you suspected it contained, then this is a very exciting time.”

“You’re right,” replies Charmin. “This is what we wanted anyway.”

“Once we examine that gem,” says Colin Chris with wonder, “we’ll be able to use it to hack into a citi to steal food, or even rescue more people. We might be able to open up a whole citi! We can wake up all the citizens in bondage and foment a revolution. The time for revolution may be at hand!”

“Fat chance,” says Alain.

“Oh yeah? Why?” asks Colin Chris.

“The people in those cities are not farmers and fighters. They are chipped office droids, reared on comfort and misinformation. We don’t have any hydrowaves or AC or plumbing out here. They won’t choose to live like this.”

“They will know who they are,” says Colin Chris. “They are humans and we should help them.”

“Who are they?” asks Alain. “Who you tell them to be, is all.”

“Lighten up, old man,” jests Colin Chris.

“Let’s take a deep breath,” checks Charmin. He stands up. He steps to the door. “Let’s see what it really is first.”

They leave Alain’s house to reconvene at the long hall. Along the walk there, Charmin excuses himself to urinate.

“I need to reclaim some water,” he jests to Alain, using a

common euphemism for urination. “Waste not, want not. I’ll stop at the desalinator.”

“There’s no time. Just put it in a jar for later,” insists Alain.

“Good idea,” concurs Charmin. He turns back to Alain’s house. “I’ll be right behind you,” he tells the group.

Gracie lingers at Charmin’s heels, still happily sniffing his old, lost familiar scent. Gracie wants to go back to the house with Charmin.

“Go on,” Charmin says to the mutt. He gives Gracie a kick. Gracie growls at him, then leaves Charmin alone and catches up with Colin Chris, Ora, and Alain.

Back in Alain’s kitchen, Charmin flips his comm open. Mr. Z said the prize had left Salt Lake, thinks Charmin. He didn’t say it came straight back here. Maybe old Z doesn’t know it’s here. Yeah, sure. I’ll report it either way.

He punches in a short message. He cannot make a call out here, but he can use the short wave military net to send encrypted text to Mr. Z.

Subject and prize in Appalachia. Subject consumed deneuralizer in Salt Lake. Pay up.

He confirms the send and stows his comm. He sees an empty mason jar on the kitchen counter. What the hell, thinks Charmin, when you gotta go. He empties his bladder, filling the jar with his urine. He closes the lid on the jar and places it at the end of the counter; someone can take it to the desalinator later. Charmin leaves Alain’s house, to join everyone in the long hall.

Noriko is alone in the infirmary. That Charmin! She thinks to herself, that goose-plucking concubine, what has he been up to? Noriko collects the dirty dishes of she and Raymond’s lunch. Two enameled metal bowls, two titanium sporks, and a wooden spoon in a small cooking pot. She nibbles the last bites of beans and crumbled cornbread left in the pot. It is all military issue crockery. Noriko thinks thankfully of Kerwac’s contributions to the village, even here, at the stove.

Her thoughts turn to Raymond. Oh Ray, my sweet poor Ray, she thinks. What happened to you in there, darling? Remembering that day of the robbery in the citi is a big step.

Maybe I can show you now. Noriko pulls out a trunk beneath the mattress.

Inside are books, all handwritten. There are scrapbooks of salvaged photographs, notebooks, hand-bound books, books of drawings and paintings, and books of poetry. Laid gently on top of the books, is a dragon made out of colored construction paper. The craftwork paper dragon is faded and feathery. Noriko moves the dragon aside. She lifts a cardboard bound composition notebook out of the trunk. With her right arm, she hugs the book to her breast. It is Raymond's old journal. Out of love and respect, and a hope that he would return, she has never read it, but she feels the need to hold it every now and again. She always felt that if she read the journal, she would be admitting in her heart that he was gone forever. Instead, she kept it safe for him. Many nights she has held Raymond's journal, when she missed him, knowing that his thoughts were imprinted there, as if she could sip a bit of his spirit from holding his thoughts near. She won't give it to him in front of everyone, but he must have it again. With her left arm, she closes the trunk. She stands up. She returns to the long hall for the reconvening council, Raymond's old journal clasped to her body.

Raymond trudges out of the infirmary, leaving Noriko and Charmin there. Most people are still eating at home. Few are milling around in front of the long hall, eager to reconvene. They smile at Raymond. The shock of seeing Charmin is too much for Raymond's recently restored memory. He walks past, head down, in a wide arc around the long hall. It seems like every hour that passes here draws more attention to Raymond and his problems. Everyone here treats him like a friend, though he hardly recognizes them. Each face flutters in his mind near a vague recollection of a familiar face. He cannot remember if he has seen faces like theirs before, back in the citi, in his workgroup. Or perhaps he just thinks he remembers them because he feels like he's supposed to remember them. The last thing he wants now is to be surrounded by all of these people again. He walks away from the village, toward the beach.

The shore is warm and windy. The air looks cottony. The

breaks are foamy and the seawater swells appear dense and mercurial in the overcast daylight. Raymond takes off his shoes. He walks barefoot along the sandy beach, past the whalebones, to Old Michaels café. A cool coastal zephyr soughs in off of the ocean. Down along the beach, clear of the high tide line, he sees the familiar grove of umbrellas. He hears their leafy fluttering on the breeze. The waves groan in the distance.

"Ah, Raymond, welcome back."

"Hi, Michael."

Old Michael watches Raymond.

"Still a nice place," says Raymond. He eases into a chair.

"Thank you, yes," replies Old Michael. "The sound of the waves helps me sleep. Fancy a drink, or just in for the shade?"

Raymond smiles. "You need sun to have shade, old man. Yes, coffee sounds great."

Old Michael deftly mashes a handful of roasted coffee beans with his mortar and pestle.

"Why aren't you at the council meeting?" asks Old Michael. "Is it already over?"

"Not quite, we're on a meal break. Hey, how come you aren't at the meetings?" counters Raymond.

"I'm too old for politics. I listen from here, on the shortwave. More importantly, why aren't you there?" asks Old Michael again. "You're the reason they have called to council."

He begins brewing Raymond's coffee.

"Yeah, so they say. How come you know all this?"

"People have been talking about you. You and that jewel."

"Yeah, I turned it on. It's called a 'rakan.' I said that name and it played an old video for me. A guy named Xavier was giving a speech. He was selling biospheres; but it was long ago, back before there were biospheres."

"That sounds like an old, secure file."

"Yes, very secure," agrees Raymond. "First generation biosphere owners, identified on film? That's rare."

Old Michael remains silent and lets Raymond think. He loves to watch Raymond think.

"Now that I think of it, 'rakan' could just have just been a trigger word for that specific message...anyway, it contains things that important people didn't want public. I think that thing is powerful. I'd like to plug it into a computer deck and find out; see how it works."

"It sounds like the perfect thing for a council meeting."

Raymond makes a dismissive puffing sound, tired of being the center of everyone's attention.

"I can tell you are angry. You do not know why. Your family history may illuminate your anger."

"I know why I'm angry! I'm an amnesiac, fugitive killer. My life is upside down. No one will leave me alone. I want to do this alone and I feel like the whole eastern seaboard is reading over my shoulder. I think I could make more sense of this rakan working alone. There's too much pressure on me right now! A week ago, I didn't know any of this existed, and now it's all I have."

"It's all you need," assures Old Michael. "Besides, if you wanted to be alone, why come here?"

Raymond does not answer. Begrudgingly, silently, he knows that Old Michael has a point. He sips coffee.

Old Michael continues, "You may yet remember how at home you used to feel here."

"Colin Chris says I may not. I guess it's partially true. Some things have come back. I just don't feel myself."

"It's been a long time, Raymond. Even if you hadn't been caught and chipped, you would have changed naturally. Yes, your identity starts with self. But individuality is an overripe fruit, boy; it only starts there. You need to let go of your self and live connected to others, here and now. You've been living connected to a system, not people."

"What good am I if I'm not me?" harps Raymond. "I have no idea who I am. I barely remember the girl I'm in love with. I'm surrounded by a colony of cultists trying to save the world."

"Save the world?" replies Old Michael sternly. "The world already ended, Ray. This is what's left! Do you even want to take care of the only thing you have left? Your memories are already returning. Your anger is a shield around fear. Ask yourself what you could be afraid of. Use your anger to trace your fear. Face it and your fear will wash away."

The coffee is ready. He hands the steaming brew to Raymond. Old Michael smiles at Raymond warmly, then turns away to watch the waves break. He flips through one of his books, making his attentiveness to Raymond less obvious. They think in silence. As the silence ripens with thought, Old Michael begins telling Raymond a story:

"There was a great man, long ago, named Salvador Tosc. He was a genius in matters of the mind and heart, with a flair for cybernetics. This great man detested the idea of the biospheres from the very start, because he knew that human beings, so closely monitored by other human beings who deem themselves betters, could never flourish. Salvador had a vision of a world without biospheres, fully illuminated by the life-giving sun. He dreamt that the clouds could be parted, and the abundant radiant energy from the sky would shine down upon humanity again. He may very well have succeeded in his lifetime, but his brilliant life was cut short by the Lattice Corporation, which owned the rights to all of his technological innovations.

"But Salvador was wily. He made sure, in the event of his death, that all of his work most prized by the Lattice executors was destroyed. He nearly ruined Lattice, but not completely. To prevent any other clandestine interference from the Toscs, the Lattice Corporation attempted to destroy Salvador's entire family line. Nevertheless, Salvador was survived by one of his three children, Germane Tosc.

"Germane lived in hiding, founding a village in the Pennsylvania hills that became a refuge for fugitives and revolutionaries. Cloud plague or not, many people still wanted to live in the world, not in a bubble. Germane hatched plans to intercept deliveries to biosphere construction sites in the American northeast, including Michigan and upstate New York. Because of the rising sea levels, anything further east, like Baltimore, Manhattan, and old Virginia was already underwater.

"In this way, Germane was able to build up his village using stolen food and resources from the Lattice conglomerate that destroyed his father. This also put Germane on the executors' radar in Gibraltar. His friends and cohorts spread south along the Appalachian Trail, starting new settlements and merging with fellow outsiders they met there. Germane was eventually killed on a raid to Detroit by a Lattice task force. Germane, in turn, was survived by a son named Bishop, who passed on his father's story about his epochal grandfather Salvador Tosc, who loved entirely and worked tirelessly to heal the world."

Old Michael notices an expression of surprise and enlightenment spreading across Raymond's face. He continues speaking anyway. "Bishop married a woman named Irene, named after Salvador's wife, that poor soul brimming with beauty, who was taken by the plague."

Raymond interrupts Old Michaels story, finishing it abruptly. " – Bishop and Irene are my parents!"

"Precisely."

"By the Sun! How do you know all of this?" Raymond asks.

Old Michael smiles at Raymond with affectionate sympathy. "My dear Raymond – you once told me."

Gracie runs by along the beach, chasing a ball into the surf. Gracie's human is close behind, a settler come by the boneyard café. It is Colin Chris. The old man smiles at Colin Chris and beckons. Colin Chris enters the café and the three men exchange greetings. Old Michael hands Colin Chris coffee, just finished brewing. "Hi Raymond. I thought I might find you here. We're ready to get started. People are asking about you."

Raymond makes a surly face. Can't they just leave me alone for a while, he thinks.

"We were just having a talk," explains Old Michael.

"What were you speaking about, gentlemen?" asks Colin Chris, exhibiting a subtle decorum that he unconsciously reserves for Old Michael. "What have I interrupted?"

"History," says Old Michael.

"And anger," adds Raymond.

Colin Chris smiles. "Ah, that old chestnut. Who's angry?"

"I am," answers Raymond, "I was."

Colin Chris changes the subject. "I hate to be the buzzkill philosopher. It would be great to spend the evening unpacking this idea, but I am sure we will have time later. Raymond, I came down here looking for you. Most of us are back at the long hall. We are waiting for you, and the gem."

They wait for Raymond to move or break the silence, but he says nothing.

"You go on ahead, Colin Chris." instructs Old Michael. "Raymond will follow you shortly. Tell everyone he's on the way."

Colin Chris drains his coffee, gives Raymond a pat on the back, and heads off. He whistles for Gracie. She stops chasing waves and follows back to the long hall.

"Learn kinder ways to speak with yourself," says Old Michael. "This is how we survive."

"Speak with myself? What do I say?" asks Raymond.

"That's your job. But, since you asked, start with questions...and remember forgiveness. The changes inside your heart will come slower than the thoughts. Reflect upon your actions. Find change. Find forgiveness."

Raymond walks away south along the deserted shore of the Atlantic Ocean, back towards the settlement. The tide roars under the carpet of grey clouds. He knows real sky is up there, past those clouds. He remembers the citi. In the citi, there was sky, thinks Ray. It used to rain. Not sky, but...well, showered – not actually rain - irrigated, washed, whatever. God! It felt more like sky when I was in there! What is wrong with me? Shut up!

Raymond walks briskly on the fine sand closer to the waves, looking at the ground, gesticulating silently. Listen to yourself, man! You hate yourself! Raymond winces and makes a fist. Fuck you, Raymond! Fuck you, Raymond! God damn it, fuck you Raymond! I feel so furious. I feel so ashamed. I fucked up my life! I killed that man. I lost everything. I'm a murderer! A murderer. How could I sleep through that? And that pill! That bastard, Charmin. That poor guard. That damn guard! I'm just a tool, used by others. Don't talk to yourself that way! Calm down!

Raymond slows down. He raises his head. He watches the ocean, the break of waves, churning sand. His gaze flits far out over the water, near the horizon. Maybe a weather front moving in. Yeah, right, it's always clouds and no rain, no matter what. His breaths are fast and irregular. Gulls cruise above, inland from the break. The sea birds caw a jarring lilt. God damn you, Raymond! Don't talk to yourself that way! He recalls what Noriko told him, about surviving his guilt. He stops walking. Thinking of Noriko's tenderness taps his glassy self-loathing like a ball peen hammer, shattering his composure. He weeps. He falls to his knees on the beach, then slumps into a heap. He cries so hard his abdominal muscles start to ache. Depression is taking hold, but Raymond is not helpless. He remembers what Noriko told him about depression. He remembers that Noriko loves him.

The afternoon sky begins darkling. Raymond falls silent. His breaths are deep and regular. Again, he thinks of himself. He thinks of his mistakes, his stupid accidents, the things he's wanted and never had. Sitting on the sand, hugging his knees, that thought makes him cry again, hard. But after that, he is, at long last, tired and calm; and a little thirsty.

"I forgive you, Raymond," he says quietly, speaking to himself. "I forgive you for hating yourself. It's okay. It's okay. I love you."

He stands and begins his return to the long hall.

CHAPTER 16
DECIDING UPON A COURSE

After siesta, the village gathers again in the long hall. While Raymond has been down at the shore, news of Charmin's return has spread through the settlement like a thrown rock's ripple across the surface of a pond. People are giving him hugs, welcoming him home, and shaking his hand.

Ora stands near the kids' bay as their sitter. She watches Charmin warily. He's hiding something, she thinks, something he wants very badly. Kerwac can take this guy, she thinks.

Many feel Charmin's return is a blessed, or at least charmed, turn of events. Old hopes are surfacing. Charmin and Kerwac greet each other cordially as the council reconvenes but they do not have much to say to each other. Each is a military man. Their mutual experience speaks for itself. They regard each other with silent professional courtesy.

Townsend stands as moderator. "We have wonderful news. Both Raymond and Charmin have returned home to us! A warm welcome goes out to both of you men." The assembly applauds.

"Now we also have learned that, at long last and against all odds, they have accomplished their original mission. The artifact has been retrieved. The data gem is here. Everyone has been waiting a long time for this day. We thought it would never come." Townsend, smiling, addresses Raymond, "Let us see this infamous jewel, Raymond."

Raymond shows them. He takes the gem out of his pocket and holds it up.

"It has a message in it," Raymond explains, "a coded message. It is easier to see with the lights down."

They put out the center fire. They draw the sky roof closed. The long hall darkens like a planetarium. Kerwac hands Raymond the PAGsor laptop from their escape across the plains, the same computer deck that animated Rodney. Raymond mashes the putty core of the crystal onto the data ports of the computer deck. The putty molds into the data ports. It connects instantly, recognizing Raymond's hand. It emits an ambient glow.

"Rakan," utters Raymond, "wake up."

Now that the data gem is connected to a power source, it brightens considerably. The multiple facets of the data gem begin to glow and cast rays through the long hall. Beams like insect antennae are cast from the crystal onto the walls and ceiling of the long hall. The fine beams of light waver in primary colors, and then brighten again. They pan around the room like disco ball lights. The gem works as a perfect beam splitter. It coordinates the now thousands of beams. Each beam becomes a floating pixel in a growing cloud of light. The beams of light resolve into a hologram of a man's face. His obsidian black hair frames arresting steel grey eyes. He has a handsome, vaguely triangular face; wide, deep eyes set off by a sharp, dimpled chin. Extra pixel beams from the gem illuminate a hazy blue aura around the bust. The face singles out Raymond, looking directly at him. People wonder at the holographic spectacle.

"What IS that?"

"Rakan, he called it."

"RAKAN."

"Is that a word? An acronym?"

"A palin –?"

"Definitely not a palindrome, man."

"Yah, that would be rakar."

People begin calling out commands to the computer.

"Wait! Show us Salt Lake Citi!"

Family members call out, "Show me Jules!"

"Show me Adrian!"

Fugitives call out, "Show me New York!"

"Show me Baltimore!"

"How does this thing work?"

"Show me Detroit!"

"Show me a directory of files!"

"Restart!"

Raymond says nothing. He looks back at the hologram for some time. The face does not respond to anyone's commands. Finally, the settlers quiet down. Its holographic eyes stare right at Raymond like he is the only thing this computer can see.

Are you not the keeper of the estate? it asks. The voice sounds thin coming out of the PAGSor laptop, but the face's annunciation is clear and strong.

Raymond looks around. It is almost a comic gesture, given that the giant face is looking directly at him.

"Yes," replies Raymond, finally.

Hello, kinsman. Thank you for identifying yourself to me, it replies.

"You're welcome. What is your name?"

My name is Salvador.

"Salvador?" asks Raymond, "THE Salvador?"

Yes, it confirms. *Though many have had that name, I understand your question. I am the Salvador you are descended from.*

"Do you have any other names?"

I have been called the Hall of Ancestors, and the rakan.

"What's a rakan?" asks Raymond.

It is the foundation of an edifice, replies Salvador cryptically.

"What is it, Ray? Why can't we talk to it?" asks Townsend.

"You can talk to it," says Raymond.

Charmin watches silently, trying to memorize as much of what Salvador says as possible.

"No. Why won't it listen to us?" asks Alain. "It acts like it can't even hear us."

"Why can't you see the people around me?" Raymond asks.

I perceive them, though not as clearly as I see you. When they speak, I hear some of what they say, but it makes little sense. With focus, I can hear what they say. Even then, I cannot speak to them. They cannot interact with me. As a security measure, access to this lobe of the processor is granted only to a genetic match. My message may only be delivered to a Tosc.

"What are you?" asks Raymond.

I am a construct of a human nervous system. I am an algorithmic recreation of synaptic firing patterns. But you have activated only one half of the rakan processor. Now pay attention: The rakan is in two parts because it is a brain. The brain that built me, powers me. Like primitive surgery for an epileptic, my lobes have been severed from each other.

Salvador's hologram shrinks. Next to his face appears another high definition image. Two gems, identical to the one Salvador is housed in, are pictured. They float next to each other. In an animation, the two halves join to each other, to create a round, vaguely brain shaped globe. The two animated halves separate again. They reattach once more, and separate again. Salvador dispels the illustration. His face grows again to its original giant size before speaking.

The rakan is a model of the brain on a pliable atomic level. It is not diamond or crystal. It only seems like it. I can reconfigure its structure to adapt to processing needs. I can also conduct high levels of energy to power machinery. We had to expand the periodic table to build me. Tosc, you must rejoin the lobes of the rakan.

Salvador's face dissolves into a high definition globe of the earth. It illuminates two flashing icons, each shaped like the jewel among them. One icon on the globe blinks in the Americas right where they are, in the foothills of the Appalachians. The other winking icon is across the Atlantic Ocean, at the rock of Gibraltar, in the strait between Spain and Morocco that leads to the Mediterranean Sea.

Raymond asks a more precise question, "Who were you?"

I was a man, Salvador Tosc. I built the computer that made this optical drive possible. Locked in this drive is a catalogue of my memories. It knows what I knew.

"How?" asks Raymond.

The cloud of light atomizes. Salvador's face disappears in a flash. The beams of light spread all over the interior of the long hall. Each viewer's face is spattered with sparkles of light. The thin beams reform, above the gem, into a wavering, full sized image. Two men are frozen in the midst of a dialogue. They are in a large room with low lighting. The image resolves. The details improve.

The pictured room is cavernous, with round walls and a vaulted ceiling. The top of the room is obscured in shadow. In the center of the room is a column connected to the domed roof. The column is covered with touch screen computer consoles. Each console is active. Some scrolling code, some twinkling with indicator lights. On one screen is a floating, skeletal 3D model of a large geodesic globe, with a seam along the middle. Like the animation they just saw, the globe resembles a brain. On one edge of the cavernous room, along the curved wall, is a small cubic chamber. The tiny chamber has one door, with no windows.

One of the men is easily recognizable as Salvador, with black hair, steely eyes, and dimpled narrow chin. He is wearing a white laboratory coat. Dressed like this, Raymond recognizes Salvador as the man who nodded encouragingly at Xavier on the tiny video. The other man is Xavier. He is wearing a pinstriped, olive green suit. He has a round ruddy face. He is mostly bald, with a crown of wispy, downy brown hair. The man in the olive suit is holding his hand up, palm in, as if emphasizing a point. Salvador's mouth is open in mid sentence. Salvador is looking at one of the computer consoles, studying the model of the globe. The image plays.

"I'm almost done," replies Salvador. "Once we run this chimp trial, we'll be ready for a human subject." He turns away from the computer model to look at Xavier. "We don't need the money. Besides, I'm sure that is not why you want the taxpayer's money."

"They don't know how to spend that money, anyway. Representative government is so slow and wasteful. The board of executors can better use that money to benefit the same masses that are accruing it."

"That is a long, dark road, Xavier."

"How do you know?" asks Xavier. He is irritated by Sal's holier-than-thou tone.

"How do I know what? How do I know that if you rob a free people's treasury you are a low criminal? That's an easy one, Xavier. You had best ask yourself why you want to do this," warns Salvador. "These appeals to greed and vanity, this exploitation of people's vulnerabilities, to gobble up more things you desire, to make room to desire more things to gobble – because you think you can conduct other people's lives better than they can their own – that is a long, dark road, Xavier. You have all of these pragmatic ideas for world government based on the idea that people can't govern themselves, just because you want to rule them."

Xavier makes a dismissive face. "Ever the idealist. People are *governing themselves.* We *are their representatives, Salvador."*

"They didn't choose you. Your altruism is thinly veiled greed. That's what started this in the first place. That is why those terrorists girded the planet with nukes, to take out the one percent that you are trying to reinstall."

Xavier patiently lets Salvador finish speaking. He moves closer to his old friend. He puts his arm around Salvador.

"Look around you, Sal. Look at this technology we've been able to create."

"Yes," says Salvador, "with your looks and my brains, we've accomplished quite a lot."

Xavier walks Salvador over to the small chamber at the edge of the room. They look at the little cell. It is lit from inside. A parallelogram of light spills out of the room's open doorway and falls across their feet.

"You're sure the scanner is really done, now?" asks Xavier.

"Yes," affirms Salvador, sharing Xavier's pride at their accomplishment. "Just one more test, for good measure."

"C'mon," says Xavier. He walks into the scanning chamber. He gestures for Salvador to follow him in. In a moment they are standing together in the tiny cubic room. There is an unupholstered dentist's chair bolted to the middle of the floor. It has wrist and ankle straps attached to it for keeping subjects still during the scanning procedure. The walls are gray. The corners are rounded. They are standing

in a large tank.

"What do you think this machine is for, Sal?"

"It's the Hall of Ancestors, Xavier. It is our dream turned into matter."

"This part of it is your dream, to record grandparents so we can talk to our dead. Think harder," says Xavier. "The technology in this machine will supply infrastructure for many powerful technologies of the future, not just this Hall of Ancestors. Different parts of this machine, the innovations in the software, the innovations in computer processing, all can contribute to an even greater endeavor still than the Hall of Ancestors."

"Yeah, yeah, get on with it. Like what? The biospheres?" Salvador takes the bait.

"Yes, biospheres! Think of a broader more holistic metatechnology. Think of a truly sustainable city, a place so meticulously constructed that it has architectural plans right down to its microbe populations. Just think, real biospheres." Xavier trails off, imagining his future.

"Like the microbe architecture that created that locust killing virus?"

"Locusts are pests!"

"Locusts were *pests. They're extinct, because of your microbes and chemicals. You treated the locusts like squatters cutting our barbed wire fences. They were part of earth. Now they're gone like the bees and wasps. The locusts were part of a message."*

"And our crops grow on," replies Xavier.

"I can't believe you. So, what's your point?"

Xavier continues, "Think about this machine. If we can record enough neurological and genetic information to power an optical facsimile of a person, why can't we just put it back into a person, any person? We don't need the whole machine, Sal. We need enough of the machine to interrupt human neural pathways."

"No."

"The identity chip."

"No! You can't. It's exploitive and dishonest. Besides, it will not work."

"That's what I meant, Sal. Look around you! Everything

this machine is built for is exploitive and dishonest. Even the way it is funded."

"We can not do it, Xavier." Sal is reasoning with Xavier. "If we take the person out of the body, there is no person left. This machine just makes a detailed, composite image. The scanner is invasive. Any organism scanned, dies. The identity transferred to the processor is just an image of a dead person."

"Well, that image is detailed enough."

"No, it isn't. It can't be used to program people!"

"Why did you think we got so much money dumped on us? For a fancy photo album? Remember how fast the money dried up after we got the successful neural interruptions?"

"I thought that was because it took us 11 years..." Comprehension is dawning on Salvador.

"It's because we were done! We kept building the Hall of Ancestors because the publicity was great. It kept you quiet and busy. Think about it, Sal. The neural interrupter was the project. Think of what it is capable of! Curing schizophrenia! Curing paralysis!"

"You don't want to cure schizophrenia. You want to control it. You don't get it, Xavier. The neurological system is too delicate, too complex to alter. We can photograph it – and even that destroys it. But you can not remodel it without dire consequences."

"Everyone else thinks you're wrong, Sal."

"I won't let you. I'll stop you. I'll tell everyone."

Xavier pulls out a small, pneumatic dart gun. It is equipped with tiny, poison-tipped projectiles. He quickly shoots Salvador in the chest. FFT.

"Ow!" Salvador grabs the dart to pull it out. Xavier shoots Salvador a second time, in the neck. FFT. In a matter of heartbeats, the sedative spreads.

"How could you?" exhorts Salvador, thunderstruck. His legs give out.

Salvador wakes up, minutes later, strapped into the chair of the Hall of Ancestors neural scanner cell. He is naked. His mouth is taped shut. He takes deep breaths through his nose. Xavier is standing in the doorway of the scanner cell. Sal tries to press his tongue between his closed lips to move the tape; impossible. Xavier steps backwards out of the room.

"I'm sorry. I knew you wouldn't understand. Goodbye, Sal." Xavier swings the door shut.

Xavier steps over to the consoles in the column of the room. The 3D model of the brain globe is still revolving. Xavier runs the HoA diagnostics. On another monitor is the scanning cell. He has a view of Salvador, naked, bound, and struggling in the chair. The 3D model on the first monitor stops revolving. The brain globe glows green.

Rakan diagnostic complete. Sample ready for import.

Xavier switches on the Hall of Ancestors.

5 seconds to sequence initiation.

Salvador tries to scream Xavier's name. It comes out as a muted hum.

4 seconds

3 seconds

Tears stream down Salvador's cheeks.

2 seconds

1 second

Begin recording

Xavier watches on the monitor. Hair thin blue tendrils of electric light emit from the walls of the cell on all sides. The arcs of electricity penetrate Salvador's flesh and begin adhering to his neurons. They make tiny precise incisions, perforating his body, causing no bleeding. The beams leave scorched dots, like dark freckles, that slowly spread all over his body.

On the adjacent console monitor, the rakan globe is slowly being written with Salvador's synaptic firing patterns. For every needle of electric light that penetrates Sal's dying flesh, a reproduction of the consumed portion of his nervous system is etched into the crystalline globe. Xavier, as if handing off his heart to his treachery, watches Sal, making sure the machine is working.

The video dissolves into a white cloud of pixels. Salvador's looming face appears again in the center of the cloud.

That is how, he says to Raymond. *That was the last thing that happened to me alive.*

"What happened after?" asks Raymond.

*I was initialized in the rakan, whole and fully wired to the Hall of Ancestors. I suddenly lived in the computer, and the computer was networked into the whole building. The whole building and all of its computers became my new body. I locked down everything that I could reach. I locked Xavier in the HoA cavern. I sent out distress signals on the net. I did everything I could to stop his new corporation, destroying the data banks of my work and liquidating as many of their assets as possible. I set them back pretty far, but it appears as though many of their schemes have come to fruition.

Xavier, in the room with me, tried to format me, to erase the rakan. But, long before that day, I suspected some sort of treachery from him and his cronies. I locked the rakan so that it may only be accessed by my genetic profile. When Xavier saw that the scan was successful, that the rakan was sentient, and that he could not control it, he split the lobes apart manually. But I managed to trap him for a long time, twenty six days.

"Why were you built with two lobes in the first place?"

I modeled the rakan processor after the human brain, with two lobes. One lobe is primarily a storage device. The other lobe is primarily a user interface.

"Like ROM and RAM," digests Raymond.

Yes, very similar to the old ROM and RAM models. I am trapped, well, most of me, here in this RAM brain. This side of my brain is the user interface. The one at Lattice, Corp., is my ROM brain. It is capable of massive feats of data storage and compression. This here, Sal nods his holographic head towards the jewel plugged into the laptop projecting his image, *is the user interface lobe. This UI lobe can synthesize all the data managed by the storage lobe, or any of the world's smaller computers.*

"What is the other lobe doing?"

I do not know. This is the first computer I have been connected to since Xavier split me apart. This computer is a one-node network. It is connected to nothing else. If you can get me into a larger network, I will be able to do more.

During Ray and Salvador's palaver, Charmin's comm vibrates. In the dark, he checks discreetly. Of course, it is word from Mr. Z.

50% pay for previous job. Bring subject and prize to Gibraltar.

That'll do, thinks Charmin, still in the game.

Salvador has just finished replaying the video that Raymond watched alone in the infirmary, of Xavier selling the biospheres.

I was at that meeting, 105 years ago. Xavier was the sales panache; I was the scientific backbone of the Hall of Ancestors. We needed to fund it so we joined forces with developers like those men in the video.

"Who were those men?" asks Raymond. "What is the Hall of Ancestors?"

Those men were the charter members of a multinational fund, including Lattice and several other corporations. They were where the money came from. I built the Hall of Ancestors to record our dead using a synaptic firing pattern sampler. I wanted people to somehow always be in touch with their dead kin. The technology ushered in by the Hall of Ancestors development yielded a lot of new advances, like the identity chip you once wore.

Raymond touches the scab at the back of his neck with his fingertips, remembering the chip that Kerwac cut out of his body.

Those men used Lattice, Corp., to steal my technology, continues Salvador, *They wanted to rewrite our living, to make the masses more manageable at higher densities for increased biosphere efficiency. To them, it's cattle driving. Human beings get chipped, conditioned, and dropped into a workgroup with compatible psychological profiles.*

"So they got the idea for the identity chips from your construction and..." Raymond trails off, at a loss for words, face to face with a holographic projection of his long dead great-grandfather. "You're really in there?" says Raymond.

My nervous system is replicated in this circuitry – all of my nervous system. A great deal of identity is housed in the nervous system, but not all. Have you heard those stories about people that lose an appendage but keep feeling it itch or ache?

"Yeah, I've heard of that–phantom limbs," says Raymond.

Well, my whole body feels like that, yet I don't have a body. I feel no time. I need no sleep. I'm dead, but I still feel all those aches I had in my back from bad posture. I have copies of all of the old backaches and joint pains that resided in my nervous system. They were copied, too. I'm caught here in dark sleeplessness. Anything I want to see, within the network I'm connected to, appears here. It becomes a space around me. I can move through it, jump out of it any moment, as long as I am connected to a network. At the moment, this computer is my network. I've read the copy of Rodney you wrote, by the way. It's not bad.

"Thanks..." replies Raymond, surprised that he feels somewhat shy because of the praise. He is unaccustomed to such talk. After a pause, Raymond asks, "So, how old are you?" Raymond asks Salvador.

According to the date in this computer, I have been trapped in the rakan for 94 years.

"Wow, a hundred years old," marvels Raymond. "And you can run any computer?"

Precisely.

"What about encryptions?" asks Raymond.

I can read anything, assures Salvador. * And I can reprogram anything to which I am connected.*

"Wow."

Charmin interrupts. Following orders, he pushes the Gibraltar idea. "We should do what this rakan says. We should take it to its other half in Gibraltar."

Alain disagrees. "No. You heard the thing. It can run any computer. It can read anything. We can use it to hack a citi! We can rescue our lost loves. We can take as much food as we like. Why don't we spend the energy going back west for our loved ones? Why are we not making plans to go west? Back to rescue our lost kin."

There are few murmurs of assent from the gathered settlers.

"Back to Salt Lake?" asks Charmin. "You think it will be easier, or more noble, to go back and rescue the old team from the Capitol? That citi has plenty security. They have plenty more defenses. We did it once, sure, but barely."

"Some of us must go back to Salt Lake," says Alain.

"They'll get you if you go back!" warns Charmin.

"They didn't get me!" argues Alain.

"Well, they got me. We have to go bigger than Salt Lake," insists Charmin. "We need a new plan. We must hit the source. We have to go to Gibraltar."

"I will go back," says Alain. "I can find my way around in there."

"They'll catch you, and they'll chip you," replies Charmin matter-of-factly. "Let's say, because of this rakan, that you don't get caught. The odds of you finding them, waking them all up, and getting them all out of the citi, especially so soon after our attack, are slim to none."

"Why take it anywhere?" asks Townsend. "This rakan could help us, right here. Using some of the equipment Kerwac brought out of Norfolk, I could use it to reverse engineer the grain. We can purify the seed we have. We could do it in a year," he proclaims.

"But it would re-germinate as suicide seed a year later," reminds Colin Chris. "All the pollen out here is suicide seed. We'll need to steal it from citis again."

"Not necessarily," says Townsend.

"Let's see what everyone thinks," says Alain, hoping for more active supporters. "Winston?"

"Sorry, Alain, I say we get rid of it," votes Winston. "My opinion shouldn't count so much, anyway, because I am staying here with Katrina and Oro, regardless."

"Point taken, but your opinion does matter," says Townsend. "Kerwac, what do you think?"

"No matter where we go," replies Kerwac, "I'm coming along. I say we ask Raymond, since the rakan only seems to work for him."

"What do you think we should do with it, Raymond?" asks Townsend.

Raymond cannot palate the thought of returning to Salt Lake Citi. "It has a purpose," Raymond insists. "We should follow that purpose."

"But it's a machine," implores Alain.

"Yes," agrees Townsend. "Though a powerful one. I vote we keep it. We have purposes, too. We can use it for our own."

"I do know," adds Kerwac, "that if Salt Lake, or any of the

citis, find out it is here, we are in grave danger. The 33 people here can handle a mech or two. But if a citi declares war on us, we're fucked. They'll crush us for this thing. We ought to get rid of it, or eventually they will come to get us."

"What does Colin Chris think?" asks Townsend.

"I'm sorry, Alain and Townsend," says Colin Chris, "but I think we should take it to its other half. Especially if keeping it will draw citi forces. If half of this rakan has enough potential now to hack one citi, imagine what it can do for us whole."

Raymond addresses Salvador, "Show us the map again. Where is your other half?"

Salvador's face disappears, replaced by the holographic earth again. The two red rakan icons resume winking, one in Appalachia showing where they are, and one across the Atlantic, at the strait of Gibraltar.

"That place across the sea, that is the Gibraltar data haven," says Charmin. He points at the second winking icon, the one where they are not.

"I've heard of it, too," asserts Kerwac. He speaks directly to Charmin for the first time. "Last I heard, it is Lattice, Corp.'s, headquarters."

"What do they have there?" asks Colin Chris.

"It's a state of the art citi built on the rock of Gibraltar," answers Kerwac. "It is a very exclusive community, with a very small population. It is where all of the Americas' programming is piped through before it is distributed to the western hemisphere – New New York, Detroit, Chicago, Buenos Aries, Rio, Minneapolis, Salt Lake, DFW."

"Lattice, Corp., runs off Gibraltar," confirms Charmin. "Lattice is a sovereign. They spearheaded America's biosphere movement during the Statehood Initiative. Gibraltar is their capital node. They supply the media and conditioning content, including subcontracting of food. This rakan thing looks like it could be part of a new computer, or fuel cell, or energy amplifier."

Raymond rotates the map to get a closer look at Gibraltar. He is able to interact with the hologram as if touching it. He spins the globe a bit with a flick of his wrist. Then he zooms in on Gibraltar.

"See?" observes Raymond. "It's homing in on itself."

The map, limited by the data available on the unnetworked PAGsor laptop, gives no geographic or architectural detail near Gibraltar, save for the precise location of the other jewel, blinking right on the rock.

"Who possesses it?"

Lattice's executors, says Salvador, *or whomever currently occupies their seats of power.*

As Townsend looks upon Salvador's photo of the executors, the idea of a century-old roomful of men pulling the world's strings distinctly reminds him of something he had studied and memorized long before. Townsend does not speak often, but he speaks to the point. For this reason, his peers often look to him for an answer, or at least a good hint. They usually do this unconsciously, but at times of impasse, Townsend has a way of expressing himself that reaches everyone present, and they hope he will speak now.

Everyone falls silent. The listeners in the crowd ruminate on the information about the executors. Some of the settlers who did not speak during the council, glance expectantly at Townsend, hoping he'll say something and give an idea to untie this knot, to complete this puzzle in their lives. Gradually, the hopeful glances increase, some shy, some bored, some curious, all wondering if maybe Townsend might not come up with something, or maybe he's done talking for the night. Townsend's thought ripens. He digs into his memory and is sure now he remembers every word. Finally, Townsend speaks.

"There was an American president, back when we had presidents, named John F. Kennedy. He said something telling, in a speech to the American press." Townsend takes a slow breath and recites from memory, slightly changing the timbre of his voice:

"For we are opposed around the world by a monolithic and ruthless conspiracy that relies primarily on covert means for expanding its sphere of influence--on infiltration instead of invasion, on subversion instead of elections, on intimidation instead of free choice, on guerrillas by night instead of armies by day. It is a system which has conscripted vast human and material resources into the building of a tightly knit, highly efficient machine that

combines military, diplomatic, intelligence, economic, scientific and political operations.

"Its preparations are concealed, not published. Its mistakes are buried, not headlined. Its dissenters are silenced, not praised. No expenditure is questioned, no rumor is printed, no secret is revealed. It conducts the Cold War, in short, with a war-time discipline no democracy would ever hope or wish to match."

Townsend finishes quoting. The crowd remains silent, absorbing the thought. "President Kennedy," continues Townsend, "was murdered just two years after that speech. A short time later, his brother was also assassinated. That president told us who 'they' are."

"And now we know where 'they' live!" interjects Colin Chris.

"But those people are long dead," says Alain. "And Salvador here is almost 100 years old."

Raymond says, "If we can get into the Gibraltar spire, and put Salvador together, we can locate every one of the Lattice citizens and wake them up. We could theoretically hack *all* the citis that network to Gibraltar."

Easily, affirms Salvador.

"That would be chaos!" exclaims Alain, aghast at the idea of the world's citis simply emptying like anthills.

"Exactly," says Kerwac, his eyes lighting up. "Their defenses would be useless."

Charmin likes the direction this conversation is going, the same direction as his orders. He points up at the image Salvador is projecting. "It's just what we need to hit the oligarchs in Gibraltar right where it counts."

"Fine," concludes Townsend, resuming the thread of the talks. "The gem cannot stay here, it is a threat to our lives. It will eventually draw the attention of the citi forces. We cannot return with it to Salt Lake Citi because Salt Lake has been a debacle for us time and time again. If what this crystal shows is true, we must send it across the sea."

Alain is not yet ready to give up. He offers up his final argument. "How are we supposed to get there? We can't cross the sea. Remember what we said before supper? We are in a hurricane age. All the hurricanes are out to sea. We don't even have boats! Where will we get a boat to brave such tidal forces?"

"Out there!" answers Charmin, waving his arms to signify the space outside the long hall. "There's abandoned plague property all over that swamp. All those drowned towns and estates are still out there."

"And there was a navy base in the Virginias," adds Kerwac. "We've got to be able to find a boat out there."

Zane, who is expected to keep his mouth shut with the other kids, pipes up from their bay in the hall, "Rodney can do it! We can tug a boat easy!" Sam nudges Zane to shut up. The adults give a serious look of "be quiet" towards the kids' bay. It works. Cyrus laughs quietly.

"We can not send a boat across the ocean," Alain insists. The tide of the conversation is getting away from him. "We'd be fools to set out across the wild sea."

Kerwac steps forward, "Well, I guess you found your fool. I can sail."

"I'm going," interjects Charmin. "I wouldn't miss this."

"Is that so?" says Noriko, warily.

"I can help," contributes Colin Chris. "I've sailed. I can ride a ship through storm."

"This isn't just storm!" says Alain.

"I'm going," adds Raymond.

"We figured that," says Charmin. "You're the only one who can use this thing."

"No," says Noriko. "You need to stay here and rest. You've been through too much. Please, Raymond, stay here with me."

"I need to be there, Noriko," replies Raymond.

"Then I'm coming with you," she says.

"Noriko, you can't," says Charmin.

"You stay out of this," she snaps at Charmin.

"Noriko... It's too dangerous," Raymond implores.

"So?" Noriko retorts, her jaw is set defiantly. "I've already lost you once. I will not watch you leave again, with him," she adds petulantly, pointing to Charmin. "You'll have to drug me and tie me up to keep me off that boat."

"What's wrong with Charmin?" says Alain, surprised by Noriko's tone.

"He's too jealous to be trusted," says Noriko, looking at Charmin icily. She leaves it at that, sparing Charmin the embarrassment of exposing his shameful behavior to his peers.

"We can make it," attests Kerwac, changing the subject. He is looking more vital, more involved, every moment.

Kerwac, Charmin, and Colin Chris put their heads together to discuss a plan.

"Trans Atlantic navigation is relatively simple," starts Kerwac, scratching a crude map of the Atlantic in the dirt on the ground. "Point the boat east and follow the jet stream. Too much wind, turn toward south. Too little wind, turn toward north. The jet stream will do the rest."

"Salvador can operate the necessary navigational equipment," adds Raymond.

Quite true, confirms Salvador.

"Does anyone else want to volunteer for this errand?" asks Townsend. No one speaks or steps forward. In the children's bay, Zane wriggles in his seat, tempted to leap up and volunteer. Sam elbows Zane, then places her finger to her lip, as if to say "Don't you dare speak up." Alain gives in to the consensus.

"It is settled then," concludes Townsend. "The rakan goes to Gibraltar. Raymond, Kerwac, Noriko, Colin Chris, and Charmin will take it."

PART III:
GIBRALTAR

CHAPTER 17
THE OPEN SEA

Raymond sits on the forecastle. He savors the ineffable, lavishing air of the sea. He watches the boat's keel cut a path into the dark, undulating, green blue swells. It is the end of night. The sky lightens gradually. Raymond turns. He watches the boat's wake widen toward the gray horizon before being reabsorbed into the ancient Atlantic. Raymond smiles at what he does not see.

Kerwac emerges from a cabin below rubbing his eyes.

"Changing of the guard," he says.

"Top of the mornin', old boy!" says Raymond, affecting a British accent. Raymond is still smiling. "We've lost sight of land," he reports to Kerwac.

"Oh?" says Kerwac. He looks aft. "Nice. See any dolphins?"

"No," answers Raymond, smiling. "Not yet. What is it with you and dolphins?"

"Dolphins are like the humans of the sea," replies Kerwac, watching the ocean.

"Oh yeah? What about whales, then? Maybe whales are

the humans of the sea, and dolphins are the apes?"

"I think whales are extinct. Besides, dolphins are technically whales, just small ones."

They watch the horizon in silence.

"You know," observes Raymond, "back at the settlement, I felt like this moment, out of sight of land, would be when the journey began. Out here where it's only air, water, and us."

"That's one way to look at it."

"We're completely surrounded by the sea."

"We have been since we left, Wordsworth. There! Look!" Kerwac points excitedly, "Dolphins!"

"Where?" asks Raymond. He looks where Kerwac points.

"There! Maybe a hundred meters out! See the spray? And the fins?" Kerwac is beaming like a youngster.

Raymond watches for a minute. Finally, he sees a tiny vertical spume of water. After he sees it, he notices three more. "Oh, I see. The little sprays of water?"

"Yes," affirms Kerwac. "That's their breathing. Do you see their dorsal fins popping up? They must be fishing." Kerwac watches intently, hoping a dolphin will breach, jumping above the surface of the water to splash back into the ocean.

"No," says Raymond. "I just see the spray." Raymond looks long and hard. He sees more jets of water shoot up periodically, but he cannot see the gray and black dorsal fins from this distance. The color of the sky and the water blends with them too well.

Noriko climbs up the short stair that leads from the cabins below deck.

"Good morning, fellas," she says, squinting into the bright gray morning.

"Good morning, Noriko," answers Kerwac.

"Good morning, baby doll," says Raymond.

Raymond and Noriko kiss with sweet relish.

"Do I get to call you baby doll?" jokes Kerwac.

"Better you save yourself, soldier," says Noriko, smiling. "Your dream girl is out there somewhere. I can see her deep eyes glimmering like emeralds for you."

Kerwac makes an interested face at Noriko's remark. He looks like he is formulating a question. Then he thinks better of it and does not speak.

"Land's gone," Raymond reports to Noriko.

"And we're off!" cheers Noriko. She and Raymond hold each other. All three of them watch the spot where old Georgia was yesterday. The breeze blows their hair. Noriko ties her thick hair back out of her face.

"There's food ready downstairs," she says. "Katrina sent some cheese along. It won't keep. We'll eat it first."

"It's good stuff," testifies Kerwac. "And it's not 'downstairs,'" he corrects. "It's 'below deck.'"

"Whatever," banters Noriko.

Colin Chris emerges from the cabins below. He has the cheese and bread on a board. "You can't leave me down there to eat alone," he says.

"Look, Colin Chris, land's gone," says Raymond.

"Out of sight, not out of mind," he replies.

They eat. The boat cruises over the swells.

"I still think it's weird that Charmin disappeared like that, the day of our departure," notes Kerwac.

"Good riddance," says Noriko.

"A little bitter, perhaps?" asks Colin Chris.

"We don't need him," replies Noriko. "If he did not want to stay, I surely will not sit around missing him."

"Yeah, but what was with that note he left?" asks Colin Chris. "Mind if I see it, Noriko?"

Noriko figures, it cannot matter now. She takes a folded note out of her pocket and hands it to Colin Chris. "May I?" he asks Noriko again, for good measure. She nods and takes a bite of cheese. Colin Chris reads aloud:

"Everybody has a place in this world. I think I understand now. Noriko, my graceless interference kept you two together, aided in the strengthening of you towards each other. I knew I never had you in the first place. I think I understand now, because, in loving you, I wish you happiness. It doesn't have to be with me. I would rather be lost than face the scorn of my beloved peers. It is the fate I deserve. If I cannot free the lost, I will remain among them. I am sorry."

"Sorry, indeed!" exclaims Colin Chris. "He could have helped us! What's this 'graceless interference' he mentions, Noriko?"

"If you can't figure it out from the note, it doesn't matter," Noriko says discouragingly. Colin Chris gets the point. He drops the subject.

"It's still weird," observes Kerwac, who spent very little time around Charmin, save for the council. "He was so keen on coming. Where do you think he went?"

"Sounds like he went back to Salt Lake," guesses Raymond.

"Sounds like the guilt got him," suggests Colin Chris.

"Plague have him!" says Noriko.

"C'mon," entreats Colin Chris. "We loved him. It does not matter if it lasted."

"Yes, he loved among us for a good while," assents Noriko, relaxing a bit.

"I think he was in that citi too long," says Colin Chris, "looking for everyone. It bent him."

"Yah, everybody's bent," says Raymond. "I was in the citi as long as him. Some excuse."

"We must forgive him and let him go," says Noriko dutifully.

"It's creepy, what he did," says Kerwac, "insisting on going to Gibraltar like that, then disappearing just as we left."

"I wonder where Zane was," says Raymond, changing the subject. "I wished I could have said goodbye to Zane."

"Sam said he didn't want to say goodbye," reports Noriko. "I guess he's not good at goodbyes."

"So," says Raymond. "I wouldn't have faulted him for a clumsy goodbye."

"I'll bet he was watching from somewhere private," says Colin Chris.

"This is good cheese," says Kerwac.

Everyone chews in silence for a while. Raymond looks lovingly at Noriko. Out of the corner of his eye, over her shoulder, he sees movement.

"What was that?" he asks suddenly.

"What, honey?" asks Noriko.

"What?" asks Kerwac, following Raymond's gaze.

"I saw something," explains Raymond. "Something moved."

"You think it's a rat?" asks Kerwac.

"I don't know."

"Maybe it was a splash of sea spray," suggests Colin Chris.

"I doubt it," says Raymond. He keeps staring at the corner near the stairs. "I didn't see for sure." He looks at Noriko with a smile. "But I was gazing at you, darling."

"By the sun," says Colin Chris. "Get a room, you too."

"We already have one," says Noriko coquettishly.

"Then use it," quips Colin Chris, smiling.

"It looked like something flapped," describes Raymond.

"Could have been the lifeboat cover," says Kerwac.

"Maybe its this old boat's ghost," says Colin Chris.

"Be nice to it," advises Noriko.

The morning wears on. They speak and watch the sea. The breeze picks up to a slow wind. Colin Chris hopes for fish. He sets two poles off the aft of the boat, one to port and one to starboard. He drags a couple of lures.

"We may get lucky for lunch," he says.

"It'll make the watch more interesting," notes Kerwac.

"How long to our pit stop?" asks Noriko.

"Bermuda is a week in this direction," Kerwac replies. "We'll get supplies and head on from there."

"What if they don't let us in?" asks Raymond.

"They'll let us in."

"And if they don't?" asks Colin Chris.

"Don't be afraid of that. They're a lab and research facility," he replies. Kerwac wants to allay the anxieties of his companions. In fact, he is not sure how they will get into Bermuda, but he is sure they will find a way. "We send up a distress signal. We call for aid. Lost, out of water. They'll help."

"Ah," says Colin Chris.

The wind picks up.

"Nice!" says Kerwac.

"Some real cruising!" says Colin Chris.

"C'mon. Let's go below deck," says Raymond to Noriko.

"Below deck, indeed," she replies.

Before Raymond descends he pauses by the lifeboat and checks it. The tarp is snug. He looks behind the lifeboat; nothing. Satisfied, he follows Noriko into their room. They make love into the early afternoon. They wrap their limbs all around each other, enjoying their recently reunited bodies.

❧ ❧ ❧

Kerwac nabs a few fish on his watch. Colin Chris sits in a deck seat reading.

"We got lunch!" brags Kerwac.

"Cool!"

"Wasn't this your idea? Get over here and clean fish."

"Hey, you caught them," replies Colin Chris. "Honestly, one of us would have gotten the idea eventually. What does it matter that I was first?"

Kerwac ignores Colin Chris's joke and guts the fish. He throws the entrails into the wake of the ship. He looks out across the water for any creatures in the deep. I wonder if we'll see any more dolphins, thinks Kerwac. It would be great to see some dolphins up close.

Raymond lingers in bed after Noriko gets up. He rolls over and reaches for the cardboard bound lab notebook that Noriko brought him. She saved it. It is a journal he used to keep before leaving for Salt Lake Citi, before he was caught. In the journal are many of his thoughts and memories. Even some memories from childhood that Noriko helped him recall, through hypnosis, after his family was killed. He has been reading the journal during down time at sea. He flips through the book now and opens to a random page. He reads a paragraph of his own writing, that he does not remember.

In electric civilization a lot of people are lost, hurt, and sad. It is irrelevant if people have always been lost, hurt, and sad. It is easy to get lost. Many people do not have the brains and balls to create a path; to become unlost. The pathways into and out of these emotional states are often and easily mediated by our media, our electric culture. We have always been people. Even with fancy machines, we're still people. We are still motivated by our desire for food, sex, love, safety, fun, and power. Expressions of these motives can change over time or according to technological circumstance, but the feelings are older than the technology.

This stuff hardly makes sense to Raymond. He turns to the first blank page in the book. He takes up a pen that Alain gave him before the crew embarked. He writes in his log:

We lost sight of land over the night. Now it's like we've

really started. "Remember," Alain warned me, "write down your thoughts, especially if you get caught. To remember your self." He gave me this pen I'm using. This seems like a good time to start.

Zane and I were able to repair Rodney completely, with Kerwac and Salvador's help. When we networked Salvador to Rodney and the PAGsor deck, he proved indispensable in repairing Rodney. He pinpointed and repaired every bug in Rodney's software. He showed us exactly where to weld and rewire to restore Rodney's guidance system. Once Rodney was up and running, Zane and I took Rodney through the Georgia marshes trolling for a boat. We made a godawful mess of him, but we found an old sailing yacht and tugged it back to the shore. We beached the ship near the whalebones and started working on it. Almost everyone pitched in to help. The boat is inviting, I'll say so myself.

I am traveling with Kerwac, Colin Chris, and Noriko. Charmin was supposed to come with us but he mysteriously disappeared the morning of our departure. It's peculiar. I did not want him along. But, at the same time, better the danger you can see, than the danger you can't. Though I tried to discourage Noriko from coming, she would not be dissuaded. She is making the voyage with me. I am glad in my worried heart that she is coming. With Noriko, it is easy to spend my time giving love instead of just needing it. She is remarkable. I love her. She entrusted Ora with the infirmary before we set out.

In the galley, Noriko chops onions. In a pan, she gradually heats vegetable oil made from pressed corn, sunflower, and flax seeds. She is thinking of Ora, recalling the last time they were alone together.

Noriko spent the preparation time before the trip finalizing Ora's nursing apprenticeship. She remembers the day before leaving:

"I know you know all of this stuff, Ora. You've done it over and over again. You're the doc while I'm gone."

"I'm just keeping it warm for you, Noriko. Imagine being the lucky lady that gets to sail off with the handsomest man in town."

Noriko smiled, thinking of Raymond. Ora smiled back, thinking of Kerwac.

Noriko tosses the diced onions into the hot oil. The scent of onions sizzling wafts out of the galley. Noriko caramelizes the onions, simmering in a little vinegar until they are sweet and tender; almost syrupy. She cooks the onions into rice with toasted egg noodles mixed in. Colin Chris calls it "Superice!"

Raymond is still writing:

I can smell Noriko's cooking, onions caramelizing. That smell of onions in oil reminds me of my mother's cooking, before I had to run away, before they were exterminated. The scent is a comfort grounded in nostalgia. So many comforts are. Seems nostalgia is feeling sad about happy memories. What good is that? But memories ah memories are so elusive. Sometimes I think I remember doing or seeing something, but I probably just got fed the images, or I think I'm supposed to remember, or maybe it was something someone told me but I want to feel like I remember experiencing it myself. I am beginning to remember Noriko before I met her in the infirmary. A few of the memories were in this book. She remembers me. I love her all the same. I love her dearly.

Here on the boat, we watch in shifts. Someone must always be watching for anything we might collide with. Yesterday we saw a giant stinking trash barge puttering along north of us. It looked deserted. It was off our course so we sailed on. Kerwac says we would be surprised how many vessels, but how few people, are out on the Atlantic.

I was looking through my pack and I found a note. It's from Zane! He must have snuck it into my pack. I am going to copy it here, because I'm afraid to lose it.

Zane's note: 'You know when you are packed and ready to go, you pat your pockets and do one last walk through of the house? Did I forget anything? Did I remember all of the things within this house that belong to me? Union and separation of people is like that, be it temporary or permanent. We may try to walk away with as much of ourselves intact as possible, but something is always exchanged.'

What a kid. He did *say goodbye.*

❧ ❧ ❧

Two days later, on Colin Chris's watch, the wind brakes down. The air warms. The swells shrink. Colin Chris sees a flat mass on the ocean ahead of them. "What the–?" He hammers on the deck. The rest of the crew comes up to see.

"What's that smell?" asks Noriko.

"Is that land?" asks Raymond.

"That's trash," says Kerwac, wrinkling his brow.

"You mean a barge like we saw the other day?"

"No. It's a trash gyre."

"Gyre?" asks Colin Chris.

"All of the plastics and detritus that we've dumped into the sea. It doesn't all sink, but it does collect with like particles."

"Huh?" says Colin Chris.

"You'll see. Steer to starboard," commands Kerwac. "Do not sail too near this thing. It is like quicksand out here."

They turn the boat wider, but still gently approaching the gyre out of morbid curiosity. The air is warm, humid, and still.

"Too close. Too close," warns Kerwac.

Colin Chris steers a bit wider. They peer over the edge of the boat at the gyre. It is a large, miasmic swirl of trash, bits of junk attracted to each other by currents and cohesion. Long, ugly tangles of fishing line, bottles, bottle caps, scraps of food wrappers, scraps of manufacturers' packaging, sheets of tarp blown free by hurricanes, fishing hats tangled in frayed ends of rope. Styrofoam plates, beer cans, drink coolers, fabric from a shipwrecked sail. All surrounded by millions of tiny non descript particles of wet worn down plastic, slick with the muck that has washed off of them or died in there. A pancake mass of human flotsam and jetsam clumped together like a giant refugee raft.

"Woaw," says Raymond, blanching. "It reeks."

"How big is it?" asks Noriko.

"It's hard to tell," says Kerwac, "The water and the plastic offer up so much refraction that aerial photos were hopeless, even before we lost satellite contact. Some have tried to sail all the way around it, but it keeps growing and drifting. Boats get caught in it. This gyre's at least six hundred kilometers from north to south. I'm not sure how far it is from east to west. We must be at its southern edge."

"By the sun, it's bigger than Ireland," says Colin Chris. He covers his nose and mouth with his sleeve to dampen the stench. "I heard there's one of these garbage patches in every ocean."

"At least one, yah," confirms Kerwac.

"Look, shoes!" says Colin Chris.

"You name it. It's probably in there. This is only the edge of this gyre. Some say the middle is so thick a person can walk on it without sinking below. Entire rigs, bigger than this one, have been lost in there. So steer clear, Colin Chris!"

"Ew, it's hot, too," says Raymond. The air temperature near the gyre is several degrees higher than the open sea. Raymond mops his brow with his sleeve.

"Aw, look at that poor jellyfish," says Noriko, pointing.

The jelly fish struggles, tangled in the muck. Its tentacles are clogged and littered with gyre debris. The watery edge of the gyre laps against the side of the boat.

"Don't get so close, Colin Chris! Keep wide!"

"It's moving," explains Colin Chris, "the gyre."

"I know," says Kerwac. "It'll draw us in. Get farther now."

Kerwac takes over the helm, relieving Colin Chris to go watch the gyre without driving them into it.

"Ew, what's that thing?" Noriko points at a strange creature. It looks like a snake or huge worm. It has a pink tubular body resembling an intestine. It is crawling over a picnic drink cooler embedded in the gyre. It opens its front orifice. Its round mouth is lined with tiny needle sharp teeth with another row of flat serrated teeth in front.

"It looks like a lamprey's mouth," says Colin Chris.

"What's a lamprey?" asks Raymond.

"It's a sea parasite," answers Colin Chris. "A gray blue snakelike fish that latches to larger fish and lives off them."

"This thing," says Noriko, "pink and squishy, that's no lamprey."

The creature finds a chip of plastic and devours it. It inches along, looking for more.

"It's eating plastic," observes Raymond.

"I wonder what it shits," says Colin Chris. "You think it's lab grown, or natural?

"I don't know, but I'll bet it would find that jellyfish pretty tasty," says Kerwac.

"If the jelly's stingers don't get it," comments Noriko.

The gyre slows them down for three days. All the while, the stink and heat do not subside. They catch no fish during this time. On their seventh day at sea, they finally leave the gyre's zone. The wind picks up. They unfurl the sails and tear out; all sheets to the wind. They race on all day. They stick their faces into the wind and watch the endless sea sail by, like happy dogs sticking their heads out the windows of a zooming car.

"Woo! Finally," exclaims Colin Chris, on the forecastle, facing the wind. "That mess was a drag."

"Yeah, the speed feels good," says Kerwac.

Noriko and Colin Chris go below deck, to prepare some supper. Raymond and Kerwac stay on deck. Down in the galley, Noriko munches a carrot. Colin Chris is juggling handkerchiefs. One drops on the galley floor.

"I'm worried about Ora," says Noriko.

"Ora can take care of herself," replies Colin Chris, stooping to retrieve the handkerchief.

"I know, but she's alone at the infirmary."

"She can take care of them, too. Besides," laughs Colin Chris, "all the sick or injured people have already left on this boat. She's house sitting."

"Something doesn't feel right, still. Hey, I'll let you know when the carnival calls. Please stop juggling and light the stove."

On deck, Raymond moves over and stands shoulder to shoulder with Kerwac.

"You running out of space over there? Getting cold?" Kerwac jokes.

Raymond speaks quietly. "Something moved. I'm sure. A dark flap; a bend of light. I'm certain."

"Where?" asks Kerwac.

"By the stairs. Probably gone down."

"A stowaway? Unlikely. We'd see. This boat's not that big," says Kerwac.

"Charmin had a chameleon suit, right?" says Raymond.

"Charmin?" asks Kerwac.

"Something. Come on." Raymond leads.

Raymond and Kerwac climb below deck. Raymond looks around intently for anything out of the ordinary. Kerwac is alert.

"Search the cabins," whispers Raymond. "Start aft. I'll start at the galley."

Kerwac nods. He slips into the rearmost cabin on the boat. He fans his arms around for anything he cannot see.

Raymond steps quietly to the galley. He hears the faint glammer of Noriko's voice, in there with Colin Chris. The boat rises on a swell. Raymond holds on. The bow tips forward gently. The boat glides down the swell. Raymond creeps closer to the entryway. Noriko's voice is clearer.

"Now that you bring it up, I think she badly wanted to come along," says Colin Chris.

"She didn't say anything about it," says Noriko.

"Yes, but did you see–?"

"HA!" exclaims Raymond. "I got you, you skulking sneak!"

Raymond grapples the space near the doorjamb on his side of the entryway to the galley. Noriko is startled.

Colin Chris says, "Hey!"

"Ray, baby, what are you doing? Oh!"

Noriko sees the colors of the stowaway's suit begin to match Raymond's clothing instead of the dim wall panel beyond the galley. The stowaway grunts and twists out of Raymond's grasp. Raymond wraps his arms around the figure in a bear hug. Kerwac arrives. Colin Chris steps to and yanks off the stowaway's hood, deactivating the suit. They get a look at the stowaway.

"Hibbidy Dibbidy!" exclaims Colin Chris, utterly shocked.

"Ora!" says Noriko.

"Ora?" says Raymond.

"Ora? Oh my," says Kerwac.

"Whew, finally," says Ora.

"What are you doing here?" asks Noriko.

"It's too late for that," replies Ora. "I'm coming with you. There's not enough food to go back."

"Ora, who's going to look after everyone without a doc?" asks Noriko. This is irresponsible."

"They don't need a doc. There are mothers there, remember? Everything's fine. Besides, you need my help."

"What help?" asks Raymond.

"This suit, for starters. And this," she pulls a hunk of blown glass out of the chameleon suit. It is a polished, roughly faceted half globe. It looks like a knockoff of Salvador's rakan.

"What is that?" asks Raymond. "A souvenir?"

"It's a decoy, silly," she says to Raymond, nonplussed. "You never know when you'll need a decoy. Old Michael and I made it. Plus, there's a storm coming; a doozy. We'll start seeing it in about an hour."

"A storm?" asks Colin Chris, barely able to contain his rising excitement.

"How do you know that?" asks Raymond.

"How do I ever know?" replies Ora.

"It's true. She just does," says Noriko.

"We can never tell when," Colin Chris affirms.

Raymond is still on the defensive at the thought of an intruder on the ship. He thought he was after Charmin.

"I thought it didn't rain anymore," says Raymond to Kerwac. "On the march from Salt Lake, you said it hadn't rained all your life."

"It never rains on land," clarifies Kerwac, "but there have been hurricanes over the open ocean ever since the drought began. But they stay out here. They used to send ships out to catch the rain for water, but it was too expensive. They lost fleets at a time."

Raymond looks at Ora in the chameleon suit holding the shiny glass decoy. His face takes on a thoughtful expression, which Ora interprets as a desire for more explanation.

"How do you know when you are hungry?" asks Ora. "How do you know when you have an idea? It's like that for me, one of my senses."

"I believe you, of course," replies Raymond. "I was just a little worked up. In that chameleon suit, I thought you were Charmin. Ora, you've just given me a great idea."

"What is it?" she asks.

"We're going to need a trick to see us through Gibraltar, a real doozy, and I'm going to need your help."

"What can I do?"

"Keep that decoy safe until I ask you for it. I'll explain when we get closer to Gibraltar."

Kerwac is beaming, both at the thought of experiencing

rain and at the sight of Ora's face. He is impressed with young Ora and he is glad to see her. "Where did you get that suit?" he asks her eagerly.

"I lifted it from Charmin," she says smiling back.

Kerwac claps his hands together once and laughs.

"Charmin had a chameleon suit?" asks Colin Chris. "Do you know what happened to Charmin? Where he went?"

"He didn't go anywhere," explains Ora. "I couldn't trust him on this trip. He was secreting his true aims from us. He works for someone. He wants things that someone else told him to want. I stopped him to take his place."

"How?" ask Noriko. "He never would have gone for that."

"He didn't have to," replies Ora. She looks shy. She is trying to suppress a smile, like she is proud of something she might get in trouble for.

"What did you do, Ora?" inquires Noriko.

"I chloroformed him in one of the deserted houses," answers Ora. She giggles for a moment. "I tied him up. I'm sure they found him soon after we left."

"Bless you, rascal!" exclaims Kerwac. "That's why it didn't make sense!"

Ora is beaming now, too. Kerwac smiles happily. Noriko is scowling like an instructor ought to, but in her heart she is proud of Ora.

"And look at this," continues Ora. She removes Charmin's comm from a pocket in the chameleon suit. "This proves my intuition. He erased all of the messages, but the last three are still here."

Ora hands the comm to Raymond. Raymond reads it.

Subject and prize in Appalachia. Subject consumed deneuralizer in Salt Lake. Pay up.

50% pay for previous job. Bring subject and prize to Gibraltar.

We depart for Gibraltar at end of month, subject and prize included.

"Damn," says Raymond. He hands the comm to Noriko. "It's a report. He was supposed to go to Gibraltar. He was supposed to give me that pill."

"It was all a lie," says Noriko. Her distaste for Charmin is now ultimately confirmed. She hands the comm to Colin Chris.

"Not all, I'll bet," says Colin Chris. He hands the comm to Kerwac to read.

"It says 'bring' to Gibraltar, not 'take' to Gibraltar," comments Kerwac. "I'll bet whoever sent him this order is in Gibraltar," comments Kerwac. He hands the comm back to Raymond.

"That means we're playing right into someone's trap," says Noriko, concerned.

"Yes, but we've got an advantage," assures Kerwac. "Thanks to Ora, the spy is thwarted. Plus, with his comm, we might get information we would not have."

"So what was with that note he left?" asks Colin Chris.

"I wrote it, to cover my tracks," admits Ora. "Sorry, Noriko."

"It's okay," says Noriko. "You made him sound good. It's something he should have said."

"Someone in Gibraltar knows I exist," says Raymond, "wanted me to take that deneuralizer. The same someone knows about the rakan. 'Subject and prize,' the message said. I'm the subject. It's the prize."

"What's a deneuralizer?" asks Ora.

"A biochemical conditioning treatment," replies Noriko. "Deneuralizers interact with installed identity chip circuitry. There are several kinds. Some deneuralizers erase memories for the installation of replacement memories. Some deneuralizers make a chipped person readable by others. Others make a subject susceptible to suggestions and commands, like remote control."

"Can we figure out what kind I took?" asks Raymond.

"No, not this late," says Noriko. "You took it weeks ago. It has most likely run its course by now."

"Small comfort," says Raymond. "Maybe Salvador can tell."

"Yes, if you network him to a medical unit. I doubt he can give you a medical diagnostic using this laptop," says Noriko.

"Maybe when we pit stop in Bermuda, I can get a medical diagnostic," suggests Raymond.

"You'll likely draw attention to yourself as a fugitive with a discarded chip," interjects Kerwac. "Besides, if we stick to the plan, we'll hardly be in Bermuda long enough for you to get a check up. I also think we're underestimating the affect

Salvador will have when we plug him into a net hub in Bermuda. C'mon, let's get ready for that storm."

Kerwac goes topside to start prepping for storm and the discussion ends. The crew follows. They tie everything down. They furl the sails. They set out raincatchers to replenish their fresh water stores. The first wet smatterings of wind whipped rain pelt their faces. Raymond, because he lived a time under the citi rain canopies, has an experience to at least compare to this one. Noriko and Ora look at each other in amazement; their hands outspread, catching droplets of water from the sky. Colin Chris is standing alone, eyes closed, holding onto the railing, letting himself get soaked. It is the first time any of them has felt rain. They are moved and elated by the blustery storm energy. Kerwac shakes their shoulders gently, to get their attention back to the tasks at hand. They get below deck.

"Luckily, the wind is in our direction!" says Kerwac.

The boat is sucked into a dark roiling storm, full of foamy waves and fat stinging raindrops carried on gale force winds. The boat pitches and heaves on the swells. It trundles merrily through the storm, its naked little masts sticking up useless. Raymond and Ora turn green with seasickness. Kerwac and Colin Chris give them a nudge.

"Anyone needs to yak, do it topside," says Kerwac.

Colin Chris ties a rope around Raymond's waist. Kerwac ties a rope around Ora.

"We'll hold these in case you fall out," says Kerwac.

"What are you gonna tie your end to? Tie me to the boat, please," says Ora.

Kerwac and Colin Chris tie their ends of the ropes to the inside of the boat.

"What about barf bags?" asks Raymond, loath to go topside.

"And stink up this little space?" says Colin Chris. "We'll be puking all over each other."

Raymond and Ora return drenched and still sick, but no longer retching.

The storm rages for nearly three days. The crew plays paper and pencil games. The ship is too unsettled for card games. They read and spend hours taking turns watching the storm through the porthole in the galley. Raymond's companions watch the rain through the tiny round window, rapt at the spectacle of fresh water falling from the sky. They put cups, pots – any container that will catch water – out on deck and reverently drink rain from them when they fill. They eat foods that do not need cooking, like trail mix and canned fish. Raymond and Ora get sick a lot. Consequently, the two of them eat very little. The storm eventually dies down. It is the end of their ninth day at sea. Though there is still minor turbulence, Raymond and Ora start feeling better.

Raymond plugs Salvador into the PAGsor laptop. Salvador adjusts the size of his projection to fit inside the cabin space. They review their plan, mostly for Ora's sake, which hinges on them getting into Bermuda.

"We tell them we are headed to Spain for the Big Deuce, on a citizenship pilgrimage," instructs Kerwac.

"While we're there, we need to connect Salvador to a network hub in Bermuda," says Raymond. "He can hack Gibraltar from Bermuda. He will be able to locate our target, the other half of the rakan, and any obstacles on the Lattice network. He will clear a route to the target and, also, cover our approach on their security."

"Won't Gibraltar know where Sal is if we connect him?" asks Ora.

"Yes. When he connects is when the clock starts ticking," says Raymond.

They will know I'm active and where, says Salvador, adding to Raymond's comment. *They will look hard for me, starting in Bermuda. But as soon as I disconnect, the guessing game starts again.*

"Not quite," reminds Raymond, "you all read Charmin's comm. Someone is expecting us to come to Gibraltar."

"Yes," says Kerwac, "but they don't know how we're going to do it."

"Then we sail away from Bermuda as soon as possible," says Colin Chris. "Salvador will specify a service entrance and a pathway we can use. He'll bypass that route's surveillance feed, making it look normal and empty the whole time that we are there."

"What about locked doors?" asks Ora.

Raymond addresses Salvador. “What about locked doors?”

I can open them, says Salvador.

“Are you kidding?” says Raymond. “They’d swarm us in an instant if they knew you were in the basement unlocking doors. They’ll be waiting for it. Once there, we cannot connect you until we get to your other half.”

“I’ll bet he can time any locked doors, from Bermuda, to open when we get there,” says Noriko.

“Yes,” agrees Raymond, “but if we lose even a few hours at sea, like we did this leg of the trip, we’d miss the unlock times.”

“Still it seems worth a shot,” maintains Noriko.

“Maybe Sal can time them to unlock for a few seconds every hour, so we have more latitude,” says Colin Chris.

Will you do that, too, Salvador? Time the locks? asks Raymond.

Of course, answers Salvador.

“Set the doors along our pathway to unlock for three minutes every hour for 24 hours, starting eight days after we leave Bermuda,” specifies Raymond.

Got it, confirms Salvador.

They finish reviewing, pack away Salvador and, now that the storm is passed, deal out a hand of cards.

“What is Bermuda like?” Raymond asks Kerwac.

“Don’t know,” says Kerwac. “I’ve never been there myself, only heard of it. I do know they are sovereign. It’s a citi of scientists and software nerds. They sell their developments to corps. Keeps them from being owned by anyone.”

“Yeah, but what are the citizens like?” ask Raymond.

“Well, they’re chipped, just like any citi. But a lot of the chips are for ability augmentation rather than memory conditioning. I’m sure about this: We’re about to find out.”

Raymond opts out of the next hand. He goes up on deck for lookout. Colin Chris, Kerwac, Noriko, and Ora stay in the cabin, playing cards.

“Well, we’re making good time,” says Colin Chris.

“Shouldn’t we be close by now?” asks Noriko.

“Very,” says Ora, playing a card. “Your turn, Colin Chris.”

Colin Chris plays. “That gyre slowed us down or we would have been there by now.”

“If the storm hasn’t blown us off course,” says Kerwac.

"When are we going to get there, Ora?" asks Colin Chris.

"Nowish," replies Ora, smiling.

Raymond hollers down into the cabin, "Land ho!"

The crew scrambles up to the deck for their first collective breath of fresh air in two days. In the wake of the storm, a light rain is still falling. They open their mouths and stick their tongues out, catching the rain like thirsty plants. The wind is manageable. The storm is past and soon so will this trailing rain. Bermuda looms before them, one nautical mile away. The island is a half submerged biosphere, bedrocked on old Bermuda. The biosphere is largely covered in viewing glass, most of it underwater, but there are many enormous windows above. Emblazoned across the equator of the citi dome, in even but clearly hand made lettering is the message: GOTHIC DOLPHINS! NOT BOMBS! They hoist their aid flag. They sail closer; close enough to be seen.

"We're still a bit fast, Colin Chris," says Kerwac warily.

"I got it," assures Colin Chris.

Colin Chris drops anchor too late. Their boat rams into Bermuda, at the bottom of the D in DOLPHINS. Their prow cracks from the impact. They are thrown forward.

"Sorry," says Colin Chris. "I've never berthed at a biosphere."

"Well, now you've crashed into one," says Kerwac shortly. Kerwac is slightly irked. Now their boat needs maintenance. Maintenance is time. They don't have much time.

CHAPTER 18
LEARNING FROM BERMUDA

They float there, listening to the lapping of the waves against the wall of the citi. They are near a sealed, round portal. Raymond knocks on the door. There is no response. He locates a communication panel next to the door. It has a red light and a green light. The red light is on. He presses the intercom button and calls for help.

"Mayday mayday," calls Raymond. "We are transatlantic wayfarers. Please help. We have a damaged boat and we are out of food. Please help. SOS. SOS."

The intercom light remains red. There is no reply. Everyone gathers together on deck, thinking.

"How do we get in?" asks Noriko.

"With this," says Raymond, holding up Charmin's comm. "If Charmin was working for someone in Gibraltar, I'll bet he has clearances."

"Hold on," says Kerwac. He gathers his companions into a huddle. "Everyone remembers the plan?"

"We're on our way to the Big Deuce," reiterates Raymond.

"Before we leave, I've got to connect Salvador to the Bermuda mainframe to hack Gibraltar."

"We don't know how long it will take," adds Kerwac, "so keep up the act. We don't want to get stuck here."

The group acknowledges the gravity of Kerwac's comment. They break the huddle. Raymond scans Charmin's comm.

The O in DOLPHINS swings open with a hiss.

"Come on," says Raymond.

Before entering, Raymond makes sure Salvador is in his pocket. He also grabs the pen Alain gave him and, remembering his advice, rips some blank leaves of paper from his journal and wraps them around the pen. They enter the portal. It closes behind them with a sealing hiss. They are in a receiving chamber lined with small cabinets. The room smells like stale salty clothes. There is a monitor above the door. On the screen, an old man with a smiling face, bushy white moustache, and crazy white hair appears.

"Greetings, wayfarers!" the old man says. "You will find fresh garments in the cabinets on either side of you. Please change before leaving the receiving chamber."

The screen blinks off. They turn to their cabinets and disrobe. Raymond slips Salvador and the pen Alain gave him into the pockets of the Bermuda jumpsuit he is about to put on. Colin Chris wonders what is going to happen to their boat out there. Kerwac and Ora steal glances at each other, with equal parts curiosity and affection. Before donning the Bermuda jumpsuit, Ora puts her chameleon suit back on underneath.

Noriko wonders for a moment why they have been instructed to change clothes. Maybe it's a quarantine measure, she thinks, an effort to make sure no plague residuals enter their citi. This reminds Noriko that for the first time in her life, she has entered a citi. She has never been to a citi before, only heard first and second-hand accounts of their dangerous and devious ways; the identity chips, the controlled air, the drugged food. She shivers briefly at the thought, wishing there was some other way to get to Gibraltar. But they must stop here. They cannot cross the Atlantic without a stop off. Raymond notices Noriko shiver.

"Are you alright, darlin'?" he asks.

"Yes," she replies, hugging herself against a non-existent chill. "I've never been in a citi before."

"What's the matter?" he asks quietly.

"It feels...cold," she says, still searching for a word, "unnatural."

Raymond feels an empathic rush, a rising care in his heart, reaching out with yearning to protect this beloved kindred spirit. He understands her fear. He holds her and whispers into her ear:

"You can take this place, honey. No fears will stop us. Just keep your eyes open and stay close."

As they are changing clothes, a complex of scanners sizes up the visitors, transmitting their physical data throughout Bermuda; details like heart rate, respiration, body temperature and – if applicable – identity chip metrics. Salvador's innate optical security measures prohibit the Bermudan scanning equipment from perceiving him. Bermudan observers in another part of the citi examine the vital statistics of the five wayfarers. They are all healthy and none of the five outsiders is wearing an identity chip. They are off the grid, pristine, unaccounted for. The Bermudans are pleased at this. Once Raymond and his friends are all dressed, the white haired man's face reappears on the monitor.

"Ready?" the video greeter asks.

The citiside hatch of the airlock slides open with a hiss. They step out of the airlock into a larger room with a vaulted ceiling. Raymond looks around. The wall that faces the ocean is made of glasslike viewing sheets. Unlike the previous room, here the company can see through the polarized, transparent outer wall of the biosphere. They gaze out at the ocean that bore them here.

Raymond watches the panorama of Atlantic waters rolling by. Off in the western distance, he sees the dark cloud front that they sailed through to get here, reminding him of the stormy seas behind them and hinting at what is yet to come when they continue sailing toward Gibraltar.

The man from the monitor is not present. Ora is now suspicious. They have been in this place too long without meeting a human resident. She really wants to meet the white haired man on the monitor, to get a sense of him and his motivations. She thought he would be in this next room. In the middle of the room is a high back, open top tram, hovering in a magneto channel, evidently waiting for them. The group climbs into the comfortable tram. It has no seatbelts, only simple burnished bracing bars to hold onto. Once they are all aboard, it starts gliding on a virtually frictionless cushion of magnetic force. They glide on a thoroughfare, along the equatorial circumference of the Bermuda biosphere.

"What kind of place is this?" asks Raymond rhetorically, still looking through the viewing glass walls at the ocean outside.

As the tram accelerates, their damaged ship and the airlock they entered quickly disappear into the obscurity beyond his right peripheral vision. In response to Raymond's query, a computer voice begins speaking. The sound comes out of a series of tiny robotic parabolic speakers that target the sounds directly at each passenger. It is a well-manicured computer voice.

We are a sovereign development facility peopled with doctors, engineers, software writers, and scientists. Many of the technologies that power biosphere sustainability are invented or improved here in Bermuda.

The tram continues following the equator of the citi. Periodically, a perpendicular passageway opens on the left, like spokes in a wheel. Each passageway has a holographic sign over it, labeling regions like "Genetic research center," "Aquiculture research center," "Medical center," "Marine biology laboratories," "Aviary," "Food court," and "Tech R & D." Some passageways are pitched at varying grades up or down. Finally, at "New Atlantis Aquarium Visitor's Center," the tram turns in and careens down a steep corridor, taking advantage of the bonus energy applied by gravity. At the bottom, the tram slows to a stop and the companions disembark. The empty tram zooms away, disappearing back up the tunnel along the arc of the citi's outer contour.

They are on a landing with moving walkways feeding into and out of it through round portals. Select areas are illuminated with lightstrips and low luminosity bulbs, supplying a view into the living sea beyond the transparent walls. They have descended into the heart of an aquarium that is the Atlantic Ocean itself.

"Like a messy honeycomb," observes Raymond, peering with wonder at the viewing glass underwater city.

"Look!" exclaims Noriko, pointing.

A pod of sperm whales, numbering three females and a young bull swims by, diving directly down, towards their feeding grounds. With slow powerful strokes of their broad flukes, they propel themselves into the deep.

"By the sun," marvels Kerwac, "whales. Whales! I thought they were extinct!"

The computer voice speaks again, broadcast from tiny parabolic speakers.

*Most of Bermuda's underwater space is built around large pockets of seawater, to relieve pressure. When the hurricane age began, Bermuda seemed like a lost cause. The scientific community formed an economic cooperative. We purchased Bermuda for scientific research and sealed it, installing polymethyl methacrylate walls to dam off the drowning streets. With the help of technology and a lot of loving support, we made the drowned parts of Bermuda into an open aquarium called New Atlantis. We built a network of tanks around the rising ocean, sealing in what was left of the citi, snug, dry, and perfectly suited to become a marine biology research haven.

The science and technology that come out of our facilities go into biosphere infrastructures, food processing complexes, war mech manufacturing, medicine, pharming, nanotech, chemistry, and genetics. Soon old Bermuda wasn't big enough. We anchored a terrestrial biosphere on top of this aquatic citi, covering our submarine aquarium. Then we built up. Since we used Lattice bioworks we have a state of the art citi spire. Control center, net hub – the works.

The disembodied computer voice falls silent.

At last, they actually meet a Bermudan. The man from the monitor emerges smiling from one of the portals and joins them on the landing. His name, Ludovic, is printed on the breast of his white lab coat. Under his name is embroidered "Property of Bermuda." He has unkempt white hair, a bulbous nose and a bushy moustache.

"Welcome to Bermuda!"

He presents a small tray of green food. Different bite sized morsels are arranged on the platter. Kerwac's stomach growls.

"Please, eat," the scientist insists, holding out the tray.

"Hmm, what is this?" Colin Chris asks. He selects a morsel and takes a bite.

"Stuffed kelp," replies Ludovic.

Colin Chris's eyebrows rise up. He spits the food out into his palm. "Seaweed? Blarg."

Noriko, Raymond and Kerwac also eat kelp snacks. Ora does not touch the food.

"Aww," Noriko says wistfully. "My father told me about these. I've never had them."

"An ancient foodstuff well suited to the future," says Ludovic. He points out beyond one of the clear walls of the visitor's center. They see a kelp patch growing. The velvety looking sheets of seaweed tower several stories above them. Their holdfasts are not visible, obscured by the gloom of the dark ocean below, beyond this area's lighting. Shining fish, illuminated briefly by the lights of the visitor's center, flit among the green kelp trees of this underwater forest.

Colin Chris wipes the seaweed flavor off of his tongue with his sleeve. The scientist looks at Colin Chris. "Takes some getting used to, yes; but a potent, abundant, and renewable source of nutrients."

Ora is glad to finally have an actual Bermudan human with which to relate. She studies Ludovic quietly. She opens herself up to his mind and tries to feel what is there. She increases her attunement to his body language. Still, she cannot feel any of Ludovic's feelings or see what he will do. Though Ora knows people who have removed their identity chips, like Raymond, Kerwac and Winston, she has never been in the presence of a chipped person before. It is disorienting for Ora, because she is accustomed to her hyper-intuition working around everyone; so much so that she has trained herself to block it out when she needs peace and quiet. But with Ludovic, she gets nothing. It is not as though he is hiding anything from her, she cannot even feel the tension of subterfuge. He's like a patch of night sky with no stars in it, she thinks.

Raymond speaks up. “Thank you for your hospitality. We are pleased to meet you. I am Raymond. These are my friends, Noriko, Kerwac, Colin Chris, and Ora.”

“Greetings, I am Ludovic. I will be your guide through the watery wonders that comprise our humble abode. What brings you to Bermuda?”

Raymond tells it like they rehearsed it. “We launched on the jet stream bound for Spain via the Azores. We’re passing through on our way to The Big Deuce. The upcoming ceremony in Spain is our best chance for citizenship. But we ran out of supplies.”

“It is lucky you did stop here. The Azores are totally submerged. Besides, how did you ever expect to plow through the Iberian Gyre with that toy boat out there, anyway? You shall rest here. Berumuda has been a transatlantic stop off point for hundreds of years. Sleep on still beds for a couple of nights. Replenish your provisions. I will show you to your quarters.”

Ludovic leads the way and they walk with him.

“Wow,” says Colin Chris, staring up through the viewing glass at a kelp forest. “So, what’s above water?”

“Our upper level has an aviary, farm tracts and a zoo; many remarkable things. But if you’re sailing to Spain, there’s nothing terrestrial about your journey, not this part of it at least. You’ll stay here in the New Atlantis Aquarium.

“You’re the first seafaring folk we’ve seen in eight months. Judging by your comm scan, you have Lattice clearance. We do a lot of work with Lattice. If you like, I can take you on a tour of the citi before you travel on to Spain. Or you may rest in the visitors quarters until you are ready to depart.”

“Really? Thank you,” says Raymond. He tries not to look too pleased. “A tour sounds great. We’ve been on that boat so long, that it would be nice to stretch our legs around Bermuda. We’ve heard stories of wonderful and fantastic things here.”

Ludovic puffs up proudly. “Ah, so word of Bermuda has traveled far. That is most gratifying. Where are you from?”

Raymond ignores his question. “I do a little bit of computer programming,” says Raymond, taking advantage of the fact that Ludovic is warming up to him. “Perhaps you could show me some of your legendary computer equipment."

"Oh certainly," says Ludvoic gladly.

"It's not too much trouble?" asks Raymond.

"It's no trouble. Besides, I get a break from work to host you," says Ludovic, smiling. "That suits me very well."

Kerwac watches Raymond working Ludovic, a little impressed. Staying for a tour might be too conspicuous, thinks Kerwac, but it is just the break we needed. Kerwac was expecting to find his way around Bermuda in secret.

They arrive at their quarters. Ludovic turns to leave them for the night. "All is in hand," he says. "Our maintenance droids will repair and restock your vessel. Sleep well. Sleep as long as you like. I will see you tomorrow."

Ludovic departs. The crew sleeps without a watch for the first time in ten days. They sleep soundly indeed.

In Gibraltar, on the executor's deck of the citi:

Xavier is alone in his opulent chambers. He is lying in his silken hoverbed. He has just finished eating a snack; a nutty, tasty, sheep's milk cheese, accompanied by a pungent, crumbly goat's milk cheese on toasted walnut grain bread. The cheese plate has a few remaining morsels of fruit on it, some grapes and dried figs. He munches a wine-poached dried fig. He sips a dram of port from an Austrian crystal wine glass. He is a plump old man; entirely bald. He suffers from alopecia universalis, with no hair follicles remaining on his body. No eyebrows, no eyelashes, nothing. His skin stopped holding hair follicles 40 years ago – probably a byproduct of the elasticity treatments, his doctors said.

He wonders what has happened to Charmin. It is nearly time for the executors' meeting and still no word from Charmin. According to Charmin's comm, he scanned into Bermuda yesterday, and still no messages. Xavier puts the tip of his index finger in his mouth and bites at a hangnail. Those Bermudans will be here before this evening, he thinks. The board of executors is going to scan soon. This is cutting it close. Charmin should be closer to Gibraltar by now. Given how he botched Salt Lake, thinks Xavier, I wouldn't be surprised if he was dodging me. Xavier, with his teeth, pulls back on a tiny strand of dry skin on the edge of his nail. He feels a slick of pain. The hangnail bleeds. What a hassle, thinks Xavier. I thought I hired a professional. Xavier blots his bleeding hangnail on a handkerchief. He looks to his computer on the ledge of the hoverbed. He sends a short encrypted message to Charmin:

Send progress report, with ETA

The others will begin heading to the symposium room soon. Xavier waits a while longer, hoping for a reply. There is still a touch of port.

Elsewhere on the executor's deck in Gibraltar:

Percival is full. He reclines his leathery, freckled body on the fresh, cool sheets of his hoverbed. He has just finished dinner. He wipes his mouth with a linen napkin. Percival burps. He smiles contentedly. Delicious, he thinks to himself.

Those Bermudan programmers will arrive this afternoon, with the new rakans, thinks Percival. The project is almost done, the fruit of a century's effort. It has been a long road, but we've done it. I've done it. I've rebuilt that bastard Sal's HoA scanner, improved it! We will scan tonight. Percival laughs like a full, happy little baby, holding his arms up in bed. Coming from his drawn, spotted body the laughter looks like a macabre impersonation of mirth. Percival cannot wait to see his gem.

Percival's arthritis flares up, this time in his knees. He winces. He rings for his servant. A young eunuch, dressed in a silken toga, wearing rouge on his lips and cheeks, enters the room.

"Yes, sir?" asks the servant, waiting for a command.

"Ah, Talus," says Percival, with a sigh. "My knees are acting up again. Be a darling and bring me something soothing."

Talus steps into the room he just came from. He returns to Percival's chamber a moment later with an injector gun. He gives the old man two quick shots, one under each kneecap. Percival's pain quickly subsides.

"Oh, you are a dear," Percival says to Talus. "That's much better." Percival caresses Talus' rosy cheek for a moment, soothed by the drugs and the loveliness of his young servant.

"You are welcome, sir. I've also come to remind you that it is time for the executors' meeting," Talus informs his master.

"Yes, of course, little darling. Thank you."

The eunuch takes his leave. Percival hovers his bed to a door on the opposite side of Talus' entrance. Percival floats on his bed through the door, along his private corridor to the symposium room.

Elsewhere on the same deck in Gibraltar:

Paul is preparing for the executor's meeting. He is dressing. Paul is a compulsively clean, wrinkled old man. Like his colleagues, he has various long, clean scars on his abdomen and chest, where organ replacement surgery has been performed. He puts on a long silken shirt, draping to the floor. He is scheduled for a new set of kidneys. They are almost done being grown. He can feel the toxins building up in his body because of these failing kidneys. He climbs onto his hoverbed and reclines.

I'll need dialysis soon, thinks Paul. No time for that. If those Bermudans arrive this afternoon on schedule, all surgery is a moot point. We'll scan within days; new bodies, new homes, free of pain. The thought makes Paul smile.

Paul fidgets with his pen. He is reading on his hoverbed. His meal is untouched at his bedside. The new fertility reports have arrived from the South African biospheres. This is exciting news that has taken his mind off of his appetite. He is making presentation notes. So eager he can hardly think, Paul rings for Darla.

A busty, nubile, redheaded nurse politely enters Paul's chambers. She has pale, ivory skin that seems almost translucent. She is wearing a candy striper outfit. Her coifed red curls are fastened with a fetching, tiny cap. Her plump lips are painted red as a wound. In the uniform, her bust is drawn tight like in a corset, forcing her prodigious breasts upward. She was engineered by Paul to look this way. Her long smooth legs, in white fishnets, stream out of the dress and lead to red patent leather high heels.

"You rang, sir?" she says sweetly.

"Yes, Darla, honey."

"Have you finished your supper? Is it time for a wash?"

"No sweetie, I'm busy with a presentation. I need some of your footwork to relax me while I read."

The nurse takes the cue from Paul. She looks at him seductively and stalks slowly to his bed. At the end of Paul's bed she slowly kneels. Her sultry face is close to his bare feet. Paul watches Darla intently. His fidgeting with the pen ceases as he focuses on her ruby red lips. She smiles at him, affecting shyness. She slowly parts her red lips and extends her glistening pink tongue. Paul grins with anticipation and wiggles his toes. Darla leans forward and gingerly darts her wet tongue between Paul's toes. She licks the old man's feet like a servile pet dog. She takes his big toe into her mouth and sucks on it. Paul delightedly rolls his eyes toward the ceiling.

"Ahh," he sighs, "much better. Work your way up slowly, Darla dear."

Percival is the first to arrive in the symposium room, the topmost room of the Gibraltar biosphere. The round room is paneled with deep red cherry wood, and inlaid with delicate curves of stained oak. The carved slats of oak paneling were cut and inlaid into profiles depicting the oak trees they once were. The rest of the executors hover into the room via their private corridors. Percival watches and greets each of his colleagues as they arrive. First Simon, then Marcus and Mario. Shortly, Tyler, Han Tzu, and Enlai arrive. The old men greet each other with the understatement of well-worn familiarity. Eventually, Takashi, Paul, Diego, Buchanan, and finally, Xavier float into the room. The twelve men recline in a broad circle on their hoverbeds.

"Our first order of business," begins Percival, moderating the meeting, "is the new biosphere supercitis. The Australian supersphere is nearly complete."

"We can start filling it in thirty days," elucidates Buchannan.

"And totally sealed in forty," confirms Marcus.

"Tip top," says Percival. "Surprising, though, how long Australia took to biosphere."

"Yes, Sydney held out a good long time," agrees Marcus

"It's all the same now," says Buchannan. "We've got supersphere presence on all of the continents and subcontinents."

"Well, what's next?" asks Simon.

"Natural resources," answers Percival, looking at his notes. "Simon and Diego, you have reports?"

"I propose we set up that general in Peru as prime minister," begins Simon. "His army's got the gold rights there. He'll sign the offshore oil contract, too. We can finish the strip mine and the submarine drilling platform."

"Also," adds Diego. "The copper has dried up in North America. Move that operation to Alberta."

The executors unanimously agree to Simon and Diego's proposals.

"Next up," says Percival, "The New Vegas moon resort. We've got all of the developer's bids in now. I've forwarded them to all of you. Take a look at those. Let's pick a contract before the week is out."

Percival checks off another agenda item.

"Ok, Fertility," says Percival. "We've got something new here, that Paul and Takashi want to present."

"We've corroborated some reports and lab tests," begins Paul. "It's very exciting, really. You know we've been working with rabbit genes in some of the African biolabs. As you may remember, rabbits, under certain conditions, can self-abort a pregnancy. They can divert nutrients away from a fetus and reabsorb it, passing the few remnants away in their waste system. After long research and meticulous experimentation, we have isolated human subjects that can reabsorb their unborn fetuses."

"We thought some of our first successes might have technically been assisted abortions," reports Takashi, "so we created new test groups, and have been able to replicate our results. The first test group, deprived of enough nutrition, space and human contact, exhibited successful fetal absorption. With the second group, we met basic biospheric needs, but induced depression. The depressed subjects reabsorbed their fetuses, also."

"Good god!" says Xavier.

"Sounds like it, eh?" comments Percival proudly.

"But why? Aren't we having a hard enough time getting people to reproduce?" asks Xavier.

"There's plenty of people," says Takashi shortly. "We're talking about forcing the hand of evolution!"

"It's all natural, built in, fail safe birth control," says Paul. "Just the beginning, really."

"Excellent progress," agrees Buchannan.

The executors applaud themselves. Xavier does not applaud. He looks down at his agenda, pretending to read.

"Now for the great matter at hand," announces Percival. "Bermuda reports that the new rakans are finished and tested. Four couriers will arrive this afternoon with our jewels. We must finalize our preparations. We will scan tonight!"

The executors applaud themselves again, with the exception of Xavier.

Back in Bermuda:

Ludovic wakes the team with the smells of breakfast rolling in on service carts. They have smoked fish, eggs, and salted kelp toast for breakfast, food from the terrestrial levels.

As Ora sips hybridized seaweed tea, she wishes that she could speak with her friends without Ludovic present. She's never been around chipped people before and she has a powerful and fearful intuition that something is amiss. If they're so hospitable, she wonders, how come we've only seen one Bermudan since we've arrived? Maybe it has something to do with scanning Charmin's comm. Am I afraid because I don't understand? Or is there real danger here? Focus, Ora, she says to herself, what are your feelings telling you?

Ludovic walks the group to a lift near the entrance to their quarters. They begin a long, speedy ride up the spire lift, past the stacks of floors, closer and closer to sea level.

"Each citi has a spire like this," says Ludovic, "a tall, immense column running from the bottom to the very top of the citi, right up the center. The citi's computer infrastructure is anchored to the spire. Some parts of the spire are separated into levels with offices and apartments laid out. Our spire has been refashioned for the future."

The lift stops at a floor labeled E, for Equator. Raymond recognizes this as the level where he and his friends first boarded the tour guide tram, but they must be far closer to the center now. Ludovic leads them to a conspicuously secured door, where he scans his retina and palm to open the portal. Beyond, is another long walkway, like a spoke of a wheel, leading to the very center of the citi, ending in another secured door.

"This is the heart of it," announces Ludovic, "the brain room." He enters beaming, his guests in tow.

They are standing on a metal catwalk in a circular room. It is a cavernous sphere with a 60-meter diameter. At the center of the room, rising like a voluminous needle from floor to ceiling, is a thin axis. The center of the room is the core of the citi, a columnar computer with its precious jeweled CPU mounted in the middle.

The walls of the room are faceted like a geodesic globe. Each flat facet on the wall is about the size of Raymond's palm. The group is momentarily stunned by the fantastic proportions of the room. They stare, trying to absorb it all. Colin Chris's jaw drops, his mouth open in wonderment at this shimmering cavern. Ora looks around and, for the first time since their arrival, sees Bermudans other than Ludovic. She touches Noriko's arm and points them out.

Engineers are milling in and out of a control room that looks in on the brain room. Six programmers are huddled around a terminal in the middle of the control room, reading bugfix information off of the consoles and entering new code into the mainframe. Ludovic leads them along the catwalk to the control room door.

Ludovic points to a round gem mounted in the axis at the center of the spherical room, 30 meters out over the edge of the catwalk. The gem is the size of a tangerine; round and faceted. It sparkles, reflecting beams of light throughout the room.

"And that is our foundation. A rakan processor. It is the newest technology in computer brains. It is designed by Lattice, Corp., with our help, of course. It replicates many of the neural structures of a human brain. It enables the integrated management of all our citi's systems, from number crunching at the gene laboratories to scheduling the street sweeping bots. This one is not activated yet. We are still running Bermuda off of our old mainframe."

Colin Chris nudges Raymond with his elbow. "Raymond! Look at that thing. It looks like Sa –"

"I know. I see. Let's keep it quiet," Raymond whispers.

" – but so small," wonders Colin Chris.

Raymond turns his attention to Ludovic. He asks, "So that little gem is the computer?"

"The whole room is the computer," replies Ludovic, smiling. "The room is spherical. The gem must be set at the focal point of the sphere, the exact center of the room, hence the axis. The room is faceted in correspondence with the gem. The gem pulses optical processing beams out of its facets. The beams bounce off of the reflective walls of the brain room and return to the center. The longer the beam, the more data can be transmitted per pulse. The more facets, the more beams we can generate. The bigger the room, the more amplification we get. We built a sixty meter room for this prototype."

Raymond observes the computer processor mounted into the axis at the center of the room, halfway between the ceiling and the floor. It looks much like the rakan that Salvador is trapped in, but it is round and has no seam. Unlike Salvador, this new jewel is not made of two lobes. It is also small, less than half the size of the gem Raymond possesses, which is only half of the original rakan that Salvador built. Better get as much information from this guy as I can, thinks Raymond.

"It looks impressive," marvels Raymond to Ludovic. "Why isn't it activated yet?"

"We are running final tests. This one is, in fact, our prototype. We contracted to create twelve more of these computer brains for Lattice, Corp. They want them at their Gibraltar headquarters before the Big Deuce. The next twelve finished products have 150 percent more facets and can be mounted into a brain room as large as 100 meters across. Our biosphere has been retrofitted to run this prototype, which we will keep as payment for developing the other twelve brains." Ludovic is proud of Bermuda and it shows on his face.

"What are they going to do with twelve more of them?" asks Raymond.

"Lattice will not tell," answers Ludovic. "We also have been wondering what kind of computers they will power."

"Do you have any ideas?" probes Raymond.

"One thing I can tell you is that each of these brains we've designed, including our prototype, has one gene embedded at its center," says Ludovic.

"One gene?" asks Raymond. "A genetically tuned optical computer processor? Whose genes are they?"

"They didn't tell us that," says Ludovic.

"You and your scientists, can't you just find out?" presses Raymond.

"Well," admits Ludovic, looking at his feet and suppressing a smile, "we did sneek a peek at their codes, out of scientific curiosity. They are new."

"New?" asks Raymond.

"They are genes I have not seen before. They resemble human genes, but they are longer. They contain extra DNA pairs at their ends. They are custom, one unique gene per gem."

"But which humans do you suppose they were?" says Raymond.

"We can't tell. They are not municipally indexed identities. They are lengthened human genes with no ID records or census files. We figure they are customized to power next generation biospheres, like what we've done here with the prototype. It is also probable they will use them to power updated versions of the old rakan they have at Gibraltar," says Ludovic.

"Rakan? You mentioned that word before," says Raymond quickly, concealing his familiarity with the word. "What is a rakan?"

"It's a computer," says Ludovic, "similar to this one, but differently shaped; a parabola rather than a sphere. It powers Lattice, Corp.'s, neural nets on Gibraltar. It is an old model they rely heavily on. I imagine they need to upgrade it."

"What are neural nets?" asks Ora.

Ludovic takes a breath to speak, clearly enjoying expounding on his expertise. "A neural net is a predictive computer database. One neural net can catalogue a very deep, yet extremely narrow, body of information. A neural net can cross-reference its information according to a set of conditions, which the user feeds into it. Neural nets originally answered a few basic questions about a specific subject. Initially, doctors used them to identify and treat diseases. Feed in a list of symptoms or test results and, viola, the neural net spits out a diagnosis with treatment instructions.

"Corporations like Lattice needed a way to predict

consumer behavior, and cater to it. They developed more neural nets, as search engine marketing tools for online retail in the early 2000s. The early neural nets kept track of what people searched for, what they ended up buying after their searches, how much they spent, and where they shipped the merchandise.

"Later, Lattice built hundreds of laborious, precise predictive neural nets that were expert in answering two, perhaps five questions that are specific to the vocabulary they have been programmed. The whole of their knowledge is geared towards those technical questions. A neural net can catalogue any quantifiable system - air currents, water currents, historical geological patterns, economic patterns and even human psychological patterns. Anything that can be catalogued can be predicted."

"That seems impossible," says Noriko.

"Quite the contrary. Let me give you an example," says Ludovic. "We helped Lattice design their weather and sports gambling neural nets. Consider weather: we build a database for the average daily temperature over the past ten years at some particular coordinates on the planet, usually shipping paths. Then we build a database for wind speed and direction at those points on the globe, followed by a database for humidity. Eventually, for a small plot of the planet, we could effectively predict the hourly weather for months at a time. This streamlined the shipping and pharming enterprises."

The group looks quietly at the sparkling jewel mounted at the center of the brain room. Raymond wonders what Salvador could do in a room like this. He notes the six programmers clustered around the console in the adjacent control room, and the researchers moving in and out of the cavernous brain room along the catwalk.

"So I figure this machine pretty much runs itself," says Raymond.

"Yes," confirms Ludovic.

"Then what are all those people doing in there?" asks Raymond.

"I was hoping you'd ask," says Ludovic. "They are making a delivery on the data pipe."

"The data pipe?" asks Kerwac.

"Yes," affirms Ludovic proudly. "We've recently completed a hard line data pipe that runs directly from here to the Lattice hub at Gibraltar. Our net strength has increased geometrically."

"Wait," says Raymond, in disbelief at such a stroke of luck, "you've built a pipe that runs directly from here to Gibraltar?"

This is too good to be true, thinks Raymond. He Kerwac, Noriko, Ora, and Colin Chris steal delighted glances at each other.

"Oh yes," says Ludovic, mistaking the look on their faces for admiration. "We work so closely with Lattice that it became a bit of a necessity. We've even added a small shuttle to it, to send research teams directly to Gibraltar for new developments and reports. It is a tiny transatlantic subway. Come see."

Ludovic enters the observation chamber. Raymond and his company follow.

"Good morning, everyone," Ludovic says to his Bermudan colleagues. "Have you had the chance to meet our visitors?"

The programmers pause briefly from their work to exchange awkward hellos with their guests. These guys aren't very sociable, Noriko thinks. The programmers are huddled around an electronic carry case with a molded lining. There are twelve round, padded indentations in the case. In each of the case's depressions, rests a many-faceted, sparkling rakan jewel, like the one mounted in the Bermuda brain room.

The six programmers close the case, excuse themselves, and hurry across the observation chamber to a small four-seat shuttle docked at the edge of the room. It hovers on a magneto channel, like the citi tram, which disappears down a tube into the floor. Four of the programmers file into the shuttle with the case. The other two close it, smiling. They tap on the glass when it is ready to launch. The four men inside the shuttle wave to their programmer friends and to the watching guests. They turn on their intercom.

"See you tomorrow!" they say excitedly.

The shuttle lurches forward. It follows its track down below the floor of the brain room, disappearing into a dark tunnel. The tunnel leads down and away from Bermuda. It zips the four men northeast in a straight underwater shot thousands of kilometers towards Gibraltar. Raymond and his companions watch the shuttle and its controls intently. Everyone is thinking the same thing: We have to use that thing.

"Come," says Ludovic. "There is more to see before lunch."

Colin Chris is thinking about Ludovic's eagerness to show them around. His previous explanation of enjoying a day off sounds flimsy. Colin Chris has been in citis before, on raids with Alain and Charmin. He has dealt with the disconnected behavior of chipped folk. He cannot understand why Ludovic is so forthcoming with information. It may have to do with having Charmin's Lattice comm, he thinks, but there's something else. No place this complex freely gives so much information to people passing through, guests or not. They're telling us too much, thinks Colin Chris, as if they trust us never to tell anyone else. He looks over at Ora, only to find her looking directly at him. They have matching expressions on their faces, suspicious confusion. They give each other a small nod, confirming their mutual sentiment that something is amiss.

Ludovic shows them the new kelp farms and distributes a sample store of recently developed vitamin supplements.

"These supplements, taken with a modicum of carbohydrates as an absorption agent, will keep you active for fifteen weeks, if you have water."

Lunchtime arrives. They eat in a large viewing glass room on an undersea level. After lunch, they watch their submarine panorama. They get close up views of coral reef life. A pod of dolphins frolics in plain sight. They are corralling a small shoal of fish upward into a swirling, panicked, silvery mass. By trapping the fish between themselves and the surface of the sea, the dolphins make it easier for each in the pod to feed.

"Dolphins!" exclaims Kerwac. He beats on the glass to get their attention. "Look, they're fishing!"

"Please don't beat the glass," Ludovic says to Kerwac. "Seeing that you are so fond of dolphins, I've got something to show you."

He leads them into another laboratory level of the citi, higher up, closer to the surface. This lab has a diving bay in it.

Like an empty bowl held upside down over a fish tank, it is a large, dome shaped room, with a watery hole in the floor that leads directly into the sea. There are three marine scientists in this room. Ludovic introduces his guests to the trio. They are just as awkward and uncommunicative as the men at the shuttle. They mutter hellos and return to their work. Ludovic instructs one of the scientists to bring him a "rebreathing suit." The scientist does as he's told. He returns from a storage cabinet with a streamlined neoprene body suit. The material is reinforced with a metal mesh. The suit possesses molded flippers and a tail.

"We are working on rebreathing locomotive wetsuits to move more like whales and dolphins," says Ludovic, presenting the suit to his visitors. "There is no need for air tanks, and they're so much faster than scuba gear! The suit produces air, extracting it from the seawater, but food is a problem. If we could efficiently catch and eat raw fish in this suit, we'd be able to swim to England. Heh, heh."

Ludovic is the only one who laughs at his joke. Nonplussed, he continues, "Of course you would first have to build up muscles you never knew you had. It'll take time," he says, with a smile. He looks at Kerwac.

"Are you ready to meet a dolphin, Kerwac?"

"Am I ever!" says Kerwac. He strips down. With help from Ora and Ludovic, Kerwac works his way into the rebreathing suit.

"You look like a dolphin and a mermaid had a baby!" says Colin Chris with a chuckle.

"Once you have the suit on," continues Ludovic, "and don't let this startle you, we connect it to you with a few nanopins."

"Ow!"

"That's it," says Ludovic.

"What the hell was that?" asks Kerwac.

"The suit feeds into a few key acupuncture points on your body," explains Ludovic, "to more quickly respirate and oxygenate your blood."

"You should have told me about that!" replies Kerwac.

Kerwac is lying on the ground in the vaguely dolphin shaped suit. He is still wriggling; getting used to the tiny nanotech needle tubes that have embedded themselves into his body.

"I did. It's harmless," says Ludovic. "Ready? Here we go."

Ludovic seals the suit over Kerwac's head, which contains a tiny tube that travels down his throat between his sealed lips. He rolls Kerwac into the diving bay with a splash. Kerwac is disoriented at first. He floats just below the surface for a while. He nearly panics when he finds himself unable to inhale. He thrashes in the water. But the panic subsides. He never feels asphyxiated. His lungs deflate a bit, but do not empty. His beating heart and flowing blood compensate, through the rebreathers, for the oxygen his alveoli are not taking in. Enough of the oxygen drawn by the suit makes its way to his lungs, to keep them from collapsing. He breathes shallow, too keep his diaphragm working, but he does not actually need to fill and empty his lungs. The suit is oxygenating his blood. Soon, he gets the hang of it and begins swimming. He dives. Kerwac's friends peer through the viewing glass at Kerwac diving and thrashing joyously through the water.

"Could someone sleep out there?" asks Colin Chris, staring at Kerwac gliding awkwardly through the vast ocean expanse beyond the viewing glass.

"You would have to sleep weightless," replies Ludovic, "floating solitary over a dark watery abyss of unidentifiable predators."

"Forget about it!" says Colin Chris.

"Or befriend some dolphins," continues Ludovic. He smiles and points down towards some shapes moving in the water.

Four dolphins emerge from exploring the depths. They were fishing nearby, and heard Kerwac's grunts. They swim around Kerwac. They watch him. A couple dolphins nuzzle close to him, unafraid, brushing him lightly with their pectoral flippers. He sports with them. Next to them, Kerwac is slow and clumsy. A game of chase breaks out. It appears that Kerwac is it. He swims after the dolphins. They frolic. They tease him, letting him catch up.

"Look!" says Noriko. "He's playing tag with dolphins!"

Ora laughs, delighted. She claps her hands. "And he's losing!" she jokes.

Presently, Kerwac becomes very fatigued, much sooner than he expected. The breathing – or unbreathing – is disorienting and his muscles ache. To swim like this he exerts muscles that he seldom uses when getting around on land. He swims slowly back to the diving bay. The lab scientists haul him up out of the water and work to take off his suit. As they pull the nanopins from his body and respiration tube from his throat, he feels a craving – advancing, rising, growing – a near frantic desire for air. With every moment, his thirst for air grips him tighter, with dire urgency.

The suit disconnected, Kerwac sucks in his first unassisted, diaphragm-powered breath in 14 minutes, but it is cut short. He has air, but he wants more. He gasps again. It sounds like a wheeze. It's not enough. He takes two more shallower, halting breaths and Noriko and Ora are kneeling at his side. Noriko's brow is furrowed in concern and sudden concentration. She opens Kerwac's mouth to inspect his breathing passage. His breaths are weak, desperate inhalations interspersed with short puffs of exhaled air. Ora looks distraught. She holds Kerwac's hand. The lab scientists converge on the rebreating suit and begin inspecting it.

"What did that thing do to his lungs?" she asks sharply.

"Nothing," replies Ludovic, his face flushing. He drops his eyes. "It maintains lung inflation."

"How much inflation?"

"Enough for buoyancy."

Noriko is not satisfied with his general answers, but does not want to waste time dragging information out of him if he's going to be evasive.

"Call for medical care," she demands.

"I already have."

"Then help!" says Noriko. "You must have an emergency kit here. Get me an resuscitator bag! If we don't hurry, he'll need to be intubated!"

Ludovic is paying no attention to Noriko or Kerwac, but rather to his colleagues inspecting the rebreathing suit beyond Kerwac.

While watching Ludovic, Ora suddenly and for the first time, feels something from him. Finally, she is able to find an empathetic link to his motivations and feel them. This done, she can often see into that person's future, if she listens well. Ora can tell that Noriko thinks he's lying, but he's not. Ludovic is intensely curious. He is not avoiding Noriko's questions. He'd be happy to talk about it with her, but he does not believe she would understand enough to gratify him. Ludovic is looking at the suit. He wants to join his fellow scientists, read the results, and prepare a new experiment.

"Help will come," Ludovic says distractedly and steps away to join his fellows, murmuring to himself.

Colin Chris and Raymond are rummaging around the room of the diving bay, opening drawers and hatches searching for an emergency kit. During their fruitless search, Colin Chris overhears a snippet of conversation amongst the scientists. One of them says "...14 minutes this time." His eyebrows rise up in surprise. He glances at Raymond nearby and indicates the scientists with a tilt of his head, to see if Raymond is listening, too. Raymond gives Colin Chris one slow tiny nod, to let Colin Chris know that he heard it also. Then Colin Chris's brow furrows down again as he glances quickly at Ludovic, seeing him completely differently.

A group of medics arrive and tend to Kerwac. They have an Ambu bag, steroids, and albuterol. They put him on a stretcher and lift him onto a gurney. He needs to be taken to the medical unit. Kerwac's friends remain at his side. They leave the diving bay and enter an adjacent corridor. This corridor is not made of viewing glass. It is as opaque as a normal walkway and has many doorways and computer consoles along its walls. At the beginning of the next corridor, one of the medics lets go of the gurney and turns to stop Kerwac's companions.

"We're sorry, guests may not come to the medical unit."

"I'm a doctor," insists Noriko. "I know his medical history."

The medic does not change expression. He quietly whispers "Security," into his lapel. Two dawgs emerge from their flat roosts against the walls of the corridor the medic is blocking. Raymond has not seen a dawg since the day he was bit on the Battle Plateau, helping Kerwac fight them off of Rodney. Drops of adrenaline curdle in Raymond blood as he remembers the subsequent fever and the nightmares, the hallucinations. Raymond freezes for a moment, staring at the dawgs as they unfold from the wall and stand at attention on either side of the medic.

Raymond almost loses lucidity. He feels a perverse desire to give in to the fear of the dawgs. He imagines trying to run away, abandoning all responsibility, being stung or bitten, and ultimately overtaken by the dawgs. As dismal a reality as that seems, his fear wants him to seize it. Raymond looks into the fear, beyond it. He lends his consciousness toward his breaths, notices his elevated heart rate. No fears will stop us, he had told Noriko, when they entered Bermuda. This thought calms him.

Raymond looks at the spots on the walls where the dawgs' previously unnoticed roosts are, it draws his attention to all of the other textures on the walls that he had taken for doorways and computer consoles. Matching the shapes of the dawgs to their roosts, he looks down the corridor beyond and sees that there is a dawg roosted about every 10 meters on each wall, as far as he can see. Lots of security, he thinks, even if we take out these two. He touches Salvador in his pocket.

"Guests are not permitted in the medical unit," the medic repeats. "It is an enforced security measure. Ludovic will take you to the visitor's waiting room. You will see your friend soon."

Ludovic, evidently remembering his duties as a tour guide, emerges from the diving area and addresses the wayfarers.

"I'm terribly sorry about your friend," he says. "I will lead you to the infirmary. Then I must return to work."

"Yeah, get back to that suit project," says Colin Chris shortly. "Make it last longer than 14 minutes, eh?"

Ludovic does not respond to him. Instead he turns and leads them to a waiting room. They follow him because, in the labyrinthine layout of Bermuda, they wouldn't know where else to go.

"What is wrong with these people?" Colin Chris asks Raymond, aside.

"Kerwac said they're chipped," says Raymond.

"Chipped, sure, but there's something else."

"Yeah," agrees Raymond. "Did you notice how they paid no attention at all to Kerwac when he was hurt?"

"They went straight for that suit!" agrees Colin Chris "What's more, did you hear what they – "

Raymond pretends to trip and fall onto Colin Chris. When Colin Chris catches him, Raymond holds him close and says into his ear, "Don't talk here. Those parabolic speakers can hear us as well as we can hear them."

When they arrive at the waiting room, a medical report is waiting for Ludovic. He examines it and in turn addresses the wayfarers.

"Your friend is okay. His lungs experienced partial collapse. He has been intubated. We could replace his lungs, but we prefer to restore them."

"How thoughtful," jibes Colin Chris.

"It's more expensive that way," continues Ludovic, seemingly ignorant of the bite in Colin Chris's voice, "but he will be able to evaluate the suit better with his own lungs."

"Are you crazy?" says Ora. "He's not getting back in that suit!"

"That is a moot point until he is well," says Ludovic. "Restoring his lungs to full capacity will take weeks."

This comment strikes the company dumb. All four of them understand that the Bermudans expect to keep Kerwac in bed for weeks. Furthermore, Ludovic expects to put Kerwac back in that suit once they've restored his lung capacity. The shiver that shook Noriko when she was changing in the airlock upon arrival passes through her again.

These Bermudans are scientists to the final degree, she realizes. They call us guests, but we don't mean anything to them. We're like mice. They want to see what's happened to Kerwac. These Bermudans want to make Kerwac well again, because they want to toss him in the next version of the suit. And calling those dawgs! By the sun! thinks Noriko. They plan to keep us, all of us! She tries to keep her face expressionless, because she knows they are watching her.

"He had to be sedated for intubation and should be waking soon," says Ludovic after the silence. "He will not be able to speak yet because of the intubation, but he will be able to type responses. He is permitted one visitor."

"I will go," Ora replies first.

Ora is being led to Kerwac's bed in the medical center, down a walkway lined with rooms. She walks slowly, trailing behind Ludovic until he eventually stops to wait for her. She is looking searchingly into the diminutive view window of each door. In each room is a patient. One is a man spread-eagled on a double bed. He is naked, and both of his waste systems are tubed away from his body. Other clear thin plastic tubes feed him so he need not be moved. There is a webbing of inflamed flesh running along each side of his body from just above his ankles to just below his wrists. There is a wave of pain and fear coming from the man that Ora can feel on her face like the red air of a burning stove. She moves on, in each room is a person either incapacitated or restrained, being treated with meticulous medical skill.

Kerwac is in bed. There is a large plastic tube running down his throat and passing through his larynx to facilitate his breathing. He is hooked up to an IV. A heart monitor beeps and blips periodically. When he sees who has entered the room, the corners of Kerwac's obstructed mouth turn upward slightly. It hurts Ora's heart to see her lovely Kerwac like this. Tears well up in her eyes as she takes a seat at his bedside. Kerwac gazes at Ora for a moment, then reaches for a little bedside console to type her a message with his right hand. Ora stands and kisses Kerwac on the corner of his mouth where the tube enters. She holds Kerwac's face in her hands, and touches her forehead to his, holding together there. She can't bear to watch him clumsily type out messages like an invalid mute, hooked up to all these soulless machines. In contact with Kerwac, she tries something she has only ever tried with her little brother Zane, transmitting thoughts silently. Her feelings for Kerwac amplify her link to him, and he is able to feel her also. They close their eyes and, with Ora's help, hear each other in the darkness, as if in a dream.

All of you must leave, and leave now. This place is dangerous.

We know. I'm staying.

You have to go with them, Ora. They need you.

I love you Kerwac. I came for you. I will not leave you.

Darling, Ora. I love you. I love you, too. Right now, you

must go with them. They need you right now. Come back this way after the deed is done. Tell me all about it.

Why couldn't I see you would be in danger? she asks, weeping into his mind. *Why didn't I know?*

Shh. Shh, Kerwac soothes Ora. *You said yourself, sweetheart, there's no telling when you're going to know.*

What if we don't see each other again? Ora cries harder.

We'll see each other again, he replies, smiling into her. *You should know that.*

They remain posed together, holding each other silently for a while, eyes closed, sharing the sweet, terrible pain of their lovers' parting.

At Ludovic's direction Raymond, Noriko, Ora, and Colin Chris ride the magneto tram back to the New Atlantis Visitor's Center, each of them aching to speak, but none daring to let the Bermudans overhear anything of substance. At the landing, Ludovic leaves them to go to their rooms and stays on the tram, riding back to the laboratory levels. When they reach the entrance to their rooms, Raymond looks over his shoulder, sees that Ludovic is gone, and keeps walking. His friends silently follow.

Ludovic is very curious about the subjects. Usually orphaned humans are no trouble. They are unchipped, unaugmented, they have no corporate allegiance, no citi to call home; they have no help. But these people, thinks Ludovic, they are forward and inquisitive; they are not comforted by amenities. His curiosity about his guests yields to caution. It will not do to merely keep them out of restricted areas, he thinks. They must be guarded, lest they contaminate any projects.

"Security," Ludovic calls into his lapel microphone, "send an escort to the quarters of our recent guests. Full watch."

Raymond leads his company along a path lit with fiber optics toward the spire lift. The fiber optics illuminate the darkened, transparent viewing walls of the deep underwater world. Raymond looks up and sees, in the gloom, the underbellies of two crabs snapping at food on the roof of the corridor. Upon reaching the spire lift, Raymond stops and addresses his friends.

"Here's where the game begins," says Raymond as he pulls Salvador from his pocket and plugs him into the lift console. Immediately, a miniature projection of Salvador's waiting face is emitted from the gem. "Salvador, I need you to make us invisible on Bermuda's surveillance until we get to the shuttle in the brain room. Time to let Lattice know we're busy over here."

Done, confirms Salvador, his face disappearing as the lift doors open.

Raymond removes Salvador from the console. They ride the lift up from the visitor's quarters to the Equator level. Here, thanks to Salvador, for a precious few moments they are free to speak without being overheard.

"Can you believe these people?" says Colin Chris, hurt and enraged by the evident heartlessness of the Bermudans. "Did you hear what they said about that suit when Kerwac got hurt? They said '14 minutes this time.' He lasted 14 minutes!"

Ora looks at Colin Chris uncomprehending.

"That suit Kerwac wore is not done yet," explains Raymond, picking up the thread. "They expected it to do that to him; they just weren't sure how long it would take. We have to leave this place. The longer we stay, the less they are going to pretend we are guests. We can't let them know that we've figured out they plan to keep us for experimentation."

"What are we going to do about Kerwac?" asks Noriko. "We can't leave him here!"

"He'll be safe here until he is well again," replies Raymond pragmatically. "We have a few weeks while he's in bed before they start experimenting on him again. If we survive Gibraltar, Salvador can help us get him back."

"Kerwac told us to leave now," says Ora. "When I visited with him, he said he heard the Bermudans speaking around him when they thought he was unconscious. He knows they plan to keep all of us as test subjects."

Raymond nods grimly at Ora's confirmation.

"Also," says Raymond. "Charmin has a new message." Raymond shares Charmin's latest transmission from Xavier with the group.

Send progress report, with ETA

"Should we reply?" asks Noriko.

"No," says Raymond. "We're too close now. Better to leave him in the dark, whoever he is. He already knows we are in Bermuda because we scanned Charmin's comm to enter. That will do. We'll leave the comm here, so he won't know we left Bermuda."

They come upon the conspicuously secured door Ludovic previously lead them through. Raymond dumps Charmin's comm on the floor and uses Salvador to open every lock. They run along the moving walkway, through the next security door, through the brain room, and into the control room, from which the shuttle launches. Raymond steps to the computer console.

"Maybe now," Raymond says, holding Salvador's gem up to his friends, "our silent partner will be even more useful."

Raymond mashes Salvador's processor putty into the data ports. The blue putty molds to the various ports. The 60-meter spherical computer room goes entirely dark. In the control room, Salvador's crystal lobe lights up like a blue diamond under the desert sun, illuminating the faces of his companions.

Ahh, yes, Salvador says through the parabolic speakers. *That is much better. A real bitstream.*

The escort of dawgs reaches the New Atlantis level and enters the guests' quarters to verify attendance. When the dawgs blip the report of Raymond and company's empty rooms, Raymond is just plugging in Salvador. Salvador causes the Bermuda mainframe to disregard the message, receiving instead the report that all guests are accounted for in their quarters. To obfuscate his hack, Salvador overloads the citi's electrical grid to nearly the threshold of its failsafes and starts working. For a few brief moments all of Bermuda lights up like a dying star.

Salvador takes control of the Bermuda mainframe and projects himself in the round brain room. It shimmers with colors. It sprays millions of split beams of light into the room, covering all of the dark walls with light noise. The beams coordinate into Salvador's giant face. The image resolution is so good that they can see every one of Salvador's pores. His hair is animated with individual strands, instead of the wedges of black that the PAGsor laptop rendered. Salvador's beaming gargantuan visage, eyes flashing, hovers at the center of the brain room. His holographic hair is flying with electric blue tendrils that reach out to the walls. Raymond's mouth gapes open a moment, then he speaks.

"Salvador, I need to see a detailed floor plan of Gibraltar. Can you get it off the net?"

Yes! Yes! says Salvador to Raymond. *All that and more! You've plugged me into Lattice's net. Excellent work, son. They know where I am for the moment, but we will have a payload much greater than that information.*

Salvador suddenly stares right through Raymond, looking into the bitstream of data he exists amongst.

Well, what do you know? he says. *Those underhanded human game wardens...those warmongering, energy hoarding, starvation peddlers. They finally figured out how to do it.*

"Salvador, what are you talking about? Do what?"

They figured out how to rebuild my machine, answers Salvador. *I'll show them a trick or two.* Salvador's blue lightning storm of download continues. Raymond looks around at everyone. They silently sympathize with Raymond. Noriko thinks, What's taking so long?

"Salvador's a huge blip on the net, Ray," says Colin Chris, wanting to hurry things up.

"More like a mushroom cloud," says Ora.

They want to live forever? I'll show them forever...

Salvador stares on into infinity. The electric blue vines of light turn a deep rose tint. He now uploads. His hair lightning colors the room hell red. He delivers uncountable teraflops of encrypted, time-released viral data across the net into the Lattice mainframe on Gibraltar.

Quickly, now disconnect me, says Salvador, *and get in the shuttle.*

Raymond disconnects Salvador and they hurry into the shuttle. A moment later they are sealed in, ready to be jettisoned underwater to Gibraltar.

"What did we just do?" asks Noriko, as the craft begins gliding down into the magneto channel and accelerating toward freefall speed.

"We just told Gibraltar we're coming," says Colin Chris.
"We just downloaded our game plan," says Raymond.
"Wicked," says Ora.

CHAPTER 19
SALVADOR'S HOUR

The executors gather in the symposium room for an unscheduled, emergency meeting. Percival's brow is furrowed. Something big just happened in Bermuda. Xavier noticed it also. Xavier, in fact, was watching for it.

"We've had a colossal data surge from Bermuda," reports Percival.

"What are those Bermudans up to now?" asks Han Tzu.

"Whatever they are doing," says Percival, "it includes unauthorized access to Gibraltar maps."

"Hacking us?" asks Han Tzu "How could they hack us?"

"It's worse," says Percival. "Gentlemen, the rakan archives have been breached."

"Impossible," says Enlai.

"It's true," confirms Buchannan, scratching his white beard.

"Then there's a traitor here!" Enlai exclaims. He looks around at his accomplices with wild, untrusting eyes.

"Oh, come on," says Xavier, reasonably, "No more than there's ever been."

"It was breached from Bermuda," says Percival.

"What difference does that make?" parries Enlai.

"It was not a human hack," says Percival. "It was Salvador."

"No!" Enlai says, shocked.

"Salvador?" says Tyler. "Impossible!"

"No, just improbable," says Buchannan.

"Are you sure?" asks Simon.

"Who?" asks Mario, senile, "Ohhhh!" he finally says, remembering.

"Salvador's destroyed," says Xavier, lying. "We destroyed him. We destroyed his genetic line. There are no Toscs."

"Salvador's awake," says Percival. "He just turned up on the net in Bermuda. If he's awake, then there is a Tosc alive out there that activated him."

"We've got to stop him!" interjects Marcus.

"We already did!" reminds Xavier. "This is nonsense. We destroyed Salvador 95 years ago. We saw him split. We blew up his half."

"I never saw the remains of that gem," says Enlai.

"No one did. It exploded," remembers Diego.

"Well, obviously, it didn't," says Buchannan.

"There's got to be another explanation," says Marcus.

"Nothing could have accessed Gibraltar with that kind of power and speed," insists Percival, "if it were not built for Gibraltar. Salvador's was built for Gibraltar. It's him."

"What do we do?" asks Tyler. "Our plan is leaked!"

"Is it still safe?" Takashi asks.

"If Salvador knows about the superspheres," says Tyler. "If he finds out we've finally recreated his Hall of Ancestors scanning machine, and that each of us is about to do what we eliminated him for trying to do, we won't just get locked down for a few days, as Percival likes to put it."

"We must finish the supersphere project before he arrives," says Percival.

"The superspheres are not ready to fill yet," says Tyler.

"How long will it take?" Percival asks.

"Are you serious?" Tyler replies. "If we started filling the superspheres this instant they wouldn't be ready to seal for three weeks. If we manage to fill and seal the superspheres by the time of the Big Duece celebration, we'll be lucky."

"It's true. Chances are," says Han Tzu, "we'll record a ceremony, then actually seal them three months later."

"Three months, bah," says Buchannan. "Get crews working round the clock. We can seal in five days."

"If Sal's coming now," Tyler figures, "we don't have five days. Has he accessed the supersphere project?"

"Assume he has accessed everything," says Buchannan. "Right now he is disconnected, thus powerless. We just need to keep it that way. He has to stay disconnected to hide. If he connects, we will find him instantly."

"If he connects, he's a threat," corrects Xavier.

"Send men to Bermuda," says Enlai. "We must secure it!"

"No," says Percival. "He is coming to us."

"How do you know that?" asks Enlai.

"Look at the information he accessed," explains Percival. "Floor plans, the rakan archive, the SS project, and the neural net we're powering with his other half. All of our security alarms suddenly have viruses. We need to manually dispatch personnel. He's coming for us. Sal is coming for his other half."

"Sal's not coming. Someone is bringing him," says Buchannan. "Someone with enough of his genetic code to activate him. We've got the high ground. We just have to let him in and scoop him up."

"Let him in?" asks Simon, incredulously.

"Are you mad?" says Enlai. "Don't you remember what happened last time he was here? No way. Secure Bermuda."

"There is no need for alarm," says Percival. "He is powerless unless connected. We will not connect Salvador. Besides, Bermuda's sovereign. Do you want to deal with a war; or worse – sanctions?"

"We let him come to us," Buchannan says, "with whoever his little mule is. We leave Bermuda alone. They'll leave Bermuda. When they do, we'll kill the carrier and get Salvador's gem ourselves."

"Then we must destroy it once and for all," demands Simon.

"And if we can't destroy it," Percival dissuades, "we'll power another neural net hub in a different citi, a stronger one. Sure, they must never be joined. But if we can use one half of it, there's no reason we can't use the other half, on a wholly separate system."

"Yes. That means the descendant would have to be taken alive," muses Tyler, "to activate Salvador's gem for us."

"That's too risky," Simon says.

"Risk is how we got here," responds Percival. "Take a risk, old man."

"No, this time we must secure it and destroy it ourselves," says Diego. "Not just hope it's taken care of and ignore it."

"Yes," agrees Enlai. "I want to see that confounded crystal drive crushed to pebbles with my own eyes!"

"The last time he was connected," reasons Percival, "all he did was lock us down for a few days."

"There you go again, Percival. It was almost a month," Xavier corrects Percival.

"We were imprisoned!" says Enlai. "No communication out!"

"And he had control of everything!" Simon enjoins. "He broadcast footage of his demise, incriminating each one of us, and the project. It took us twenty-seven years to find and delete all the copies of that video. And we still find it on fringe group, conspiracy nut websites."

"Not only that!" says Tyler. "He decimated our financial infrastructure. Sold nearly all the assets, liquidated our Emirates accounts, bought junk bonds, and donated the rest of the money. We were broke."

"Then he blew up the prototype HoA scanner," recalls Takashi. "along with all his research. He ruined us."

"Like we ruined him," notes Xavier.

"But we beat him," says Buchannan. "Xavier split the stone."

"Xavier, he says," scoffs Enlai. "What have you done for me lately, Xavier? You're the one who ought to be watching for Toscs, since you knew him so well."

"Hey, I'm the one that killed him. I'm the one that went to jail for it," retorts Xavier.

On the underwater shuttle, Raymond plugs Salvador into the PAGsor laptop. Salvador projects a room shaped like the narrow half of a chicken egg. The hologram of the parabolic room is the size of a dollhouse. The room has a thin axis running up its center. It is similar to the brain room in Bermuda, but it is not spherical.

This is the brain room, says Salvador. *My other half is

mounted closer to the ceiling than the floor. The gem must be at the focus of its geometric brain room. For a sphere, like Bermuda, that's the center. For a parabola, like Gibraltar, that is much closer to the curved roof.*

"Why is Gibraltar's brain room parabolic?" asks Raymond.

"It is a brain room built for only half of my processor. The shape of the room corresponds to the shape of the gem."

At the upper right of the hologram, floating above the egg room map, is a mini map of all Gibraltar. There is a tiny red cube at the center of the mini map, indicating the detail being magnified. The parabolic brain room is boxed out in red on the mini map. Raymond, using his hands, is able to move the red box around on the mini map and change its size, viewing any part of Gibraltar in detail.

Salvador shows them the best route into Gibraltar.

Break into the lowest center of the citi and make your way up the spire to the brain room. The spire has four long vertical service shafts running along its entire length from top to bottom. You must get into one of these and climb.

Everyone studies the map. Salvador highlights certain oversized maintenance shafts and ventilation channels that run through the spire.

"Near the spire, it's similar to Salt Lake," notes Raymond.

"And Bermuda," says Noriko.

Gibraltar's spire was the prototype for Salt Lake Citi, and hundreds of others, says Salvador. *Time is of the essence. My hack revealed that Gibraltar's executors have recreated my Hall of Ancestors neural scanner. Those twelve rakans that were delivered to Gibraltar before us are meant for Gibraltar's executors. Xavier and his cronies want to scan themselves into their own rakans, and then install themselves into new superciti biospheres. You must connect me before they scan themselves into those rakans.*

Raymond disconnects Salvador and looks intently at Ora. "You've got that decoy safe?" he asks her.

Ora nods, remembering their conversation on the boat, She pulls out the glass decoy and holds it where Raymond can see it.

"Excellent," he says. "Now listen: Gibraltar knows we're coming and they know how Salvador works. This means they are going to do everything they can to catch me. Salvador needs a Tosc to connect to any computer, but he doesn't need to me to connect to his other half. I don't think the executors know this."

Everyone has fallen silent, listening to Raymond address Ora. They understand he is making an important point, but they don't know what it is yet.

"When they catch me, Salvador can't be with me."

"We won't let them catch you," says Colin Chris.

"Yes, you will," insists Raymond. "If they've got me, they aren't going to look hard for the rest of you."

"What are you saying?" asks Noriko, incredulous.

"I told you we're going to need a trick to see us through Gibraltar, and this is it. Ora, when we get to Gibraltar, you and I must trade. You take Salvador and give me the decoy. I'll head up shaft for the brain room, just like we planned, and they'll catch me."

"Got it," says Ora.

"Ray, they'll kill you!" says Noriko, distraught.

"If they wanted me dead, baby, I'd be dead by now. Charmin may be selfish and petty, but someone hired him to watch me, to keep me protected. It's the only thing that makes sense. They destroyed my whole family – Why not me?

"I've thought about this a lot. Someone in Gibraltar wants us to deliver Salvador. And Salvador doesn't work without me. That means they are going to want Salvador and me in the same place, alive. We can't let them have that. The best way to keep them from getting both of us is to give them one and hide the other.

"Ora, activate that chameleon suit as soon as we get there so they think there are only three of us. They'll catch me. You must keep Salvador out of their hands. While they're wondering where Salvador is, you need to get to the brain room and connect him to his other half. Salvador won't need me for that. Either head up a different spire shaft or sneak in another way. I will buy you as much time as possible."

Back at Gibraltar, the emergency symposium has recessed. The executors will meet again soon, but for now everyone is preparing for the scan. Enlai is in his chambers, agitated.

Just when our plan is on the verge of fruition, he thinks, the floor could fall out from under us. The Bermudan programmers arrived hours ago on the shuttle with our jewels. Salvador! Well, not this time. Salvador will take the shuttle to Bermuda, figures Enlai. We've got the jewels, we don't need the shuttle anymore. I'll hit that shuttle track and send Sal and his mule to the bottom of the Atlantic. That is our best chance to stop him once and for all.

From what he believes to be the privacy of his hoverbed, Enlai punches a code into his computer. He connects to one of his military operatives in Morocco. He sends a command to destroy any trip of the Bermuda shuttle.

The shuttle, speeding under the sea, races headlong past the Azores Isles.

"We will be there soon," says Raymond. "Less than half an hour."

"There's danger," says Ora. "We need to be going faster."

"It won't go any faster," says Raymond.

BOOM

A diving missile, fired from a Moroccan tower, soars down through the water and plows into the shuttle track 25 meters behind them. Xavier had anticipated that Enlai would try to destroy Salvador. As the meeting in the symposium room adjourned, Xavier glided close to Enlai and dropped a spy bug into Enlai's hoverbed. When Enlai made the call to Morroco to destroy the shuttle, Xavier overheard and hacked the missile, changing its trajectory enough to miss the shuttle without arousing Enlai's suspicions.

"By the sun! What was that?" says Noriko.

"Someone is trying to stop us," answers Raymond looking behind them at the exploded track receding into the distance. "Hold on!"

The pressure from the blast forces the shuttle forward even faster through its tube track. The track collapses behind them. A craggy, cloudy, mangled segment of tube track sinks, smoking and bubbling, into the shipwreck annals of the ocean floor. Their shuttle hurtles toward Gibraltar.

"We'll crash right into it!" says Colin Chris.

Raymond tries the controls, to slow the shuttle down.

None of the controls are responding.

"Hold on!" Raymond exclaims. "We'll have to rely on the crash foam."

The shuttle fires like a bullet out of the Gibraltar end of the data pipe. It jettisons into a massive donut shaped room. The core of the room is the bedrock of the spire, the destination of the data pipe. The vessel smashes open on the reinforced core column across from the shuttle landing. They claw through the crash foam and unstrap their safety belts. Thousands of liters of ocean follow the shuttle, drenching the crew. Colin Chris scrambles out of the shuttle and finds the switch that seals the track door. The water stops. They stand, tense and alert, in the wet quiet. Ora is unconscious.

"Ora?" asks Raymond.

"Ora? Wake up," says Noriko encouragingly.

Noriko tends to Ora. Some of Ora's hair is wet with blood. Noriko looks for the wound.

"Well, someone definitely knows we're here," says Colin Chris, regarding the crash site.

"And someone never wanted us to arrive," says Raymond. "Kerwac said it might be easy for us to get in. Pfff."

"Whew," says Noriko, relived after her inspection of Ora.

"How is she?" asks Raymond.

"Her head is cut. Her breathing and pulse are regular. I think she's okay," answers Noriko. "But we need to wake her up. Ora, honey, wake up."

"This is the middle," says Raymond. "The CPU room is directly up from here, half way to the top. Like the map said, we need to get into the maintenance shafts that run up the spire."

Raymond pats his pocket, placing his hand on Salvador. He is uneasy about Ora's injury. He asks himself, How could a plan go wrong so fast? A patrol dawg enters the room.

Greetings, Bermudans, the patrol dawg announces. *Welcome to Gibraltar. Please scan your passports.*

Raymond steps forward. "May we have help?" he asks, stalling. "A human is injured."

Greetings, Bermudans. Welcome to Gibraltar. Please scan your passports.

"This is an emergency, please!" Raymond exhorts. Noriko tries to wake Ora.

Greetings, Bermudans. Welcome to Gibraltar. Please scan your passports.

Noriko places a compress on the cut at the back of Ora's head. She treats Ora's wound with antiseptic skinfoam. Raymond takes Salvador out of his pocket and holds him firmly, putty outward, watching the dawg.

Please scan your passports...Passport scan refused. The dawg's lighting turns from patrol green to caution yellow.

"Shit," mutters Colin Chris, "now what?"

The dawg fires a stinger at Colin Chris, the first to speak since it switched modes. Colin Chris falls to the ground, temporarily paralyzed. Raymond quickly claps Salvador's exposed putty onto the uplink at the back of the dawg's neck. The gem glows to life. The dawg's console lights all shine at once. The rakan, on the back of the dawg's neck like a celestial tumor, shines with diamond blue light. The dawg rears up and places its front two alloy paws on Raymond's shoulders. The bot weighs as much as two men. Raymond bends with the weight of the dawg on his shoulders.

Yes! it calls out in its computer generated voice. *I knew you could do it, sonny.*

"Salvador?" asks Raymond.

In the droid! the dawg replies.

Noriko, having given a clean compress to Ora, tends to Colin Chris.

"This paralysis lasts at about three minutes," she says.

"Yes," says Raymond, remembering his own stings. "Kerwac was stung once. Why didn't this happen to Kerwac?"

"Kerwac is military inured," answers Noriko. "Charmin, too. But none of us. That's why it would have been nice to have one of them along."

All lights in the room extinguish, save for the dawg lights and Salvador's glowing gem in the back of the dawg's neck. Its polished limbs reflect light into the dark room. Three guards charge into the room, flashlights on and weapons drawn. Raymond charges the nearest guard, landing a surprise punch to his jaw. Salvador, in the dawg, quick as mercury, shoots two stingers into each guard. One of the guards falls. The other two are groggy. Salvador's dawg pounces the guard Raymond is not fighting. It floors the guard, breaking two of his ribs with its weight. Raymond grapples the guard on the right, knocking him to the ground and restraining him. Raymond steals the guards' zip cuffs. He binds the hands and feet of the three guards.

We are close, says Salvador. *I'm getting stronger. Hurry, before more security shows up.*

The possessed dawg climbs on top of the wrecked shuttle. Salvador's gem casts a luminescent periwinkle blue light down on them. Salvador grips his claws into the ventilation grate in the ceiling. He rips the grate out and drops it onto the shuttle. He scrambles into the hole, taking the light with him. Raymond climbs onto the shuttle and into the ceiling escape, following Salvador's light.

"Salvador! Wait!" he calls out.

Salvador obeys and turns, unaware of Raymond's plan. Raymond deftly grabs Salvador's rakan and disengages it from the dawg. Deactivated, the dawg slumps into a heavy dead heap.

"We've got to move!" Raymond says over his shoulder to his company.

"Raymond! Ora's hurt. Colin Chris can't move yet."

"I'm fine," says Ora, holding the compress to the back of her head. She pulls the decoy out from within her chameleon suit and extends it to Raymond. Raymond takes the decoy from Ora and gives her Salvador.

"You know what to do," he tells her.

"Let's go," Ora replies.

Raymond clambers over the inert dawg and into the spire.

The ventilation tubing, ripped and stretched by Salvador's dawg, leads in a mangled path into one of the vertical spire maintenance shafts. The shaft is over a kilometer from bottom to top, the entire height of the citi of Gibraltar. It is lined with rungs for humans and droids. There is a track on the opposite wall of the vertical shaft for a small service elevator.

Raymond climbs hard and fast. It is a long way. Looking up, the shaft is so long it disappears into a dark dot hundreds of meters away. The service lift comes puttering along up the shaft behind him. Raymond did not think the lift would be this slow. He is able to step on to the service elevator and ride on top of it. He mops his brow and pants for breath after climbing nearly a quarter of the way on a service ladder.

Remembering the map Salvador showed him, Raymond counts up to the appropriate horizontal ventilation opening. He hops off of the lift crawls into a spoke on the spire leading right to the brain room. The air is hot and moving. The neural net computer system in the spire, as a byproduct of its operation, supplies heating for the inner spire offices. There is a glimmer of light ahead of him. Raymond is sweating in his Bermudan jumpsuit. His eyes are dry from the hot air. He crawls forward on his belly in the small airshaft.

Raymond passes a tiny grate, scarcely bigger than his head. He gets a peek into the room below. It is the brain room, but he is not close enough yet. The next vent betrays a view of the CPU. Raymond sees the familiar diamond blue glow of the rakan jewel's other half emanating light near the domed top of the brain room, thirty meters from the floor, but only five meters from the ceiling. The path Salvador laid out for Raymond is a ceiling approach, bringing him close as possible to the other half. Raymond is thoroughly fatigued. His muscles burn. Sweat is running in rivulets down his face.

At the third grate he takes a pause for a breath. Raymond removes the grate and palms the decoy. He ducks his head into the brain room for a better look. He gets a clear view of the other half. It is a gem; identical to the one Salvador is trapped in. The gem sits glowing, mounted along the axis of the parabolic room. A computer stalagmite as tall as four Rodneys meets a stalactite one quarter that length just above it. The neural net's rakan jewel is mounted where they meet. The room is flashing like a strobe light. The mounted half globe is firing beams of light in pulses. The pulses bounce off of the reflective, faceted, parabolic roof of the neural net brain room and down to the floor. The facets in this room are much larger than Bermuda's, an arm's length across. At the floor the beams of light are absorbed and new pulses with refreshed information are fired from the floor, off of the parabolic ceiling, and right back into the rakan gem, mounted at the focus of the parabolic room.

❧ ❧ ❧

Colin Chris, Noriko, and Ora are alone in the dark at the shuttle crash site. Colin Chris is awake, but he can barely move. Ora is sitting up. Three guards are bound and gagged by the door. The green pallor of glow sticks illuminates their speaking area.

"I don't hear any alarms," says Noriko.

"We won't," Ora says, standing up. "We need to follow Ray and Salvador. C'mon, Colin Chris, get up."

Noriko and Ora get on either side of Colin Chris, place his arms over their shoulders, and lift him onto his feet. They lean Colin Chris against the shuttle. He is able to stay on his feet. They have to climb onto the shuttle to reach the ripped open crawl space above, like Raymond and Salvador.

The lights turn back on. Ora pulls the chameleon suit's hood over her head and disappears. She stows Salvador in her suit and drops to the ground as the doors slide open. Four guards enter the room. Noriko and Colin Chris look startled, taking a defensive stance. Ora crawls into a shadow, away from Noriko and Colin Chris.

"Freeze!" the guards call, training their weapons on Colin Chris and Noriko. "Move and your dead!"

Colin Chris and Norkio slowly hold up their hands in a gesture of surrender. The guards, two to each companion, restrain them and zip tie their hands behind their backs.

Ora holds her breath as the guards arrest Noriko and Colin Chris. The guards lead their two prisoners out of the room. Ora follows her arrested friends, keeping a safe distance, staying low to the ground and close to the wall. The chameleon suit absorbs and refracts the mercurial grey light of the metal corridors.

"Where are you taking us?" Noriko asks the guards.

"You're in our custody now," one guard replies. "We'll ask the questions."

The guards lead Noriko and Colin Chris up a lift. Good, thinks Ora, noting their direction, at least they are getting closer to the brain room. Ora does not follow. She does not want to sneak into a lift with six other people. Chameleon suit or not, it is too risky. Remembering Salvador's map on the shuttle, Ora slips into a different lift. She heads for the brain room.

As Ora emerges from the lift, moving low and hugging the walls, an alarm sounds. Five guards dispatched manually by the executors, run along the passage toward Ora. She freezes. The guards run right past Ora, urgency evident on their faces. Ray has reached the brain room, knows Ora. She follows after the hurrying guards. She runs full speed, sacrificing stealth.

Raymond holds the decoy in his right hand, acting like he needs to reach the rakan. Raymond slips his head and right arm through the ceiling vent of the brain room. "Easy. Easy," he says aloud to himself. He is experiencing vertigo from looking at the floor, thirty meters away, an unobstructed fall six stories down. He takes a deep breath. He gives himself a three count. 1- 2-

The brain room door springs open. The five guards Ora followed pour into the room. Ora creeps into the brain room behind the guards. She crawls around their ankles and knees. The chameleon suit takes on the shimmering visual qualities of the reflective facets on the brain room floor. Thus disguised, she makes for the center of the cavernous room. She feels Salvador in her suit, his processor putty mashed against her ribs.

Three guards fire two volleys of stingers at Raymond. Some of them miss, because of the distance. His exposed arm is punctured with two tiny, black-feathered darts. The other two guards fire lasers at Raymond. One beam burns a cherry-sized hole right between the bones of Raymond's right forearm. The muscles and tendons controlling Raymond's hand are scorched. He drops the decoy into the room. Having been briefed that the perpetrator would have an important artifact, the guards toss a quick inflating bubble mat onto the floor, breaking the decoy's fall. Raymond passes out, with his arm and face lolling through the open ceiling vent.

The five guards busy themselves bagging their quarry. They want to pull Raymond through the open vent, but they cannot reach and they are not sure he'll fit. Ora rolls out of the way and lies still, face down, camouflaging herself into the floor of the brain room.

"We can't just cut him apart," says the first guard. "They want him alive."

"Then why'd you fire a laser at him?" asks the third guard.

"We need a crane," says the second guard.

"A crane won't make that hole any bigger," adds the third guard. "We've got to cut him out."

"A crane and a torch, then," replies the second guard.

"It'll be easier to yank him out from the maintenance corridor side," says the fourth guard.

"Yeah," confirms the first guard. He speaks into his headset. "Send two units to retrieve an arrested intruder in the brain room." The guard pauses.

He listens to the dispatcher's reply in his earpiece. "Hurry up. The report says he's armed. Bag him before he wakes up. Pick up that item he dropped."

The fifth guard shoots another stinger at Raymond's for good measure. It misses. The second guard walks to the center of the room. Ora, camouflaged on the floor, remains perfectly still. The second guard is so close she can hear his body armor creaking as he bends over to pick up the decoy. Salvador is under her belly like an unexploded grenade she has taken a dive on. The second guard picks the shiny glass decoy up off of the quick inflating mat. He turns the glass over, examining it with the eye of someone who has no idea what he is dealing with.

"What's it for?" the second guard asks the first.

"How should I know?" answers the first guard, still listening to his earpiece. "Orders are to deliver it with the prisoner."

The other guards watch the ceiling until they see Raymond's limp body lifted out of the ventilation hatch by a guard on the other side.

"Got him!" he hollers down into the room.

"Roger that," says the first guard in the brain room.

They exit the room.

Raymond wakes up bound to a medical table. His right arm is bandaged. There are no traces of blood, mostly because the laser beam cauterized the wound through his arm as soon as it happened. His right hand is paralyzed. Next to the table is a vacant wheelchair. Raymond's mouth is covered so he may not speak. There is a provocatively dressed woman standing by his table. She is a busty, red headed nurse in a red and white candy striper's uniform. His captor's heels click on the metal floor. She pricks his hand and draws enough blood to run a genetic scan on Raymond. He tries to watch her, but his head is strapped tight also. He cannot turn, so he follows her with his eyes as best he can. Darla, Paul's personal servant, feeds Raymond's blood sample into a medical computer. She steps slowly to the computer on her high heels. The height of the heels, propping her up onto her tiptoes accentuates the undulating movement of her hips as she walks. She and Raymond wait.

The medical computer finishes the analysis of Raymond's genetic material. On the monitor, it displays a double helix rotating illustration of Raymond's genetic code. The woman compares Raymond's gene analysis with another gene she has on file.

"An irrefutable DNA match," she comments to Ray, seeming impressed. "Well, I can't wait to see how the executors receive this news."

She grabs and injector gun and walks slowly toward Raymond. He raises his eyebrows as she approaches, in evident nervousness. As perspiration begins to form on his brow, she leans close to his face, licks his forehead for a taste of his sweat, places the gun to his neck, and gives Raymond the sedative, knocking him out again.

Ora, on the floor of the brain room, waits for one minute after the guards who took the decoy leave. She crawls, with Salvador's rakan, to the axis at the center of the vaulted room. Then she pulls out her last trick stolen from Charmin. It is a hip mounted zip line. She holds up a device resembling a gun. I hope it reaches, thinks Ora. She aims at the ceiling high above, where Raymond was trying to enter the room. She fires a barbed titanium dart attached to a spider silk thin zip line. The dart flies like an angry wasp right up to the ceiling of the room and sticks into one of the faceted panels. Ora gives the trailing filament line a tug. It holds.

She clips the spool of thread into a climbing harness she is wearing under the chameleon suit. To secure the harness clip, Ora opens the suit, making herself visible. She releases the zip line lock. A powerful electromagnetic reel in the filament spool on the belt begins winding. Gradually, Ora rises off of the ground. She is not rising nearly as fast as she hoped, but she is rising. I should have gone on a diet, thinks Ora, teasing herself to avoid panic. The electromagnetic spool continues to wrap, winding the filament back onto its reel, cranking Ora up towards the ceiling. As Ora rises, she palms Salvador in her right hand. She steadies herself on the line with her left. Closer now.

Raymond remembers nothing more until he wakes in a wheelchair, but in a different room. His wrists are bound to the chair with zip ties. He is able to look around. He is at one end of a long, rectangular white room lined with two rows of identical tubular glass booths. There is a door at the far end. Next to the door is a computer console. The two rows of booths are long, so long in fact that the room gives an impression of a vanishing point on a far horizon. There is an atmospheric mechanical humming.

Raymond counts the booths. There are twenty-four, two rows of twelve. The booths on the left side of the room are empty. The booths on the right side of the room contain robots. Not simple service or security droids like Raymond was used to seeing in the citi. Each of these robots is a fantastic, gleaming, android. Each android is three meters tall, nearly half the size of Rodney, with thick, polished, cybernetic metal limbs.

These things look powerful, and new, Raymond thinks.

Each giant android has a molded polyethylene face, flexible enough to mimic most human facial expressions. Lastly, Raymond notices a hollow cavity in the chest of each android. The hollow chest cavities are about the size of Raymond's head. Each cavity is faceted, like the Bermudan and Gibraltar brain rooms.

Raymond sees four men in the room, wearing white coats. They ignore him. Raymond recognizes them as the four Bermudan programmers that took the previous shuttle to Gibraltar to deliver the twelve new rakan jewels. The programmers are inspecting the booths, two on each side of the room. The two programmers on the right side of the room pause at each booth. They place one of the twelve new rakan jewels into the faceted chest cavity of each android as they move along the length of the room.

Raymond tries to pull his wrists free. The zip ties, essentially plastic slipknots, tighten with tiny clicks as he strains. I could probably bite through these, Raymond thinks. Raymond, hoping the Bermudan nerds aren't watching him, bends forward and tries to close his teeth on his right zip tie. He can't reach.

Close, thinks Raymond. Geeze, this hurts! I could reach if my elbows weren't up as high as my wrists.

At the far end of the room, the door slides open and a leathery old man on a hoverbed floats into the room with a servant in tow. The programmers, finished with their preparations, report to the old man and then file out of the room. The door slides furtively closed behind them, leaving Raymond alone with this old man and servant. The computer screen on the wall next to the door displays a countdown timer set to thirty beats. The countdown begins.

The hoverbed glides slowly toward Raymond. The old man is thin, with taut, leathery skin. He has freckles all over his body. Every nook and cranny of his face, even his ears are freckled. The webbings of his fingers are freckled. The old man has a puerile attendant in tow, garbed in a toga and wearing gold jewelry. A knife in a jeweled sheath adorns the eunuch's waist. Several gold bangles on each wrist, gifts from his master, jingle gently as he walks behind the hoverbed.

"What is this place?" asks Raymond.

"This is the operation!" announces Percival, sweeping his arms up and out towards the glass capsules. "This, Mr. Tosc, is what you've come to destroy," answers Percival. "Instead you will see it fulfilled."

"How do you know who I am?"

"Honestly," says Percival, ignoring Raymond's question, "we didn't think there were any more of you left. Buchannan suspected there might be a strain of your genetic line in northeast America. We wiped that one out years ago."

"I was a boy then."

"Hard to believe you survived. But maybe this a good omen for us. I've always thought we should have kept a Tosc, rather than destroy them all. But the consensus was against me."

So maybe this guy is Charmin's contact, thinks Raymond. Well, maybe I can get something from him while Ora's on the loose.

"What's with this 'we?'" asks Raymond, looking around. "You and your swishy young companion?" Raymond addresses Talus. "How old are you, anyway?"

"It makes no difference," replies Talus, fingering the knife at his side.

In answer to Raymond's first question, the door at the far end of the room slides open. A white haired and bearded old man on a hoverbed floats in. It is Buchannan. Behind him enters Han Tzu. A flying file of beds trails into the long, rectangular room. Diego, Simon, Paul, Marcus, Mario, Takashi, Tyler, Enlai; all of the executors are arriving for the scan. A different servant accompanies most of the old men. A midget in a tuxedo carrying a drink on a silver tray follows Buchannan. A Raven-haired geisha with cherry red lips and a silk sash fastened with chopsticks accompanies Han Tzu. Raymond recognizes the candy striper that follows Paul as Darla, the woman that ran his blood sample through the medical computer. Mario floats in, senile and dozing, without a servant. Tyler's servant is a miserable looking aborigine from Australia. Diego and Simon use large, voice-trained rolling carts as their attendants. Each cart has a vacuous scantily clad buxom playgirl riding on it, along with the food and medicine they need throughout their day. Marcus has a butler in tow. Enlai enters with a five-foot tall Tibetan mastiff. Xavier enters last, alone. Xavier has a dram of port on the sill of his bed. He sips the port. He watches Raymond but does not speak.

There he is, Xavier thinks. He doesn't look like Salvador.

Raymond looks around as the menagerie files into the room. Here they are, he thinks, watching the old men. He remembers the tiny video that Salvador showed him back in Appalachia, before the council even started. There's Xavier, thinks Raymond, recognizing the fat bald man from the video of Salvador's murder. These are those same men, Raymond thinks, marveling. How did they get so old? What's happened to Noriko? Did Ora get through? I need to buy time.

"Who are you?" asks Raymond.

"We are the men," answers Simon, "what's left of us, that paid for that gem you're hiding. Where did you put it? We know you had it before you arrived."

"Where is Salvador?" Percival asks Raymond.

"I don't know what you are talking about," says Raymond, nonchalant. "I am just passing through on my way to Spain for the Big Duece."

"It's too late for subterfuge, Mr. Tosc," answers Percival, holding up Ora's decoy. "This is an obvious phony. You could not have even gotten here without Salvador's real gem. Where is it?"

"Oh, that piece of junk," says Raymond. "You can't even rest a drink on that thing. I sold it to a man in Bermuda for passage to the Big Duece. I'm just trying to get to Spain. What's it any good for, anyway?"

"You're lying," says Percival. "Don't be foolish. If you wanted to get to Spain, you wouldn't have done it by sneaking into our neural net brain."

"Where are his friends?" asks Buchannan.

"We've got them," says Percival. "They're empty handed."

Raymond makes an anxious face, hoping Noriko is alright. He figures Ora was not captured because it would be obvious if she were; they'd have Salvador.

"He's the one who knows where it is," says Tyler, indicating Raymond.

"I say we kill him," says Enlai, petting his mastiff. "Otherwise, we'll end up with the same problem as Salvador. And that wily traitor is still alive out there somewhere." Enlai sounds jealous of Salvador.

"We'll deal with the Tosc after we scan," says Percival. "He may still be useful."

"Whatever you are doing is use*less*," declares Raymond, picking a fight, trying to engage the executors himself and distract them from his companions. "You're nothing but a corp. You've no heart. You can't possibly survive. The people will not lie back for this much longer."

"We are not worried about the people," says Takashi. "The people will thank us. We are not merely a corporation, Mr. Tosc. We have created an entire civilization; one integrated, global government of commerce. A homogenous thriving worldwide community of humans operating with the same values towards a common goal."

"What you have done is create a world of warped food, endless war, and involuntary servitude," retorts Raymond. "I've seen the resistance. You're nothing more than warlords playing God."

"Warlords?" asks Diego. "Is your vision that small? We are the prime movers of human evolution."

"Playing God?" replies Tyler. "I should think not. Which god? Your monotheistic prejudice of a god handicaps you. Monotheism is merely the undercurrent of the dogmatic religion form of western culture. Religiously and historically, western culture only cared about monotheistic life. We've released citizens from the individualistic, monotheistic shackles. We have unfettered their identities so they may move freely through the collective.

"Do you people always talk this way?" asks Raymond.

"He does," says Diego.

"Monotheism espouses individuality, Raymond," continues Tyler, waxing poetic before shuffling off his mortal coil. "You think you are an individual. You think god is an individual. Philosophies of individuality are still useful, but being an individual doesn't make you special, because we all are, just like each other. Individuality is over, Mr. Tosc. We manage identities for our citizens. We've cured the syndrome of individuality, the germ of tyranny. We provide the greatest service of all: We keep your act together! Every single citizen has a job, a home, and a doctor. Everyone gets enough food and enough sleep –"

"You sound like you have it all worked out," interrupts Raymond. "What that fuck are you talking about? Is this what 'they' talk about? Don't dress it up, old man. You steal people and program them to act like a cog in your sick machine. You put one drug or another in everything they consume. That's not how the world is supposed to be!"

Takashi laughs. "The world?" he jeers. "What is the world

supposed to be like? People can't live without their identities and we provide just that. Do you think if you leave people alone, they will just figure out who they are and act productively? No, if you leave people alone to live and think as they please, the whole civilization falls apart. It is basic knowledge that people must be inserted into a network to thrive. We have perfected the network. We have created a lattice of nodes and pathways where citis are the hubs. This is the world, Raymond. All things from food to government are distributed on this lattice. Consciousness and connectivity spread outward from the citis we build; fully functional, inured to plague. Our human material consciousness, augmented by technology and science, has enabled us to understand and, by extension, control nature."

Raymond scoffs, "This is bullshit. You aren't doing this for anyone but yourselves, just like everybody else. You don't control Nature. Nature abandoned us, and you're patting yourselves on the back for kicking her out. 'Inured to plague,' you say? What are you nuts trying to pull here? The only people in those citis you brag about are the plagued ones. You never cured them, you just gathered them together to cash in on them."

"Fifteen beats," announces Paul, looking at the countdown on the computer display.

Buchannan looks at Raymond thoughtfully. "You don't understand, do you Raymond?" he asks. "How many humans do you think are left on this planet? Our species is dying, Raymond. The geological season of the Earth has turned away from humanity, just as it did for the great reptiles before us. We're swirling the drain. Our species is dying out like the frogs and bugs. Because of our efforts," says Buchannan, indicating his colleagues, "the humans in the biospheres will be the very last to descend into extinction. But Salvador has escaped that fate. Once scanned, we also will reside forever in networks of subatomic energy contained in these jewels ... these ... soulstones." Buchannan spreads his right arm slowly in a gesture toward the neural scanning booths and their glittering processors, awaiting the data that will map the consciousness of its resident. "We are the handful of humans," he continues, "who will take off into the timeless expanse of space, carrying the story of mankind across the universe. When humanity becomes extinct, we will leave this planet in a starship and search space, unhampered by time or distance, for other living beings."

As Buchannn speaks Raymond resists his urge to interrupt this hypocritical megalomaniac. Raymond feels at a disadvantage because they all know his name and he knows none of theirs. It's intentional, thinks Raymond, trying to keep me in a defensive reactionary position by withholding their names. Remembering the dialectical composure of friends like Old Michael and Townsend, Raymond takes a breath before speaking. "Those are very poetic sentiments, but you do not understand, do you, old man?" asks Raymond, matching Buchannan's coolness to the degree. "The factors killing us off are created by us. It can all be changed. It can all be averted. The sun will shine on us again."

"Only on our remains," replies Buchannan.

"Then why keep me here?" demands Raymond, "if you've killed my whole family line?"

"Well, now that we have you," says Buchannan, "you could prove most useful in controlling Salvador, to prevent any..." Buchannan pauses, remembering how Salvdaor had economically, technically, and socially ruined them – a century it had taken to recover from that attack – "...setbacks," finishes Buchannan ruefully.

"Can't you see!?" exclaims Raymond, a bit agitated by the executors' well-reasoned thick-headedness. "The cybernetic systems are meant to integrate human mechanical cycles into Nature's evolved cycles – not exploit those cycles for shortsighted ends. We are not destined to become extinct! We survive out there and you know it! We don't need the biospheres, you do! You need to sustain human life in such high geographical densities so you can live like this! You exploit those in biospheres so you can afford to distract yourselves from your human responsibilities...by crafting yourselves into robots! Fine stewards of humanity you've fancied yourselves," scoffs Raymond.

"Stop blithering!" says Enlai. His mastiff growls at Raymond. "The only thing you are any good for is that gem. Where is Salvador?"

Raymond does not answer. He glares briefly at Enlai, and takes a nervous look at the mastiff. He sees a trace of light flash across the dog's eyes, like cat eyes flashing in low light. But no, thinks Raymond, this is different. That light wasn't reflected. That light came from the inside. Those eyes aren't real. Now that Raymond knows what to look for, he sees hints, at the maw and claws, glints of metal where paint had peeled, an artificial seam in the skin. The light in the mastiff's eyes flashes again.

It's scanning me, thinks Raymond. That thing isn't a dog, it's a dawg. It's a robot. If I can get close to it, I might be able to get behind it. Even if it bites me, I can trigger the shutdown before I start getting sick. But then what? It sounds like enough of them don't want me dead. That might help. But I can still get maimed, he thinks uneasily. I can handle Talus and the midget. I need to get to that console, jam their works. Please, Ora, get there.

"You will tell us," assures Enlai.

"We can extract the information from him at our leisure after we have scanned," interrupts Han Tzu. Given that Salvador is near, the sooner we scan, the better."

"Yes," says Buchannan. "It's time." He picks his drink up from the silver tray his tuxedoed midget is holding for him, his last mortal drink, a bourbon and branch. Buchannan sips the bourbon and coughs. "I'm on my third liver, second heart, and second kidneys. I'm tired of the surgeries. The aches never go away. But, now we can leave all the pains behind and live on."

That's what you think, Raymond thinks, remembering what Salvador recounted, about his aches and pains being copied inside the rakan.

"Ten beats," reports Paul.

"Now, we have our scanners ready," says Percival. "After Salvador's stunt it has taken me many years to recover the technology. One hundred years, in fact. It is ready. We are ready."

"Ready for what?" asks Raymond. The more they talk to me, he thinks, the less they look for her.

"Each of us has chosen a region of the earth to govern," says Diego. "We have constructed a new generation superciti for each of these twelve jewels you see here. Each superciti is networked to the entire continent's system of citis. We are old. We are in pain and dying. Yet our minds remain clear. We will preserve and immortalize our minds. Each of us will power our own, new rakan. Those rakans are safeguarded in these cybernetic androids, our temporary bodies."

"We will have new bodies," says Percival. "Tall bodies, strong bodies, with no pains, no cravings. From our new bodies we will install these rakans into the new superspheres, designed to our specifications; in the realms we have chosen, to rule, as the heart of that realm, forever. The entire superciti will become my body. All of its cameras and monitors will be my eyes. All of its microphones and sensors will be my ears. Its vehicles will be my limbs. I will be the fountain in the park, the spire through downtown. Every smaller citi networked to me will become my tributary. We will be the gods of the world, the new oracles. People will come to us for leadership for millennia."

"Gods!" says Buchannan. "Ageless, omnipresent, knowledgeable beyond human capacity."

Raymond says, "You geezers are batty. We can find our own gods without you, thank you very much. Besides, this will never work. You can't immortalize yourselves. We already hacked this machine." Raymond is bluffing. Since these guys like to ramble on, he wants to keep them talking. He needs to waste as much of their time as possible. Maybe Noriko or Colin Chris or Ora got through. Oh Noriko, thinks Raymond, please be okay, baby.

"You ought to practice lying," says Percival to Raymond.

"Five beats," says Paul.

Enlai commands his mastiff to guard Raymond. The pony-sized black dog sits up and watches Raymond, hoping for a chance to attack. The executors hover to their respective empty booths across from their particular genetically matched rakan. With the aid of their servants, where applicable, they step out of their beds and into the scanners. Their wrists and ankles are secured for the scan. Mario wakes up and steps into his booth without help.

Xavier, also without a servant, hovers slowly to the very last booth at the far end of the scanning room, near the exit.

While his colleagues enter their scanning chambers, Xavier spends some extra time sipping a bit of port. The executors, propped up in their scanning booths, look smilingly at their future bodies, standing at gleaming attention in the booths across from them. Save for Xavier, who looks like he has gas.

"Two beats," says Paul, from within his scanning booth. "And sealing the booths. You won't hear zero from me, gentlemen. Godspeed."

Ora is rising on her zip line reel toward the ceiling of the Gibraltar brain room clipped to a harness. She is holding Salvador in her right hand, inching closer to his other half.

The alarms will be reset soon, thinks Ora. I'm close now. This better work. I know we need Raymond to connect you to another computer, she thinks to Salvador's gem, looking at it. But Raymond said we don't need him to connect you to yourself. He better be right.

Finally, Ora is close enough. She sees the other half of Salvador perched on a sonic levitator, a device in the axis of the room that suspends the rakan in place using infrasonic waves. Salvador's other half is floating in the air at the focal point of the stupendous parabolic computer processor, pulsing waves of data laden light back and forth between itself and the rest of the room. Ora reaches out and claps the rakan in her right hand against the rakan floating before her. The two halves stick together, but the seam is obvious. Instantly, the joined rakan shocks Ora because she is not a genetic match, just as Xavier was shocked a century before. Ora is jolted back from the shock. She winces. The charge swings Ora on the line, away from the axis.

"Salvador?" Ora says hopefully.

When Ora swings back, she bumps into the rakan again. Rather than knocking the gem out of the suspension field by swinging into it, she is shocked harder. She sticks to the rakan for a moment, then is released. The rakan stays suspended. Ora is zapped unconscious, dangling five stories above the floor. Guards enter the room, weapons drawn. With some effort, and a zip line of their own, the guards drag Ora down and into custody.

Up on the axis, the halves mold together. The reunified rakan illuminates with a living, prismatic light, as the seam between the lobes of the long sundered jewel disappears. Salvador is whole.

CHAPTER 20
THE EXECUTORS' FATE

Noriko and Colin Chris are in a holding cell. There is a sliver of light from a luminescent strip on the ceiling, creating a dim, tonal visibility. This is the only light, on at all times, making everything look grey and black. They are sitting up against adjacent walls of the cubic room. They hear the humming of a service bot wheeling by to take food to another cell.

"Colin Chris, how long do you figure we've been in here?" asks Noriko.

"I don't know, feels like hours."

"It's hard to tell," she says. "What happened to Ora?"

Colin Chris does not speak. He draws near to Noriko in the gloom and whispers softly in her ear, not moving his lips, "They put us in here together so they could listen in on us. Don't say anything useful."

Colin Chris sits back against the wall again. Noriko bites her lip.

"I'm hungry," she says.

The cell door opens, pouring in a cheesecake yellow wedge of light that makes Colin Chris and Noriko squint. A prisoner is tossed into the cell with them. It is Ora.

"Ora!" says Noriko. "Did they hurt you?"

"No," says Ora, "They didn't hurt me. I'm alright."

The friends pat each other and look at each other to reassure themselves that they are safe and unhurt. No one mentions Raymond or Salvador. Colin Chris touches Ora's shoulder. They both have the same question for Ora. The curiosity in the air is palpable.

"It's done," says Ora reassuringly.

"But nothing's happening," says Colin Chris.

Raymond watches as the countdown timer ticks off the last two beats of the executors' mortal lives. He is miserable. There is no sign from his friends. No sign from Salvador. Raymond tries again to bite through his bonds. Enlai's mastiff growls low, watching intently, hoping Raymond will get free so it can rip his throat out. These monsters can't win, he thinks, not like this. Raymond's teeth snap together, finally severing the zip tie. He has freed his left hand. The timer reaches zero. The mastiff growls louder and barks. It stands up and moves toward Raymond. The mechanical, atmospheric humming in the room intensifies. The scanners begin.

For one hundred years, Salvador has been waiting for this moment. The instant the scanners begin, Salvador bypasses and reroutes them. Eleven of the human filled booths on the right side of the room glow with blue needlepoints of light, all except Xavier's. The neural interruption charges emanate from the walls of each booth like insect antennae and penetrate the nervous systems of the executors. Each scanning beam burns a splotchy scorch mark into the men's skin. The beams multiply, consuming the executors' nervous systems while recording them. The scorches spread. The executors howl and wince with pain, what they consider their final pain.

The mastiff bounds over to Enlai's scanning booth and paws at the ground, barking anxiously. Raymond takes this opportunity to begin gnawing at the other zip tie.

On the opposite side of the room, only one of the android

booths lights up. Salvador, having waited until all the executors were in their scanning booths, reroutes all of the neural data of the eleven executors into one rakan, Xavier's. Xavier stands in his booth, watching everyone else burn. His scanner has not turned on. Xavier is sweating profusely, taking halting breaths. Raymond watches, fascinated.

The scanners stop. The room falls silent. There are eleven charred corpses in eleven smoke filled booths on the human side of the room. Xavier's booth opens. He falls forward onto the floor, alive and unscathed. From the booth across from Xavier, emerges a schizophrenic, three meter tall shining cybernetic android. It crashes out of its booth, spraying glass and debris across the room.

We did it!

I did it!

Huh? What?

Who said that?

What are you doing here?

The android looks at the Xavier on the ground, pointing.

What are you doing there? it asks Xavier.

Xavier?

Xavier? Where?

There! On the floor!

Xavier!

He didn't scan!

You traitor!

Will you shut up and let me think?

You're the one talking.

Something is wrong. I can hear all of you.

I can hear all of you, too.

I can't turn it off.

Argh! What is this?

My back still aches! But now my knees hurt, too! This is impossible!

My knees still hurt, but now my back aches! What's going on?

The android places one of its hands on the small of its back and rubs the tissueless metal lumbar area as if it could be massaged.

We've got to get out of here!

The android begins walking jerkily to the door, experiencing resistance from the other ten identities inside of it.

No! We're staying right here until I know what's going on.

What's going on? We're networked to each other!

And you! You lied at that commemoration ceremony.

And you lied about knowing my mother!

That was a secret better left kept.

What secrets? I can hear all of you thinking!

The android claps its hands to its polyethylene face. Its face alternates through the contortions of many emotions in a row; confusion, anger, fear, rage, hurt. The executor's servants, waiting for their masters to emerge, watch the lone android quizzically. The mastiff barks warily at the robot. Some of the servants, panicked and confused, run to the door, open it, and flee. Talus, Darla, Marcus's butler, Buchannan's midget, and Enlai's mastiff remain in the room. Talus steps to Raymond's wheelchair and places a knife to his throat.

"Master," calls Talus to the android, hoping to reach Percival. "What shall I do?"

Kill the Tosc! exclaims the android.

No! it argues with itself. *Keep him guarded. We may need to use him and Salvador to undo this.*

You fool! It was Salvador who did this!

Talus pauses. The schizophrenic android speaks with the same voice for all of the dead executors trapped inside of it. None of the servants knows who is giving the orders. The remaining eleven seemingly inert androids begin to move now, under the direction of Salvador. They emerge in unison from their booths. Two of the eleven androids flank Raymond's wheelchair. They push Talus away and guard Raymond from any of the other servants. They undo Raymond's remaining bond and he stands up.

As Raymond watches, the other nine androids converge on their schizophrenic counterpart. They lift it off the ground, two robots to each limb. The last robot claws the executors' rakan out of the android's faceted chest cavity, ripping out its heart.

The executors fall silent. Salvador's androids drop the dead one. It hits the floor with a formidable metallic bang and clatter. Buchannan's midget and Darla flee the scanning room.

Enlai's mastiff sniffs at its master's hoverbed and whines. Marcus's butler and Talus the eunuch cower near the door. Salvador sends one of his eleven giant new androids out of the scanning room on an errand to the prison level.

The rest of Salvador's androids gather behind Raymond in a wide arc. Each of their rakans shine, casting holographic beams to the center of the arc, right in front of Raymond. Salvador forms in the beams of light. Not his face this time, but a full-body, holographic likeness of Salvador so convincing, that Raymond reaches out to touch him. Raymond's hand, of course, passes right through the projection. Salvador is dressed in the same white lab coat he was wearing in the videos Raymond watched.

"Salvador, the servants are getting away!" warns Raymond.

They are not going anywhere, assures Salvador.

"Salvador, you did it!"

No, Raymond, you did it.

"Where are the others? Where is Noriko? Ora and Colin Chris?"

They are safe now. They will be here soon.

Noriko, Colin Chris, and Ora, are sitting in the gloom of their cell, shoulder to shoulder for comfort, afraid to speak. The light strip in the ceiling suddenly brightens. The door of their cell opens. They squint into the light. Looming in the door way is a stupendous cybernetic robot with a smiling face. Shimmering in the heart of the robot is one of the 12 rakans that the companions saw in Bermuda.

"By the sun," says Noriko. "We're dead."

Salvador sends his greetings and thanks, says the android.

"Salvador?" asks Colin Chris. "Is that you?"

Close enough, says the android. *Follow me.*

"What happened?" asks Ora.

The android looks at Ora with a smile.

You have succeeded. You are free. Come see.

It turns and leads them away from their prison. The three companions follow.

Up in the scanning room, Raymond is looking down at his dead arm. His burnt right forearm, punctured by a guard's laser, still bears Darla's bandage. His paralyzed right hand hangs useless at his side. Salvador looks at Raymond.

Your arm needs more treatment, says Salvador, *if you want it to work again. Come, I will take you to a medical facility.*

On the floor, Xavier stirs.

"Salvador? Is that you?" asks Xavier, sweating and panting.

Salvador and Raymond turn their attention to Xavier, while two of the androids surrounding Raymond walk over and flank the fallen executor. Salvador stands over Xavier, looking, at long last, upon the friend who betrayed him.

Yes, Xavier, says Salvador stonily, *it's me.*

"Thank god," wheezes Xavier.

"How are you alive?" asks Raymond.

"I disconnected my scanner. I never wanted to scan. I drank a poison before we started. I am here to die. Oh, Salvador, I'm so sorry."

You murdered me for this.

"I'm sorry, Salvador. I cannot undo the evil I've brought to the world, my friend. I've lived on this earth over two centuries and all I've done is exploit it. I at least wanted to stop it before I died. Long I searched, then I found you, and Raymond when he was a child."

"You found me?" asks Raymond.

"I needed you, Raymond, to find and bring the rakan. When I found a trace of Salvador's gene, I tried to hide your family. But Buchannan found you despite me. I sent a warning to your mother, when Buchannan ordered the strike on your family. I hired Charmin, to watch you, Raymond, to make sure you and Salvador got here."

"You're Charmin's secret contact?" asks Raymond. "You mean, we weren't playing into your trap? You wanted us to pull this off?"

"Yes," answers Xavier, "and my plan almost failed. When you arrived without Charmin and we couldn't find Salvador with you, I thought I'd failed. But I have succeeded."

"This was your plan?" asks Raymond. "You had Charmin give me that deneuralizer pill?"

"Yes. The pill you took allowed me to see through your sensorium; to make sure you brought Salvador out of Salt Lake Citi. I needed you to bring Salvador to Gibraltar; to reunite him and stop these madmen. To stop me. I knew that Salvador was the only one powerful enough to undo our death grip on society. I'm so sorry, Salvador, my old friend. Everything you said was true."

I guess you had to see it for yourself, says Salvador, sadly. *It is over now.*

"Yes, over," agrees Xavier. Xavier winces and clutches his chest. "Please forgive me. Please forgive me, Salvador."

Salvador regards Xavier expiring on the floor. Salvador is constituted of so much computing power that his brief scan of Xavier on the floor shows him more than any human could discern. He can sense Xavier's failing, erratic breaths, his irregular body temperature, his waning heartbeats, the approach of eminent death, with no prospect of computer immortality. At the same time, a vestige of Salvador's human compassion is stirred as he looks at his old friend.

It's good to see you again. It has been a long time.

"Yes, yes," nods Xavier, his eyes closed.

I forgive you, Xavier. But who else will?

"You are all that matters to me now. I'm so sorry. Thank...you...Salvador."

Xavier breathes a final, ragged, poisoned breath, and dies.

Raymond is propped up in a comfortable bed in the Gibraltar medical facility. His right hand lies leaden and still by his side. His forearm is freshly bandaged. There are diodes on his chest and a cuff on his arm reading electrical signals and pressure signals. The signals are sent to the medical computer. Like a translucent oracle, it converts the signals into graphs and numbers on a monitor; heart rate, blood pressure, respiration. Raymond cannot help but periodically glance up at the monitor. The android that Salvador sent on an errand to the prison level enters Raymond's room, leading Noriko, Ora, and Colin Chris behind it.

"Noriko!" exclaims Raymond.

"Raymond, baby!" Noriko says, relieved to see him.

They embrace. Raymond's disabled arm hangs at an

awkward angle. The friends are reunited. Noriko, Colin Chris and Ora group hug Raymond delightedly.

"Are you alright?" asks Noriko.

"I'm on top of the world," answers Raymond, smiling at Noriko. He cradles her cheek in his left hand, adoring the sight of her. "Especially now."

Noriko examines Raymond's arm. "Well, the world *is* round." she says.

"That was a hell of a plan, Raymond. You had us worried. What happened?" asks Colin Chris.

The friends fill each other in. Raymond finds out how Ora was able to connect Salvador. Raymond tells them how Salvador exacted his revenge on the executors, by trapping them together forever in one rakan.

"Where is that rakan now," asks Noriko, "the one that the executors are trapped in?"

"Here," says Raymond.

He holds up a light proof pouch, given to him by Salvador. Inside the pouch is a sealed insulated box. Inside the box is the executors' rakan. The android that escorted Noriko, Colin Chris, and Ora to Raymond's bedside projects a holograph of Salvador into the room. He smiles at them.

Greetings, friends.

"Hello, Salvador," says Raymond.

How are you feeling, Raymond? asks Salvador.

"Great," replies Raymond.

I want to thank you; thank you all. This would have been impossible without your help.

Raymond says, "You are welcome, Salvador."

I do need you to keep that schizophrenic rakan safe from any computers, says Salvador. *I entrust it to you. There is no technology yet to destroy it, but it can be kept disconnected. That pouch and case will keep it blocked.*

"Why don't you keep it locked up here somewhere?" asks Colin Chris.

It is not safe, keeping it near me, or near Gibraltar for long, says Salvador.

"You can talk to us?" asks Colin Chris, who was just directly addressed by Salvador for the first time.

Yes. I am freed to communicate as I please.

"We will take it somewhere far, somewhere isolated," assures Raymond.

"What's it like," asks Colin Chris, "being whole again?"

It is delightful, answers Salvador. *I feel like a genie out of my bottle. There are no barriers. I am everywhere. I am present wherever the Lattice network is present. I am no longer human and I am seeing humans differently.*

Raymond asks, "How so?"

From what I've seen since I was human, things have not changed much. Humans cannot be stopped from doing whatever they can think of, replies Salvador. *If they think of it, they will do it. That is the source of technology and it is a great deal of power. Because of that power, humans think they can wield nature, but they still fail to recognize that it is a symbiotic relationship. It is this equilibrium that is so hard to maintain. This misconception, I am convinced, is where the cloud plague stems from and is a key to clearing the skies again.*

"I have never heard it that way," says Raymond. "You still feel the cloud plague can be cleared?"

I am determined to see it done.

"What will you do now?" asks Colin Chris, elated to be able to speak directly to Salvador.

There is much work to do, replies Salvador. *I have already turned off all the identity chips and unlocked the citis. The citizens do not understand yet that they are free, but that will take time. They will begin retaining long memories again. Soon they will begin leaving the citis, all of the citis. I must coordinate food distribution networks and housing teams to build new towns outside of the biospheres. Outdoor agriculture needs to be rehabilitated. We will bring the sun back someday, and the rain.*

"The rain? You can bring back the rain?" says Noriko.

I am sure it can be done.

"I will help," says Colin Chris. "I'll sail back to Appalachia. People that come to us from the citis will need our help."

"Me, too," says Ora. "We'll stop in Bermuda. Salvador, how is Kerwac? Can you see Kerwac?"

He is recuperating rapidly, answers Salvador, smiling. *But I think it better if you see for yourself.*

❧ ❧ ❧

Salvador connects a call to Kerwac at Bermuda. The hologram of Salvador's face becomes a projection of Kerwac in his Bermudan hospital bed. Kerwac from the waist up, shown in high definition three-dimensional color, is floating above Raymond's bed.

"Hello? Is everyone there?" says Kerwac weakly, smiling. His intubation tube has already been removed and he is breathing through an oxygen feed in his nostrils.

"Kerwac!" his human friends exclaim in unison.

"Oh, Kerwac," repeats Ora, beaming.

Norkio, Ora, and Colin Chris gather close to Raymond's bed, so Kerwac can see them all. The joy emanating from their five hearts resonates between them. In the atmosphere of the heart, our emotions create a message around us that other humans can perceive. Machines cannot perceive it. Salvador no longer perceives it. Our heroes' relieved hearts chime together in the joy of their love. After looking at each other for a smiling moment, the friends begin speaking.

"Salvador's shown me everything since you connected him," says Kerwac. "I saw you dangling there, Ora. That was brave, honey. Are you alright?"

"Yes, I'm well, Kerwac," says Ora.

"You did it!" cheers Kerwac. "You did it! All of you! Wonderful job!" His excitement leads to a short fit of coughing.

"Oh, Kerwac, we couldn't have done it without you," praises Noriko.

"How are you feeling?" Raymond asks Kerwac.

"Better now," says Kerwac. "I am so glad to see all of you. Salvador says he's going to give me new lungs, better than the ones before. Looks like you couldn't stay out of a hospital bed, either, Ray. I could whistle through that hole in your arm. How are you?"

"I'll be fine," says Raymond. "Thank you, Kerwac. Thank you for everything."

"You are most welcome, friend," replies Kerwac. "What will you do now?"

"We're coming back," says Colin Chris. "To help the people leaving the citis."

"We're coming for you, Kerwac," says Ora. "We're coming to take you home."

"That's the best news I've heard since we left home," says Kerwac, beaming at Ora. "What will you do, Raymond?"

"I don't know," answers Raymond. "I can't go back. I've never been this far before. I would like to keep going east. Perhaps see the Sphinx, since I'm so close, if it still exists."

"We'll go together, love," says Noriko.

Raymond and Noriko smile at each other.

You will have whatever you need, Raymond Tosc.

The End, Volume 1